"I've changed," he said, and a corner of his mouth twitched. "What are you going to have to eat?"

"You haven't changed. You're too old."

"Gee, thanks."

"I don't want you to change." She did want to know what was really on his mind, not that he'd tell her until he was ready or made a slip.

Aaron paused, his eyes on hers. "None of us stays exactly the same, Libby. The world makes sure of that."

"Yes." She felt watched, and glanced at the woman behind the counter. "I guess I'll have tuna on rye. I used to like that."

As she stepped away, Aaron caught her arm. He bowed his head. "You and I will always be the same.... We'll always be the same for each other, won't we?"

She blinked rapidly and told him softly, "Yes."

"That's what matters, isn't it?"

"Yes."

"Stella Cameron is sensational!"

—Jayne Ann Krentz

D0197853

Stella Cameron

SNOW Angels

MIRA

ISBN 1-55166-840-8

SNOW ANGELS

Copyright © 1991 by Stella Cameron.

The longest journey
is from the head to the heart...
This story is dedicated
to Colleen Fox, Barbara Mains,
Lynette O'Neill, Shirley Underbrink
and Kathy VonDerLinn—
my dear companions on the trek
De Colores!

1

"**N**o! Go away!"

The man was there above her on the ski trail. Libby crouched lower, picking up speed, and looked back again. He shot down the slope after her, skiing with a fluid grace that showed he was an expert. And he was gaining on her.

But this was *her* place. No one came here.

Every mogul, every dip, was an old friend, as familiar as the warm little rooms in her stone cottage at the foot of this beloved Italian mountain.

Rushing a bump, she shifted her weight away from her skis, picking up still more speed. On either side of her the scrubby conifers blurred as she raced past—faster and faster.

She mustn't lose control.

The tall man was still coming, still closing the distance between them. A tourist wouldn't risk a side run like this. He had to be a local from the village, someone with a chance to watch her movements, then choose his time to follow. She tried to remember some Italian words that might discourage him. *"Mi…lasci…in pace!"* she tried.

But he didn't leave her alone—if he could even hear her shouted words through the dark cap pinned to his ears by the band of his goggles—black-lensed goggles that gleamed like huge predatory eyes.

Icy breath sawed past her burning throat. He must have

waited above, watching the lift, watching for her to come.
Then, after giving her a few seconds to start down the
piste and cut away from the main run—away from the
few skiers who ventured on *any* part of this treacherous
area—he'd known he had her…alone.

The end of the trail was too far. She couldn't keep up
this pace and not fall.

Libby skidded to a slithering half stop. Jumping off the
marked trail, she launched herself into deep virgin powder. Only a fool would come this way. There were trees
everywhere.

The wind whipped her hat away and tossed her long
hair across her face. As Libby continued her headlong
race down the mountain, the trees rose up in her path,
seeming to claw at her with their branches, tugging her
toward their trunks, then faded as she skimmed past.

"Hey!"

Her heart made a giant, suffocating leap. She hadn't
lost the man. But she wouldn't give up.

Several yards ahead stood a clump of gnarled firs.
Hunching, tucking her poles against her body, Libby shot
straight toward the trees. When she judged they were hiding her from the man's sight, she made her turn, throwing
her weight toward the evergreens. There was no time to
think…or pray.

She fell.

The powder rose slowly around her, a soft, wet white
cocoon. Catching her breath after the bone-jarring fall, she
wiped a blinding film of snow off her goggles and saw
the dark shape of the skier hurtling toward her. He was
skidding, too, but still in control.

Bracing herself on her knees, Libby yanked a pole free,
grasped it in both hands and pointed the steel tip toward
the man.

"WHAT THE HELL!" Aaron Conrad stared into the sharp, glinting center of a yellow plastic star—the lancelike tip of a ski pole aimed straight for his rocketing body.

He threw himself sideways, twisted onto his back as the snow enveloped him and slid beneath the scrunching surface.

"Libby—!" His mouth was full of snow and he spat viciously as he struggled to sit up. "Libby, have you lost—? Scratch that. You have lost your mind, haven't you?"

But his quarry had already grabbed a barren lower limb of the closest stunted alpine. Fascinated, he remained still while Libby hauled herself up and herringboned her skis.

She was trying to get away again.

"That's it." Fury carried him far enough to snake an arm around her legs.

Tumbling on top of him, arms swinging wildly inside her faded green windsuit, Libby yelled those words again. But the words were Italian and totally incomprehensible to Aaron.

It came to him then that she didn't know who he was. "Libby," he said, pinning her before she could think of another mode of attack, "it's me, Aaron."

The struggling didn't stop. "Help!" She hit him, a painless blow that glanced off his thick parka. *"Aiuto, polizia!"*

Police was a recognizable word in most languages. Aaron freed one hand long enough to flip his goggles on top of his head. "Darn it, Libby, shut up! And hold still!"

Her body suddenly flopped against the snow. "Oh." Pulling her own goggles beneath her chin, she swept back the long tangles of her magnificent hair and stared up at him.

At the foot of the first lift Aaron had asked the attendant

if he'd seen Libby Duclaux. A ski instructor had interpreted the man's response: "You mean the silent lady with red-gold hair?"

"The silent lady?" Aaron had wondered about that description. But it didn't surprise him that the lift attendant had noticed Libby—any man would.

"Libby, it's me, Aaron. What's the matter with you?"

She continued to stare, the wildness fading from her tawny eyes much more slowly than made sense to him. "You don't come in January," she said at last. "Not until April."

"So I changed my plans." He smiled at her. Staying angry with Libby wasn't possible, never had been for him. "Come on. Time to stop making snow angels. We should get out of here before we freeze to death."

"Never in January," Libby muttered as they scrambled to stand.

No, never, Aaron thought—until this time. A little earlier in the afternoon as a second, then a third chair lift had borne him steadily up this spectacular slope among the Dolomites, he'd known that when he finally stood face-to-face with Libby, he'd be looking at one of the toughest challenges of his life. That moment had arrived and he wasn't ready.

"Why are you here, Aaron?"

He saw her red hat lying in the snow. "Just a minute." Grasping at the chance to delay the inevitable, he lunged away to retrieve the sodden lump of wool. Suddenly all the words he'd rehearsed fled. What he could remember of his carefully planned speech sounded contrived.

"I left my things at your place—with Mme. Sedillot," he said, stuffing the cap into his pocket. "You can't wear this. It's wet. Use mine." Before she could respond he tore off his own hat and crammed it onto her head, pulling it down to rest halfway over her eyes. "Oh, dear." He laughed and readjusted his efforts.

"Aaron—"

"Mme. Sedillot said you were up here somewhere. A lift operator remembered seeing you…and an instructor. He said I'd best wait at the top because you come down to the bottom in different places, but you always use that lift several times in an afternoon. He called you an American-style skier. 'Like the yo-yo,' he said. 'Up, down. Up, down. Not like the European who knows to enjoy the beautiful run, then take as much time with the beautiful wine.' I think the good folks of Madonna di Lago are disappointed that they haven't civilized you yet."

He was gabbling. And the silent lady wasn't laughing, wasn't even smiling. A frown formed a line between her brows. Looking at Libby now, in this setting, he had to remember other times when they'd all skied this mountain together—he and Libby and Georges Duclaux, Libby's French-Swiss husband and Aaron's best friend. But the three of them would never ski together again. Georges was dead—murdered by his own nephew.

"Aaron, please, why are you here?"

Libby was a tall woman and appeared more so since she'd become too thin. For the past three years, since Georges's murder, she'd haunted a space in Aaron's mind. She was right. He shouldn't be here now. He had a ski lodge to run back in Washington State, and January was one of his busiest months. But other considerations were pushing him toward doing what he should have done long ago. He had to find a way to get Libby away from this mountain and back to the world, back to life.

"Why—?" she pressed.

"I decided to take a break. Simple as that." He made

himself smile. "Where else would I spend some extra spare time but with you?"

She bowed her head. "I'm not a fool—"

"Why did you run from me like that? I almost missed you coming off the lift. You got ahead of me. But I called out and you just kept going like a bat out of hell."

Libby raised her face. "I'm sorry. No one…I'm always alone, so I thought—" She shrugged, leaving the sentence unfinished.

What a beautiful face she had. With smooth olive skin, a full, soft mouth and big light golden eyes that couldn't hide what was in her heart, Libby only seemed to become more stunning as time went on. And after three years it was time for her to be over mourning for Georges and to stop hiding away in this Italian backwoods with only a middle-aged French housekeeper for company.

Aaron slipped a pole from one wrist and put his arm around her shoulders. "What did you think, Libby—when you ran away from me?"

Defiance was in those limpid eyes now. "You wouldn't understand. You'd say I'm paranoid."

"Try me." For Georges, he told himself. He was doing this for Georges and for Susan Kinnear, Libby's sister, who needed her only sibling back in the States. But most of all, he was doing it for Libby.

"Men don't believe a woman isn't interested," she said quietly.

"Interested in what?"

"You know what I mean. Since Georges died, I haven't wanted…I want to be left alone."

As far as Aaron knew, Libby *was* very much alone. She'd made sure of that. He felt her tremble. "You're cold.… Libby, what do you mean? I'm not getting this."

"Yes, you are." She tried to twist away, but he held

her fast and she pressed a fist to his chest. "You're pretending to be obtuse. You make me mad when you do that."

Aaron looked skyward through a dazzling sheet of fine snowflakes and shifting mist. "Are you telling me you thought I was some ski bum on the make? Libby—"

"No. I'm not talking about it anymore. I knew I shouldn't tell you, and I'm sorry I behaved the way I did. It was stupid."

"Slow down. Let's talk about this."

"No." She swung one ski to flip a turn, then stopped. "It's Susan! Something's wrong with Susan. Tell me now."

Aaron's heart did unpleasant things. "Susan's fine." Damn his cowardice, but if he sprang everything on her now, they'd never get off this mountain.

"What is it, then? Mike? Anne?"

"Mike and Anne are in great shape." That was an absolutely true statement about Susan's husband and stepdaughter.

"My folks." She looked aghast that she hadn't thought of them first. "Of course. It had to happen. They shouldn't be driving all over the country in that motor home in winter. The roads get slippery and—"

"No. As far as I know, your parents are in perfect health. And Mike's dad's okay, too, and my mom and dad." But Libby had given him yet another indication of why she kept herself wrapped up in an insular world. While she was far away and mostly out of touch, she was less likely to imagine horrible fates for the people she loved.

She crossed her arms, and a spark of the old stubborn Libby showed. "Aaron Conrad, I know you'd love to sit by the fire in my cozy cottage."

"I would." He nodded enthusiastically.

"And have some of Mimi's fantastic stew and home-made bread. And a few glasses of that terrible local red wine that you imagine is a great undiscovered vintage."

"You are so right."

"Yes. And I'm so right that a man who owns a chain of sporting goods stores and a resort rarely has spare time."

He shrugged. "He has some. Everyone does."

"Not in January. Not if that resort is a ski resort in the good old Washington Cascades in the good old U.S. of A. where the season is short. Right?"

"Well…"

"Short and sure of about one thing—the best snow, whatever that turns out to be, will be in the first couple of months of the year."

She had him. "Everything you say is true." Breaking eye contact, he adjusted the wrist locks on his gloves. "The truth is that we're having a phenomenal season, and I have plenty of people I trust to do a good job while I'm away. Also, this may be a long way from home, but a couple of plane hops and a car ride and here I am in little more than a day. The rest of the truth is that I do have some important things to discuss with you, Libby. That's why I'm here."

"You could have phoned."

His blood pressure simmered. "You don't *have* a phone, remember?" One more way to shut out reality.

"You could have got hold of me through the guest house."

"It's getting dark and it's so cold that my face is falling off. I'm going down," he said, starting uphill. "By the shortest—and safest—route. You coming?"

She didn't answer, but when he rolled over the snow

ridge and plopped onto the trail, Libby passed him, a flash of green in her windsuit, skiing back toward the main run.

"Go to it, silent lady," he murmured, setting off in her tracks.

By the time he copied her sharp turn from the trail to the narrow and very expert downhill piste, the surface of the packed snow was glittering in the gathering dusk like millions of starbursts dancing on shimmering blue-white satin.

He let her set the pace. She would be mulling over the possibilities of what he'd come to say, but she wouldn't guess, or not completely.

The revelation that she was afraid of direct human contact troubled him deeply. Her fear would have to be brought into the open and dispelled.

Libby carved her way down the mountain with the kind of style that would make an average skier drool. Aaron smiled and tried to ignore the pain in his ears from the arctic wind. He made several sharp turns, catching moguls and lifting into each snatched moment of airborne weightless power. His blood sang. It had been on snow like this on another European mountain that he and Georges Duclaux had first met over fifteen years ago. They'd both been in their early twenties, Aaron two years younger than Georges, and they'd both been competing for one of the world's biggest downhill titles. That had been only one of many races they were destined to share. Neither of them had ever become more than talented also-rans, but the thrill of racing had been a prize in itself.

"Yip! Yip!"

Libby's high-pitched cry startled and pleased him...then made him thoughtful once more. The shout meant she could forget anything up here, even the scrambled shadows of ideas she must be forming about his reasons for coming. It also helped confirm his growing suspicion that she'd chosen to become a recluse for that reason—because she could only forget when she was alone.

A final curving cut through sparse trees opened onto the broad area at the foot of the mountain. The lifts and the gondola had stopped running and the last skiers of the day had converged, forming shouting, neon-garbed clusters. Aaron stopped beside Libby, his skis throwing up a spray of icy clumps.

Without a word she released her bindings, stepped out and popped open the top buckles on her boots. He followed her upward glance to where the first of the ski patrol members, their orange jackets iridescent flags in gathering gloom, descended from their final sweep of the day.

"Half an hour more and we'd have been bringing up the rear guard for those guys."

"Wouldn't be the first time," she said, then closed her mouth firmly.

Aaron eyed her sharply but decided to save his lecture on prudent ski behavior for another time. He also thought better of offering to carry her skis. With poles banded on top, she already had them over her shoulder. By the time he'd followed suit, she was plodding toward the yellow lights of the village square, only a few hundred yards from the lifts.

The snow had been cleared from the cobblestones, which shone wet. Around the square, shop windows glowed, vying with one another for most-jammed or most-colorful awards. On his normal schedule Aaron saw this old-world scene every six months when he visited Libby to discuss her finances. Actually they never really "discussed" anything. He talked and read aloud…and finally showed Libby where to sign. She showed no interest.

"Mike's business isn't failing?" Libby asked suddenly without checking her clumping stride.

"Nope." Aaron looked down at the side of her face, the thick downcast lashes against a rounded cheek, the line of her slightly tilted nose. "Mike's got more business than he can handle."

"He was always too picky about commissions. Even Susan said that."

Aaron blew out an exasperated breath. "Mike prefers to choose the boats he refurbishes. It's the individual attention that makes every boat owner—around the world these days, not just in the States—want Michael Kinnear to look after their floating babies. I'm a silent partner in that operation of his, remember? I believe in his philosophy."

"Good." She halted before a window that looked like a still life painting of every variety of sausage in the world. "I promised Mimi I'd get…a sausage. Which one do you think?"

"Don't ask me. Could we just get home?"

"Did Susan lose the lease on the salon?"

Aaron ground his teeth together before responding. "The salon is clicking—or should I say clipping?—along nicely. Jeff's in charge while Susan's off during her preg—"

"Red-and-green wrapper," Libby blurted out, cutting him off. She pushed open the shop door, and they passed beneath a jangling bell that announced their entry.

A bald, red-faced man swathed in a dark blue apron came forward, rubbing his hands. He smiled at Libby politely but said nothing. She merely inclined her head.

Puzzled, Aaron breathed in the rich, spicy scents of the

meats that hung in swags from ceiling hooks and crammed marble-topped glass cases.

Libby pointed to a sausage with a red-and-green band. The man nodded, wrapped it in a sheet of paper and gave it to her. No money changed hands, and all Libby said before leading Aaron back outside was "Thanks."

"Weird," Aaron muttered, taking the package.

"What?"

"All that talking could make a man nervous. Is the guy deaf or something?"

"In the shop? No, I don't think so." They turned, side by side, down a narrow street echoing with the laughter of rowdy après-skiers.

"Why didn't you speak to each other?" He left the sidewalk to dodge a strolling couple.

"I thanked him. He doesn't speak English or French. I don't speak Italian or German."

Aaron stood still. "You've lived here for years."

"I don't need to learn the local languages."

"Why?" He was amazed. When she'd been married to Georges and living in Geneva, she'd learned to speak a very passable French.

Libby had stopped, but she didn't turn around. "There's no one here I want to talk to."

No wonder she was known as the silent lady. She didn't speak to anyone because she didn't want to, didn't own a phone, always skied alone. Aaron sighed, stuffed the sausage inside his parka and caught her hand firmly in his. She glanced at him quickly and smiled…and his heart turned.

Aaron had never failed at anything important in his life. He prayed his record would hold in the next few hours.

2

Without being sure why, Libby was certain she should keep talking. Throughout dinner, whenever Aaron and Mimi had been quiet, she'd felt as if something terrible were about to happen if she, Libby, didn't shut it out.

"Let's have the fruit and cheese by the fire," she said brightly, getting up from the heavy oak table at one end of the cottage's big kitchen. "Help me, Aaron. You bring the wine."

The kitchen was warm, and on any other night she would have been content to sit among its hanging copper pans, talking to Mimi and inhaling the yeasty aroma of the next day's bread rising atop the black wood-burning oven. Tonight she needed to be busy, to be moving and filling any silent spaces until she went to bed—to the safety of sleep.

The sitting room fireplace, rough-hewn stone topped with a thick and shiny wooden mantel, almost covered one wall. Brass—andirons, wood box, pots for dried grasses, a scuttle filled with books—glimmered in the light from the flames that curled up the blackened chimney.

"Put it here," she told Aaron, referring to the stone jug filled with red wine and the three glasses he carried. "On the chest." And she dragged forward the old brass-cornered sea chest that had been one of Georges's treasures.

Mimi set a cheese board and basket of bread beside the wine and busied herself helping Aaron move the deep, chintz-covered chairs to form a circle around the fire. Libby avoided the bright brown eyes of her housekeeper and friend. The woman had worked for Georges before he'd married and stayed on to become Libby's trusted helper. Mimi understood her employer well enough to sense how troubled she was.

"I'll pour the wine," Aaron said, bending over the chest. A dusting of gray showed at the temples of his brown curly hair. "You'll both have some?" He smiled up at her. The lines fanning from the corners of his dark eyes were deeper than Libby recalled.

"Yes, please."

Aaron must be thirty-eight now, she realized. A tall, rangy man, he was good-looking in an unconventional way. His sharply boned face, dominated by deep-set eyes and arched brows, had a reflective quality. But when Aaron smiled in his distinctive way, turning up the corners of his wide mouth and holding his bottom lip in his teeth, any mystery was dispelled and his devil-may-care character showed clearly. Libby had the sudden revelation that, next to Susan, Aaron was the most important person in her life. She sat down abruptly and looked into the fire.

"You'll have more wine, won't you, Mme. Sedillot?" Aaron asked.

"Er, no. There are things for me to do in the kitchen."

"No!" Libby cleared her throat and passed her tongue over her lips. "We wouldn't hear of you not staying with us, would we, Aaron?" If she were alone with him, he'd say something she didn't want to hear.

He shook his head, and the distant, troubled look was back. "Please join us."

"Very well, but—if you don't mind—I'd prefer you to call me Mimi. I may be a gray-haired old lady of sixty-five, but perhaps I don't feel so old." In her chic red silk blouse and black skirt worn with flat black boots, Mimi might be considered plump, but she appeared anything but old. The long gray hair she'd mentioned was worn in a smoothly shining plait wound at the back of her head.

Aaron bowed. "Mimi it is," he said, and offered her a glass.

Libby picked up her own wine and glanced from Aaron to Mimi and quickly away. They had exchanged a knowing look. She was sure of it.

"I love your cottage," Aaron said, settling himself in the chair opposite Libby's.

"So do I. Georges called it a nest." She thought of him often, but the memories were sweet now, resigned, not sharp and binding as they'd been for so long.

"It's a great vacation place. The next time you come home, you should try to get Susan and Mike to come here."

Libby drew up her shoulders. He always talked about the next time she went home. "This is my home now."

He drank deeply of his wine, but his eyes never left her.

He'd discarded his parka and turtleneck liner in favor of a heavy black polo-neck sweater. But he hadn't changed out of his black ski pants, which were like a second skin on his long, powerful legs. Aaron was more comfortable in such ski clothes than in any others, as Georges had been and Libby had become.

Mimi twirled her glass in her worn fingers and stared resolutely at the fire.

"When Georges bought this place he never intended it as a permanent residence," Aaron remarked.

Libby glanced at the white plastered walls and exposed wooden beams that shone darkly. Antique farm implements and old paintings of country scenes were scattered on the walls. "We spent our honeymoon here."

"I know, but that doesn't—"

"Did I tell you the orphanage near Lyons has two more employees? A doctor visits twice a week."

"No. Libby—"

"I'm considering adding another wing. The director wrote to me. She says conditions are crowded." The orphanage she was financing was in France, north of Lyons. Through an old acquaintance of Georges's she'd been approached for help by the order of nuns who operated the institution. For almost two years Libby had poured money into the orphanage—and into similar establishments around the world.

"Libby loves children," Mimi said quietly.

Libby flinched. She was infertile but had planned to adopt children with Georges. But then... "There's so much work to be done at the Lyons orphanage. It keeps me very busy."

"Have you visited the children there?" Aaron asked.

"I...no. There's always more to consider for them, and for others. In Korea and South America the needs grow every day."

"And you can't deal with them all."

She let out the breath she'd been holding. "I can try."

"Others have to try, too, have to spend their money, as well."

"They do. There are many helpers, but never enough." A shivery coolness washed over her. "That's it, isn't it,

Aaron? You're here to discuss money? The way I spend it?''

"No." His features turned rock-hard and he leaned forward. "That's not it. Will you let me talk to you?"

"I've been spending too much." She wanted to know what he was trying to say, but she didn't want to know. If there was something wrong with someone she loved, it would be unbearable. "This house is paid for. Georges paid for it. And I don't spend a lot on clothes—"

"Libby." There was warning in his voice now. "You don't spend anything on…clothes. You don't spend much on anything else, either. Georges was a highly successful financier. The fortune he left makes you a very, very wealthy woman. Anything you want, you can have. Anywhere you want to go, you can go."

"I don't want anything. This is where I belong. Everyone knows me here, don't they, Mimi?" She reached a hand toward her housekeeper.

"Is that why they don't speak to you?" Aaron asked.

"It's because she doesn't speak to them," Mimi said gently, rubbing Libby's fingers.

"Mimi!"

"Don't blame Mimi for telling the truth. You already admitted as much. You didn't even pay that man in the shop. What way is that to behave?"

"We've got an account," Libby told him miserably. "Mimi takes care of it."

"Because Mimi has learned to communicate the way normal people do. She's learned to function."

"I'm normal. I function."

"Libby, you're hiding here, walling yourself off from everyone who cares about you. It's got to stop." He rose to loom over her. "If you don't speak Italian, what was that you yelled at me on that mountain?"

"I don't speak Italian. Just a few words. I had to scramble to think of them."

"Sure."

"Don't you believe me?"

"I believe you've mourned long enough, my friend. It's time to stop and move on. You're important to me. I can't see you wasting the rest of your days in this hole-in-the-wall."

An explosive sensation in her head rocked Libby. No one could force her to change the life she'd chosen. She got up and found Aaron standing so close that she could see his pulse beating in his temple.

"I'm not leaving." She edged past him, avoiding his burning gaze. "I'm staying here forever."

"Libby, please listen to him," Mimi said.

"Even you." Libby scrubbed at her face. "I thought you were my friend. I thought you understood that I can't...I can't..."

"You're needed at home," Aaron said intensely.

He didn't know anything. "I'm not needed anywhere anymore. Except here. Except by the children."

"I've booked your flight to the States—"

"Cancel it." She turned wearily toward the stairs and walked away. "I'm tired. I have to sleep."

LIBBY'S FOOTSTEPS FADED on the stairs before Aaron began to think clearly again. He started after her.

"Not yet," Mimi Sedillot whispered. "Soon, but we should talk first."

Reluctantly he returned to his chair and sat on the edge of the seat. "I'd like to talk to her before she goes to sleep."

"Tomorrow will be soon enough. Or tonight, if it's

possible.'' She leaned her head back, raised her glass and studied its ruby-colored contents.

Aaron hadn't had more than brief conversations with Mimi in the past. In Geneva she'd been the swiftly moving administrator of a busy household. Since she'd come to Madonna di Lago, he'd come to view her as Libby's self-appointed protector. He'd analyzed possible reasons for Mimi taking on this role and decided the woman's loyalty to Georges had made her determined to look after his widow. Aaron's visits were always short, and Mimi invariably chose those times to pay a speedy call on her daughter in Paris.

"I'll always do what I think is best for Libby," she said, still swirling her wine. "Please understand that nothing will change that."

Aaron spread his hands, about to speak, then thought better of it and poured more wine into his glass. Diplomacy came naturally to him, and in this situation he was going to need plenty of that commodity.

"You're determined to take her back to America, aren't you?" she asked him.

Cupping the glass in his hands, he swung it between his knees. "Yes," he said carefully. "I take it you don't approve."

"I didn't say that. I only said that my own actions are dictated by her needs and best interests."

What she didn't say, rather than what she did, made Aaron uncertain. "You don't believe I have Libby's best interests at heart?"

"Oh, but of course. I certainly do. What I wonder is if you fully understand her needs—all of them—and what is actually happening here."

He looked up sharply into amazingly brilliant dark eyes. "What's happening...apart from the obvious?"

Mimi sat forward. "And what is obvious to you, Aaron?"

The temptation to pour out his concerns almost undid his restraint. Taking a drink, reaching to cut a slice from a wheel of thick yellow cheese, he bought time. The room had the power to relax the most tense of souls. Beneath his sock-clad feet, a beautiful old rug in shades of burgundy enhanced the polished, dark wooden floors. Heavy red velvet drapes had been drawn across the bowed window, but he knew snow was falling softly on the cobbled street outside, while they were warm and protected within the thick walls of the cottage.

Protection, Libby's self-protection, was what this was all about.

"Aaron?"

"For the first year after Georges died, I expected her to be devastated. I never saw a love like theirs." He swallowed, surprised by the emotion he felt simply remembering how Georges and Libby had lived for each other. "The following year, the second one—well, I still understood, but I kept expecting to see her returning, if you know what I mean."

"I know."

Aaron extended a hand. "You really do know?"

"Oh, yes. And I've been waiting for this day that had to come."

Her serene manner confused him. "This day?"

"Yes. But go on. There's still much for us to say. Last year? The third year?"

"Mmm." He sensed he was somehow on trial. "I've become very worried. You see how she is."

"How is that?"

He wasn't accustomed to interrogation, even in this gentle format. Shifting uncomfortably, he ordered his thoughts. "The sweater Libby was wearing tonight is...there are holes in it. And in the jeans. The windsuit she wore on the mountain is one of only two she owns, right?"

"Correct. She insists she doesn't need more. They can be cleaned, one each week, and then there's more money for the children. Logical, yes?"

"Logical like hell!" He couldn't restrain the outburst. "Libby's an incredibly wealthy woman. She could buy—"

"I know. I know." Mimi held up a hand. "But Libby has every reason to disdain money and what it can buy, no?"

"Because her husband was murdered for money." He felt as flat as his voice sounded.

"Of course. She trusted Jean-Claude Duclaux. After all, he was Georges's dutiful nephew, his right hand in business yet, for money, he became a madman."

"Yes..."

"For money and the power it could bring him, a supposedly charming young man murdered Libby's husband and also tried to kill her." Mimi pursed her mouth. "I think she wishes she and Georges had been poor so that he might still be with her."

"You think very clearly, Mimi."

"I've had much opportunity for close observation. But I must also tell you that, in my opinion, money has little to do with what she, er, doesn't do for herself anymore."

Aaron flexed muscles in his jaw. "What are you trying to tell me?"

"Libby's very beautiful."

"Yes," he agreed. "Probably the most beautiful woman I've ever known."

"You'd think she'd want to make the very best of herself, no?'' Mimi shook her head when he started to respond. ''Libby doesn't care anymore. And I believe she almost doesn't want to look good because she feels guilty that she's alive and Georges isn't. If she can't look good for him, there's no one else for whom she should make the effort.''

He stared. ''I see. I hadn't thought of that.''

''She wears no makeup. Her hair grows longer and is never styled.''

Aaron felt a protective rush. ''She's beautiful as she is.''

Mimi smiled and nodded. ''Very. But not because she wants to be. If a man smiles at her, she looks away…if she notices at all. She's shutting out everything and everyone she thinks might pull her away from the safe place she's made here.''

''I want to change that.'' For some reason he held back from explaining what was happening in Friday Harbor. Libby should be the first to hear. For a few seconds he felt himself moving away, back there to Washington State and to San Juan Island, where wild seas and almost daily storms thrashed the shore beneath the house where Mike and Susan Kinnear were living out their own quiet, personal drama.

''Libby refuses to have a phone,'' Mimi said, sounding remote. ''She checks the locks on doors and windows several times every night.''

''I noticed. Do you have any idea how she might react if a man actually approached her?''

Mimi shook her head, frowning. ''Not really.''

''I do. She raced away from me on the mountain.'' He wouldn't tell her all the details. ''Afterward, she more or less told me she'd thought I was some stray male who'd decided to follow her. That was before I caught up and she recognized me.''

''Ah, it's time.'' Sighing, she drank and swirled the wine some more.

Aaron didn't like the direction his thoughts were heading. ''Do you think I should encourage her to find professional help?''

''Therapy?'' Mimi laughed shortly. ''No. That's not what she needs.''

''What then? I'll do whatever has to be done, by whatever means.''

''Will you? I have your promise?''

''Yes. Yes.''

''Then persuade her to leave this place. What our Libby needs is to be loved.''

''She is loved.''

''She needs someone to love her again as she doesn't believe is possible, hasn't even considered as possible. Someone must love Libby back to what she was, by loving her as Georges did. And although she can't have children of her own, she should be close to some little ones, not simply caring for them from a distance.''

Aaron nodded. ''Exactly. And that's part of my plan.''

Mimi raised her brows.

''I mean...uh, well, getting her back with her family will show her how much she's needed.'' He'd almost spilled the part of his plan that he'd confided to no one, except Mike—who had laughed. Aaron winced.

''You have pain?'' Mimi asked.

''Oh, no.'' His face didn't usually betray any uneasiness he felt. ''I was just thinking about how I'm going to persuade Libby to come with me.''

''I see.'' Mimi looked unconvinced. ''Libby needs more than the affection of her sister.''

Aaron contained a smile. "You're right. But one step at a time will do for a start." He'd already worked all this out, but his one enthusiastic attempt to share his own brilliance had taught him caution.

"I'll do whatever I can to help you in this," Mimi said with audible resolution. "What date are you hoping to leave?"

"As quickly as possible. The tickets are open."

She cleared her throat. "It's possible—no—it *will* be best if I come, too."

Aaron hadn't considered this angle, but it made sense. "Yes, yes, of course. In fact you could be the one to insist—"

"No." She interrupted him. "I can't insist or she'll doubt I'm to be completely trusted. You must be the one to persuade, and I'll then do what she'll expect—continue to be with her at all times for as long as she desires it."

Doubting his own abilities was unusual for Aaron, but he did at this moment. "What if she won't agree?"

Mimi smiled secretively. "You have something to tell her that will force her to agree, I think."

Her insight didn't surprise him. "Tell me how you know."

"Men aren't very good at hiding some things."

He smiled. "Certainly not from some women. Libby knows, too, but she's burying her head. She's afraid to let me have my say because I'll probably confirm fears she already has."

Mimi regarded him seriously. "Exactly. That's why she wanted so badly to escape to her room. She's hiding and hoping the trouble will go away."

"She's likely to keep right on avoiding me," Aaron said. "I can't make her listen."

"Can't you?" The bright eyes pinned him. "Oh, but I think you can—and will. You have to."

A ripple of cold apprehension climbed his spine. "I'll try."

"Yes, you will. Go now. Aaron Conrad, I know one thing—Libby cares more for you than for any other human being."

"There's Susan..."

"Even more than Susan. You have become her only link to the outside world. If you don't act, and soon, it may be too late."

Aaron stood. "Too late?"

"Yes, we're starting to lose the Libby we knew. It could take a short time or a long time, but if you don't do something about it, Aaron, Libby will end up as nothing but a hollow shell with no life at all inside."

THE NARROW STAIRS to the third floor creaked beneath Aaron's feet. Upon leaving Mimi, he'd gone to the room always kept in readiness for him on the second floor above the kitchen. His plan had been to think and sleep and give Libby time to become less suspicious of him.

But he couldn't sleep and he was tired of thinking. Libby might be asleep, but if she wasn't, there would never be a better time to talk.

She still used the bedroom that had been an unfinished attic before Georges had bought the house. The uncarpeted flight of stairs was narrow and unlit. He felt his way upward and opened the door at the top. The first door inside, to a storage area, was closed. The second stood open to reveal the dim shapes of bathroom fixtures.

Under the last door, at the end of a short hallway, a slice of light showed. Unless she slept with her lamp on, Libby was also having difficulty falling asleep.

Aaron still wore his ski pants and heavy sweater, but he shivered. The cottage had no central heating, and warmth from the kitchen stove that was kept burning at all times failed to reach this floor. He didn't have to wonder why Libby insisted on staying up here instead of in one of the cozier rooms below: this had been where she and Georges had slept. He squared his shoulders and walked quietly on. Plan A was about to be set in motion, and then all this reclusive nonsense would be quashed.

He tapped her door.

"Mimi?"

"No, it's Aaron."

She didn't answer.

Aaron waited, counting to a hundred. "I'm coming in now."

When he opened the door, there was no rustling, no sound at all. Against one white wall the headboard of a simple, dark wooden bed almost reached the base of the steeply sloped ceiling. The pillows on the double bed were propped up, the covers thrown back.

Aaron ventured farther, looking around.

"I'm over here."

He jumped and opened the door fully. Libby sat on the wide sill of a window that faced the bed. Wrapped in a threadbare navy blue terry-cloth robe, her knees were drawn up to her chin.

"May I come in?"

"You already have."

"Is it all right though?"

"Oh, Aaron." She held out her arms. "It's always all right for you."

He only took time to smile before rapidly covering the small room and bending to hold her. "Libby, Libby. I'm so glad to be here...to see you. I miss you when you're so far away." The odd turning in his heart made him swallow.

"Me, too," she murmured against his chest.

Her body was too slender, her neck where he rested a hand beneath her hair, too fragile, but she felt wonderfully soft, and holding her blew away his doubts about the future.

"Sit with me." She shifted her feet to let him join her, then crossed her ankles on top of his thighs. "Do you like my little glass elevator on the world?"

He looked over his shoulder. The window was a dormer arrangement with small square panes, some as thick as the bottoms of bottles. Snow fell steadily, catching in soft, lopsided hammocks against the corner of each leaded frame.

"It's a beautiful place, Libby. I've always thought so." The cottage, at the edge of the village, was set slightly higher than the other buildings. From the window, in the glow from streetlights, he could see across white-mounded rooftops to the belfry of the minute Gothic church close to the square.

"I feel so safe here."

Absently he rubbed her ankles and turned to see her face. Her beautiful reddish hair, waist-length now, was caught forward over one shoulder. Aaron touched it with the back of his fingers, lifted some of its weight and tugged lightly.

"What are you thinking?" she asked.

The room's one small bedside lamp cast shadows beneath her cheekbones and outlined her full, parted lips. And he knew well that the goodness on the inside outshone the exterior beauty. He wouldn't let her waste herself here.

"I'm thinking," he said finally, "that you and I have shared more than most people could imagine."

She took a shaky breath and her hand went to her throat. The top button of her faded flannel nightgown was open, and Aaron didn't need a closer look to identify what sparkled there. Gold and diamonds, the last gift Georges had given Libby. She wore this fantastically expensive necklace with her old nightgown and beneath the worn-out clothes in which she skied and went through her days.

Aaron leaned back against the cold windowpanes, keeping his eyes on her. They were comfortable together. He gained even more confidence from the thought. The ghosts were going to be packed away.

"Aaron." Libby scooted her bottom along the sill until she sat very close with her arms clasped around her knees. "How long can you stay? I'd love us to ski some more."

"I can't stay," he said, and didn't allow himself to look away from the tense expression on her face. "Two days is the most I have. The day after tomorrow I'm driving back to Verona and flying out." His rented Alfa Romeo was parked in an old stable behind the cottage.

She put her forehead on her knees. "You do understand that it's not because I don't care about all of you that I have to stay here?"

"No."

"There are the children. I've got so much work to do."

"You can write checks anywhere."

When she raised her face, the stricken glitter in her eyes turned his stomach.

"This is where they write to me." She wound a lock of hair around a finger.

"You're needed on San Juan Island. Now."

"No!"

He didn't want to do it this way, but she'd forced his

back to the wall. "Libby, Susan's your only sister and she needs you."

The hand stilled, then it was tugging at his sweater, the fingers digging into his flesh. "Why? You said she was fine. Why?"

Aaron tried to capture her hand but failed. Libby anchored her grip behind his neck and brought her face near.

"This is a critical stage of pregnancy," he told her, willing his voice to sound level, unconcerned. "Six months always is, so I'm told."

"No. I knew this was wrong. I knew she should never have gotten pregnant again. Why didn't they go ahead with the adoption like they said they would? There are so many children who—"

"Libby, listen to me, please." He prayed she couldn't sense his own encroaching panic. "They're going ahead with the adoption once this baby's born. Remember they had to be married two years before they could apply, and they applied as soon as they could. But then Susan got pregnant. That happens, you know."

"Mike shouldn't have allowed it to happen. She lost three babies when she was married before, and she was told it wasn't a good idea to try again. Susan gets toxic and that's dangerous."

"I don't know about all that," he lied. "She'll probably have to have a cesarean section, though, and everything's being very carefully monitored."

Libby thought about that. "Yes, of course it is. And you said it only takes a couple of days to get there." She scooted back to her corner and wrapped her arms around her middle. "I'll come when the baby's born."

Aaron bit back the retort that he knew she'd find another excuse then if he let her. "No you won't," he said, moving her feet and standing up. "Libby, I've tried to put

this every other way I can think of and it isn't working."
Her hand found his, and he laced their fingers together.
"When I left Susan, I promised I'd bring you back with
me."

"Is...what's wrong with her?"

"You were right. She probably shouldn't have started
this pregnancy, but she did. And now... Now she *needs*
you."

"Why?"

Where their hands joined he felt spasms of shuddering.
There was no pretty way out anymore. "Because she's
afraid she might die."

3

Libby sat resolutely still in the middle of a yellow plastic-covered bench on the ferry's enclosed passenger deck.

"It's beautiful scenery," Mimi murmured. "Such seas. So magnificent and terrible."

Libby nodded. The descriptions were apt.

"These are all the San Juan Islands ahead, but the one where we're going is called San Juan, correct?" Mimi said, touching her arm.

"Yes."

"And they're part of Washington State."

"Yes." She wished she could show enthusiasm and be glad at coming back to a place she had once loved.

Aaron stretched his jean-clad legs out to cross his feet on the opposite bench. "The San Juans continue north until they join Canada's Gulf Islands in British Columbia."

Libby turned her head away. Waves, topped with what looked like splatterings of heavy cream, rolled past the green-and-white vessel's broad windows. Nothing about this—the boat, the wild seas, the distant humps of gray-green islands rising on the horizon—nothing held beauty for her. She pictured her cottage at the foot of her mountain, and snow, and the warmth of the fire.

"It's okay," Aaron said. He sat on her other side from

Mimi. "I know what you're thinking, but this is different. No Jean-Claude on this boat. No guns and threats."

She pushed her hand into his. "Don't talk about it." On a terrible night, in the hold of a ferry like this one...perhaps even this same boat, Georges's nephew had tried to send her to her death in the dark sea. He'd died instead, dragged beneath the car deck to be sucked into the propellers. And all because of his greed, his mad determination to inherit the estate of the man who had befriended and cared for him, the man he'd lured aboard a yacht in Hawaii a few weeks earlier and murdered.

"You must be excited to see your Susan," Mimi said with a cheerfulness that sounded unnatural. "It's been too long for both of you."

Libby sank lower on the seat. She and Susan hadn't been together since Libby had left Friday Harbor for Europe two and a half years ago, two months after Susan's marriage to Mike...six months after Georges's death. "I'm looking forward to seeing Susan. Things are going to change at the Kinnear house when I get there."

She felt Aaron look at Mimi, but ignored them both. "I'll do what has to be done to make sure Susan comes through this pregnancy healthy. Then I must get back to Madonna di Lago. I'm needed there."

Aaron sighed loudly. "Whatever you say. But try to enjoy the three months you have to spend here first, please. Maybe more than three months."

"It won't be longer." Grimly determined, she shook her head. "Definitely not. They'll probably set a date for the baby's delivery. Everything will go perfectly well, and I'll be able to leave Susan in the good hands of her family here."

"You won't want to stick around? Maybe spend a little

time with your new nephew?'' Susan already knew her baby was a boy.

Libby chewed her lip and studied her hand, thin in Aaron's broad tanned fingers. ''He'll probably be delivered early.'' That tan of Aaron's came from spending a good portion of his life, winter and summer, in the open air, overseeing his business. She and Susan were keeping him from that business, and it was time that stopped. As soon as possible, she had to thank him as deeply as he deserved to be thanked for all he'd done and tell him to stop worrying. He must be anxious to be free of them.

''We're almost there.'' Aaron got up. ''Let's go down to the car hold. I told Mike we'd meet above the marina.''

''They didn't need to come,'' Libby said, regretting her snappishness too late.

''I know,'' Aaron said, apparently unconcerned. ''He insisted. You really are very loved around here, you know.''

Mimi squeezed her arm again, and Libby managed a smile at her. ''I'm glad you're with me.''

''Where else would I be?'' Mimi said. ''Or Aaron?''

''Yeah. Don't forget me, huh?'' He smiled at her and started toward the stairs to the car deck.

The flight from Verona to London, then across the pole to Seattle, had seemed long. Libby shut out the recollection of how many times she'd wanted to flee, to get out of crowded places. Once in Seattle and inside Aaron's Peugeot, some of the claustrophobia had fizzled. For a while, on the drive north to the ferry terminal in Anacortes, Libby had almost relaxed as she watched the evergreen-blanketed hillsides roll by beneath a predictable downpour of early January rain.

But she didn't want to go into the hold of this ferry—never again.

As if he'd heard her thoughts, Aaron slipped an arm around her and held her tightly at his side as they clattered down the metal stairs.

"Don't go so quickly," Mimi called, her voice rising. "It's slippery."

Aaron laughed. "We like slippery, don't we, Libby?"

His attempts to divert her weren't working, but she said, "Yes," as loudly as she could.

"This isn't a mountain," Mimi complained. "These bumps don't have snowy cushions."

Libby allowed herself to be bundled inside Aaron's car. Mimi got into the back seat, and Aaron ran around to climb behind the wheel. Immediately he turned on the engine and the heat. Then he tuned in the radio—without appearing to notice that the only result was loud static—and whistled while he rubbed his hands together. "Whoa, it's a damp one. We'll have to get you to bed and rested up as soon as possible."

"I'm not sick. And I'm no more tired than you and Mimi." Libby avoided adding that since Mimi was much older than either of them, she was probably exhausted.

"Of course not," he said. "How are you doing, Mimi?"

"Tired," she said with characteristic candor. "But excited. This is all new for me. I've always wanted to see America."

Apprehension overwhelmed Libby. She sat straighter and crossed her hands in her lap. Some people might question the way she chose to deal with adversity, but she always did deal with it and would again.

Sitting still became harder. "How's Lisa?" she asked Aaron abruptly. Lisa was the woman he'd been seeing when Libby was last here.

He frowned down at her. "Lisa's now happily married

to a very nice guy with a guest house and a tulip farm in Mount Vernon.'' Craning around to look at Mimi, he added, ''That's a little place north of Seattle that's famous for its tulip fields.''

Libby was momentarily nonplussed. ''You were still dating her when you came to visit me in September.''

He shrugged. *''C'est la vie.* We were great friends. Now we're good friends. She needed a husband and children and I was too slow getting around to doing anything about that. Carl, her husband, was someone she'd known for years, and he gets around to things quicker than I do.''

Which was why he was thirty-eight and had never been married, Libby thought, irritated. Aaron needed a family. He'd be good at that sort of thing. ''I'm sorry, Aaron. You should have told me.''

''I would have if it mattered.'' He glanced at her, a smile in his eyes. ''It did matter in a way. One can come to rely on having someone there when you need them. Lisa was there for me, and I enjoyed that. But relying on someone the way you would a faithful dog isn't right, is it? And it isn't enough for the other person.''

He was fair, always fair, but even if his business interests did absorb him, Libby didn't like to think of Aaron going through the rest of his life alone.

A grinding bump meant the ferry had connected with the dock. Within minutes rows of cars were being waved ashore, and before long Aaron drove the gray Peugeot over the landing and onto the streets of Friday Harbor.

Libby looked to the left at a two-story building housing an assortment of small gift shops, a florist and an ice-cream parlor. On the upper level, undeterred by the rain, brilliant nylon windsocks twirled bravely outside the Island Clipper Company, Susan's beauty salon.

In summer the town of Friday Harbor teemed with tour-

ists and boaters. Today only a few hardy souls swathed
in a variety of rain gear leaned into the wind to stroll or
go about their business.

Aaron steered right along the street above the marina
and pulled in behind a dark red truck with a canopy.
"Here we are."

"The Blue Heron?" They'd parked beside one of Friday Harbor's best known restaurants. Painted blue, its ve-
randa was a summertime favorite with diners who flocked
to eat here, where they could overlook the harbor and the
islands beyond.

Libby was waiting for Aaron's response when her door
was yanked open. She turned to look into Mike Kinnear's
startlingly green eyes.

"Get out here now," he said, offering a hand.

She undid her seat belt and climbed from the car to be
enfolded in a bone-crushing embrace.

"It's damn good to see you," Mike said, holding her
away. "I can't tell you how much I prayed you'd come
this time."

Libby narrowed her eyes. Already she was being reminded of her supposed shortcomings. "Aaron said Susan
needs me." Looking around, she was surprised to find that
Aaron had remained in the car, but then these two saw
each other regularly.

"She certainly does," Mike said. "Wait till she sees
you."

He was a big, rugged man with sun-streaked brown hair
and clear-cut features. Libby remembered what he'd
looked like eight years ago when they'd first met. The
epitome of the impeccably dressed, executive row
"comer," Mike, still married to his equally smooth first
wife then, was undeniably very good-looking but stiff and
unapproachable. By the time he met Susan, he'd changed

professions and been divorced for two years. Firmly entrenched in his exclusive boat refurbishing business, his persona was now that of a casually successful rake. There was no mystery about why Susan found Michael Kinnear irresistible.

"Hey, Mike." Aaron had opened his door and stood with his arms folded on the car roof. "I'm going to give Mimi a little tour of the island. Then we'll be over."

"Yeah," Mike said.

"Just a minute—" But Aaron didn't hear Libby. He'd already slammed his door again, and the car swerved rapidly away. "You haven't met Mimi."

"I will at the house," Mike said. "I want to get you to Susan."

Libby looked all around. "Is she in the restaurant?"

He frowned and bent over as if fascinated by his worn running shoes. "Aaron told you how it is with Susan?"

A pulse thudded in her head harder and harder. "I'm sure there's nothing to worry about. Let's go in."

"Susan's at the house. I thought you knew I'd be coming alone."

She opened her mouth to take a deeper breath. "When Aaron said you'd meet us, I assumed..."

"Susan has to rest a lot. Her blood pressure—"

"She'll be fine. I'll see to that."

"Of course. I'll take you to her. She was so afraid you wouldn't come." Mike opened the passenger door of the red truck and helped Libby inside.

She felt she would choke. Trembling, she watched him walk from the curb, sorting through a bundle of keys. He wore an unsnapped yellow oil slicker with the hood thrown back. His hair dripped and his jeans clung to his thighs, but he didn't appear to notice.

Mike climbed behind the wheel, slammed his door and

started the engine. The windows fogged and he turned on the defroster. A sharp odor of wet rubber and wool filled the cab, and Mike wiped at the windshield with a big, rough hand. "This weather isn't helping," he muttered.

Libby crossed her arms tightly. "The weather isn't helping what?"

"If it was nice, Susan could sit outside. She's going stir-crazy in the house."

She didn't want to ask the question, but she had to. "How bad is it?"

The engine roared. Mike maneuvered a U-turn and drove away before answering. "If she does exactly as she's told, they'll both be okay. Pregnancy Induced Hypertension they call—"

"I *know* what they call it. I asked how bad it is."

Mike was silent for a while as he peered past the wipers, which barely coped with the downpour. "It isn't bad and it won't be if she continues to be careful."

Easy for him to say. "What does that mean?"

"Special diet, monitoring blood pressure—and rest. That's the rub. She's got to rest. If she doesn't, they'll hospitalize her, and she says she won't do that."

"She'll rest. I'll make sure of it."

"I knew you'd help. You wouldn't have believed what it took to stop her from coming with me today." He slowed for a stop sign, then drove on toward the west side of the island. "I'm not sure I shouldn't have brought her, anyway. She'll be uptight waiting, and that doesn't help a thing."

Libby's fingernails dug into her palms. "You can leave everything to me now."

She felt him look at her. "This is my responsibility, Libby. Thanks for wanting to take over, but Susan needs me, too. And I need her. We *both* need your help."

Whatever happened, she must keep some perspective. Mike should have made sure this pregnancy never happened, but Susan loved and trusted him; Libby couldn't allow her anger with the man to show.

"Aaron said...he said Susan was afraid. I expect he meant nervous."

"I doubt it."

Libby fixed her eyes on Mike's face. The corner of his mouth turned sharply down.

"What happens if she doesn't rest and...what could happen?"

"You want it word for word?" His voice was tight and low.

No! "Yes."

"What did you say?"

"I said, yes, tell me." The beating in her throat was suffocating.

"Severe headache, drowsiness, loss of memory. Those are called dangerous symptoms that things are getting worse. Also vertigo, vision disturbances. That can progress to nausea and vomiting, breathing difficulties, rapid heartbeat and so on."

Libby grabbed the dashboard with both hands and held on. "But even if that happens she'll get over it."

"Oh, hell! Damn it all to hell!" He accelerated, and the screaming of the truck's tires ripped at Libby's nerves.

"Mike?"

"The doctors say any stage is reversible, but Susan thinks they're just trying to keep her quiet. And so do I. If she doesn't remain stable, the final stage is convulsions." His voice rose, pounding Libby's ears. "And then, if we get real unlucky, she'll die."

Libby saw his knuckles, white on the wheel, the rigid lines in his face. This was Mike, Susan's Mike, who had

been so good to Libby when she'd needed all the help
she could get.

She took several calming breaths and put a hand on his
arm. "Nothing bad's going to happen. Trust me. I won't
leave Susan's side until the baby's born."

"IS IT JUST FANTASTIC in Italy?" Anne sat on the floor
beside the den stove.

"Italy's wonderful," Libby said, sounding distracted.
"I think you should be in bed, Sue."

From her spot in Mike's leather recliner, Susan's attention switched from her stepdaughter to her sister. She
didn't much like what she saw. "Rest doesn't have to
mean horizontal. Just having you here makes me feel
rested." And she'd feel even more rested if Libby weren't
skinny and apparently wearing thrift store rejects.

"Tomorrow I'm sending Mimi over to Seattle," Libby
said. Her wrists protruded from the sleeves of a pink-and-
white striped sweater. Probable instructions to "dry clean
only" had obviously been ignored. "We'll get the latest
books written on this sort of thing."

Susan didn't dare to do more than let her glance pass
Mike's. "We have all the information we need, Lib."

"Yeah," Anne said, shifting closer to Susan. "I can
tell you anything you want to know about what's going
on. Can't I, Susan? It'll be great for her to have you here
while I'm at school, though."

Susan eyed her stepdaughter with amusement. Three
years ago, at age twelve, Anne had been a budding punk
rocker, complete with semishaved head and an all-black
wardrobe. Today, still diminutive, but definitely more
woman than girl, Anne wore her smooth blond hair in a
short angular wedge. Subtle shading had replaced the
black circles that used to ring her bright blue eyes. Mike's

daughter had inherited the best of her father's and her mother's looks. She was a knockout, and an unshakable free spirit. Anne had also decided to adore, protect and, if possible, to own her stepmother.

"Come nearer the fire," Susan told Libby. "You look cold."

When Libby arrived, she'd kissed Susan, holding her as if she might break, and promptly retreated to a straight-backed chair against a wall.

"Come on." Susan motioned. "I feel as if I'm shouting at you across a canyon."

Libby rose instantly and moved to an ottoman beside Susan's chair. "You look..." Her eyes went to Susan's abdomen. "Does every woman...?"

Susan chuckled. "No, every woman doesn't blow up like a blimp. I've gained too much weight." She deliberately kept her smile in place. "I'm afraid it's one of the symptoms of this darn toxicity. I feel ugly and too big for my skin."

"You're beautiful," Mike said predictably, coming to stand behind her. He massaged her shoulders, and she closed her eyes. "We think she's more beautiful than ever, don't we, Anne?"

"Yup. Sure do." The lighter touch on Susan's knee was recognizable as the girl's who, when she wasn't in school, hovered in almost constant attendance.

Susan glanced at Libby. "I'm looking forward to meeting your Mimi."

"Yes." Libby checked her watch and sucked in her bottom lip. She jumped up and went to stare out the window at a darkening late-afternoon vista. "They've been gone over an hour. The roads are slick. I hope Aaron's being careful."

Susan tilted her head back to catch Mike's eye. He

raised a brow and said, "Aaron spends months of every year driving on packed snow, remember? And he's damn good at it. Relax Libby. Anne, go and ask Connie to make us some coffee."

Anne hooked an elbow over Susan's knees. "She'll only say dinner's in an hour."

"Anne—"

"I don't feel like coffee," Libby said, still peering through the windows toward the first terrace of grounds that rose in tiers to the street above. "And I read that caffeine isn't good for pregnant women."

Susan stifled a groan. "Nothing's good for pregnant women."

"You should have thought—" Libby spun around, her face paling beneath her mountain tan. "You have to think of these things, Sue. You have to be guided."

"I know. You're right." Indeed, she had to be guided—by Mike, by Aaron, by Anne, by Connie Bangs, their housekeeper, and even by Mike's dad, Lester, who left his cottage on the bluff behind the main house several times a day to make sure she was "behaving herself." Susan sighed. Everyone had to guide her, even Aaron's well-meaning mother, Marjorie, who'd engineered two outrageous excuses for coming from Seattle to Friday Harbor in the past month.

Now there was Libby. But Libby was here for special reasons known only to Susan. Oh, Mike and Aaron guessed some of it, but not the most important elements. Aaron had swallowed the bait Susan had given him and fed it neatly enough to Libby to get her to come. Now it was up to Susan to do the rest of the work.

She covered one of Mike's hands on her shoulder and guided him to her side. He knelt, arms crossed on the arm of the chair, and smiled into her eyes.

Susan's love for him brought tears to her eyes, and she buried her face against his neck. "I'd like to be alone with Libby for a while," she whispered.

When she raised her head, Mike kissed her gently and mouthed, "Okay." He got up. "Anne, the photos of the Dutch schooner came. I saved them till you could look at them with me."

"Yeah?"

"Yeah." Fascination with old vessels was a passion he shared with his daughter. "Let's go through them now. There's time before dinner."

"Great." Anne stood, but turned back to Susan. "Is it okay?"

Susan found herself avoiding Mike's eyes once more. "Absolutely, kiddo. Libby's here and I'm not going anywhere." In concentrating so intensely on Susan and the sibling Anne could hardly wait to possess, the girl was steadily excluding her father. So far Mike had made little comment, but Susan hadn't missed his bemused and sometimes exasperated reactions.

"Libby," she said when they were alone. "Please sit where I can look at you. We need to talk, and something tells me we're not going to have much time alone."

"I wish Aaron would get back." Libby approached, glancing over her shoulder at the window.

"He will," Susan said gently. "I'm sure he's trying to give us some time together."

"I worry about him."

So Susan was beginning to notice. "Libby, you don't see him for months at a time. He travels constantly and—"

"I know. I just wish he'd get back now, that's all." She sat on the ottoman again.

"We have some things to discuss," Susan said. The

baby rolled, thrusting out some small extremity, and she rested a hand on her belly. "You already know that if things go badly—"

"They won't. We won't let them."

Susan shifted to a more comfortable position. "We'll try not to."

"Is the baby moving?" Libby asked. She reached tentatively toward Susan's abdomen and, when Susan nodded, splayed her fingers in a light touch. The serious expression on her face cleared, transformed by a delighted grin. "That's wonderful. What does it feel like?"

"Ooh, like a thousand elephants shifting wood in a Thai logging camp." Wiggling her head, she pointed to a moving bump. "Maybe that's an exaggeration. More like a bunch of birds heading south for winter."

"A little boy," Libby whispered.

"Mmm. Michael Georges."

Libby bowed her head. "Oh, Sue. He would have loved that."

"I've got something big to ask you." She'd intended to be more subtle, to take more time, but she didn't know how many chances they'd have to talk. "Mike doesn't relate to this. He won't even talk about it. But someone has to."

"What?" Libby drew back, sitting stiffly upright.

"If something happens to me—"

"It won't. Mike's right. We don't have to talk about it."

"You're probably both right. But I do have to talk about what will happen if the baby lives and I die." She couldn't tell this sister who loved her that the baby mattered most.

"They won't let you die," Libby almost shouted. "Mike said they'll take him if you start to get worse."

She wouldn't dwell on Mike now. Not so many years ago, she wouldn't have believed there could be as much love as she felt for him. Now she felt that same overwhelming emotion toward this child of theirs, and he had a right to his chance at life.

"Susan, they'll schedule a cesarean section, and it'll be done as an emergency if necessary."

"Not unless they can assure me the baby's developed enough to survive."

"Sue!"

"I mean it. Nothing's going to change my mind. And if… Libby, if necessary, will you look after my baby?"

In the silence that followed, Susan watched Libby open her mouth as if short of oxygen.

"Mike has to work. Anne's got school and, anyway, she's too young. Connie would do her best, and I'm very fond of her, but I want to know my baby will be with someone who'll love him the way I would."

Libby got up slowly and bent over Susan. "Stop it! Don't talk like this. I'm going to look after you, and you're going to be looking after your own baby in a few months."

"I hope so." Susan lowered her eyelids wearily. "Please, I can't keep on fighting with this. If you don't want to do it, say so. I know you'll eventually marry again and—"

"Never." The retort was vehement.

"We won't talk about that now. But, Libby, regardless of what you decide to do with your life, would you tell me you'll always make sure my little boy's okay…and try to help Mike and Anne if they need it?"

"I…Susan, in Italy…" Libby's voice trailed off.

"Will you at least promise that if I die, you'll stay and look after the baby until Mike marries again?"

"Susan, I can't believe this." Libby sat down with a thump. "You're thinking your life away, and I won't have it. Do you understand? You are not to think or talk like this again."

Not again? Not talking about it was possible. But for now she would get her way. "Fine. But humor me. Agree to my request and we'll drop the subject."

"I…yes. All right. Yes!"

A FEW HOURS RESPITE from the rain had slowed the dripping from the eaves outside Mike's office. He scooted his chair and himself toward the corner of the window where he could look down on one of the boat sheds. Workers moved around the shadowed hull inside.

"I thought you'd have left us by now," he said to Aaron. "Mission accomplished with flying colors and on your way."

"Soon."

"Aren't you anxious to be in the thick of things again?"

"Mmm."

Aaron was facing the first serious threat to his control of Alpine Ridge. A tip in the delicate balance he'd established since issuing private stock placements and he could end up without the resort that had been his life for years.

"Any further approaches by Falk?" Dennis Falk was the empire builder who wanted to add Alpine Ridge to his chain of resorts.

"Not to me."

"Do you think he's buying blocks of stock?"

"Probably."

The uphill work this conversation represented began to grate on Mike. "You'd know if he went after the big chunks." These were owned by Aaron's two most trusted employees, the men responsible for the hands-on running of the company.

"Mmm."

Mike was used to Aaron's long bouts of silence and his penchant for working problems through alone, but in the four days since he'd arrived with Libby, his air of preoccupation had become oppressive. It was that damn irritating reserve that had caused Mike to engineer time alone with Aaron this morning, that and the way he was hanging around, which was very odd for a man beset by potential heavy business battles and whose most common phrase even in the best of times was: "Well, got to get on."

"Susan and I really are grateful to you for managing to get Libby here."

Aaron grunted.

Mike began to simmer. If he didn't keep his temper in check, he'd be blurting out that, although he was very fond of Libby, he was already getting sick of falling over her every time he wanted to be with his wife.

"I do think Libby's going to be good for Susan in the weeks to come." Not that she had to sit at her elbow *every* minute of the day…and evening. "I've promised her we'll have her back in Italy as soon as we can."

"Not if I can help it."

"What did you say?"

"I said—I said, over my dead body, buddy."

Mike let his feet slam onto the floor. "Cute. What does that mean?"

"Don't pretend you don't know Susan and I have both been worried about Libby."

"No," Mike agreed cautiously.

"You don't know her as well as we do. What's happened since Georges died hasn't been healthy. She's become a recluse, bordering on eccentric.''

"I'd noticed the eccentric. I wouldn't have said the recluse bit fitted. She's under my feet every time—'' He stopped on a silent whistle and felt heat flood his face.

Aaron shot him a malevolent stare. "You agreed it was a good idea for Libby to come here.''

"It was. It was.'' Mike held up his hands. "Sorry about the slip. It's only that I'm not used to sharing Susan *all* the time. Amend that. I'm not used to sharing her with anyone other than Anne all of the time.''

Aaron sat on the desk, one booted foot on the floor, the other swinging. "Libby will be good for Susan. But I also hope Susan will be good for Libby. She's grieved too long. And shut herself away too long.''

"And maybe been coddled too long,'' Mike muttered. "Time she did something useful on a full-time basis. Hands-on variety of useful.'' If Libby weren't a wealthy woman, she'd have been forced to make her way in the world again.

"Damn it,'' Aaron said explosively. "Don't talk about her like that. Not to me. Is that clear?''

Mike rocked back in his chair, startled at the reaction.

"I asked if you've got that straight.'' Aaron leaned closer to Mike. "Libby means a lot to me. I intend to make sure she's happy again. And I know she needs to be actively involved in something. I'll see to that, too.''

"Right,'' Mike said faintly.

"Do you remember what I talked to you about a couple of months ago? About Libby?''

Mike searched his overcrowded brain. Two months earlier had been when Susan first showed signs of pregnancy complications. "Not really.''

"You laughed.''

"Oh, yeah, sure. Some nutty scheme to get her involved with friends back here so she'd leave Italy."

"Damn you, Mike." Aaron began to pace. "Not just friends. *A* friend. Someone she'd enjoy doing things with."

Pointing out that Libby was obviously not interested in doing anything but hovering over her sister would probably be ill-timed. "She's determined to return to Madonna di Lago and carry on working with the orphans."

"Libby's orphans aren't in Madonna di Lago. They're all over the world. You and I know that all she does there is write big checks and mail them. She can do that here or anywhere." Aaron paused for breath. "And she's not going back. Not for a very long time, if ever."

"I see." Intrigued, Mike tented his fingers. "And how do you intend to accomplish that?"

"I'm going to find her a husband."

4

Aaron walked ahead of Libby up the wooden steps leading to the second floor of the little shopping complex that housed Susan's salon. At the top he stopped and looked back.

Libby smiled at him and forced light into her eyes. She didn't want to be here, but coming as far as Friday Harbor on Susan's contrived errand had been one way to help make up for not agreeing to go with Aaron to Alpine Ridge.

"Come on. Hurry it up there, or we won't have time for lunch." Aaron smiled back at her and, as usual, the glint in his eyes, the glimpse of very white teeth catching at his lower lip, warmed Libby.

She held the hand he extended and climbed up beside him. No rain today, for the first time in the five days since she'd arrived, and Susan's garish wind socks twirled and flapped in a dry, brisk breeze.

"Maybe this would go faster if you went into the salon and I waited for you at the sandwich shop." They had decided to buy picnic food and eat in a wind shelter above the marina.

"Nothing doing," Aaron told her. "Jeff and Molly would never forgive me—or Susan—if we didn't make sure you saw them today. Susan promised you'd be in."

She should be with Susan now. The instructions from

the obstetrician were that she should have total rest and absolutely no stress. Libby felt stress in the Kinnear household, and she had to figure out how to make sure Susan remained oblivious.

Aaron's big, warm hand tightened around hers. He pulled her close to the salon windows. "We're blocking the way."

"Mmm." She stood, facing him, and rubbed a finger up and down a flexed tendon in his wrist. In a heavy dark green parka over a navy blue polo shirt and jeans, he was solid and reassuring—and he must be tired of trying to understand her reactions.

"Are you really having a hard time with all this?" He spread wide an arm. "Coming back?"

Libby tipped back her head to gaze at a gray sky. "I'll get over it," she told him. "Each step I take for the first time is tough. But it's not so hard the next time I take it."

"That's my girl." Aaron pulled her close, held her face to his chest and rested his chin atop her head. "I knew this was what you needed. You're going to be just fine. Leave it to me."

She closed her eyes. "Yes." Let him feel good, whatever it cost her to go through the motions. Eventually Susan's baby would be safely delivered and it would be time to return to Italy, wonderful, gentle, safe Italy…and the cottage beneath the mountain.

"Why don't you change your mind and come to Alpine Ridge with me?"

"I can't."

"You can. We'll call the house and say you'll be back tomorrow morning. I have to look in at the offices in Seattle, then we could drive straight to the Ridge in time for dinner. You'd enjoy staying at the lodge. We could take a few runs this evening and—''

"I don't have any clothes or equipment and—''

"Anything you need we can get. In case you've forgotten, ski equipment's part of my business. And you always loved night skiing.''

He was so dear, so important to her. "Not today, Aaron.'' Another moment and she'd be asking him not to leave, telling him how much it had meant to have him close by in the past few days.

"It would do you good to get away.''

"I'll come soon, okay?'' She looked up at him and rested her fingertips on his square jaw. His lips parted. Each feature, each mannerism and expression was familiar. When they were apart, she saw his face in her mind often—and wished for a moment like this when she could touch him.

"Libby, please come.'' Flecks of black showed in his dark eyes. He took her hand from his jaw and held her fingers against his chest. Smiling, he said, "For me? I could use some time with someone I don't have to be anyone but myself for.''

"I…'' She wanted to go. She could. Whatever he said, no matter how emphatically he declared himself content, Aaron wasn't happy. Libby drew in a breath that seared her throat. She must help him, but not today, not when Susan expected her back in a couple of hours. "Let me go at my own pace, Aaron. I'm not ready to leave Susan yet, not till I'm absolutely sure she's stable.''

"I'll let you off this time,'' he said slowly, but he sounded disappointed. "But don't try to get out of coming into the salon. Not that you're going to get the chance now.''

Before he could turn, Libby heard a whoop, and a

young blond woman was beside them, her arm snaking through Libby's. "There you are! Susan just called to make sure you'd arrived. Jeff!" she called over her shoulder. "Tell Susan they're here."

"Hello, Molly," Libby said, unable not to smile into the woman's guileless blue eyes. "We'd better get inside before you freeze." Molly wore a loose pink corduroy dress that didn't begin to disguise that its wearer was very pregnant. Not, Libby was sure, that Molly wanted to hide the fact.

Libby was drawn away from Aaron and into the warm little salon with blue-and-gray decor and a lovely old wooden reception desk that Susan had refinished herself years ago when she'd first opened her doors here. One change Libby immediately noticed was the addition of two new stations, in a central island, where operators she didn't recognize worked. Pearl and Lynne, both in their thirties, stood in their old spots along the back wall of the room, smiling broadly at Libby. She returned the smiles and waved.

Jeff, Susan's manager and, as she frequently said, a very talented hairstylist, waited beside the desk. "She's here, Susan," he said into the phone. "Yes. Thanks. Wonderful. I'll have the staff look through the catalog. Yes. See you soon. Bye." He hung up and gave Libby a shy smile that she knew wasn't in keeping with his personality.

Everyone—with the possible exception of Molly, who was renowned for her sunny disposition—treated her carefully. She hated that, but although any awkwardness was her own fault, there was no way to change what had gone before or what had resulted from old horrors. And the drama had unfolded before these people. They remembered, were thinking about it all even as she looked at them.

The door closed behind her and Aaron stood at her shoulder. "How're the mom and dad-to-be?" he asked lightly.

Jeff put an arm around Molly and looked her over with a deep fondness that filled Libby with sad-sweet nostalgia.

"We're making the best of a difficult situation," Jeff said, and Molly punched his flat middle playfully. Undeterred, Jeff continued. "It isn't easy having our manicurist insist on afternoon naps. Then there are her moods. Pregnant women have the worst moods, y'know."

Libby took a deep breath. "Still roaring around on the motorcycle, Jeff?" Tall, thin and dark, physically Jeff didn't look any different than he had three years earlier.

He grimaced. "Are you kidding? A man allows himself to be tricked into marriage, and the next thing he knows the Harley's gone and he's chugging around in a station wagon. Can't face any of my friends."

"Tricked!" Molly's voice soared and her eyes became round. "What does that mean?"

"Nothing, my love." Jeff held up his hands and tried unsuccessfully for an innocent air. "Absolutely nothing."

"Doesn't sound like nothing," Molly retorted. "Sounds as if I got pregnant to make you marry me. Well—"

Jeff swept her into his arms, closing off the rest of whatever she'd intended to say. "Molly always speaks her mind," he said, grinning over her head. "She was going to try to say that I chased her until she caught me. And probably that we were married before she got pregnant. You know how they defend themselves."

Aaron laughed and Libby glanced at him. His broad grin made him look like the carelessly happy man she'd met ten years ago. She narrowed her eyes. What was he thinking as he joked with Jeff about becoming a father? And when he was with Mike, what then? Aaron, perpetual "uncle." Libby set her jaw. He should be married by now, with children of his own, and as soon as the timing was right, she'd tell him as much.

Molly didn't hurry, but finally struggled free, her short hair mussed. "We were married before—for months. And engaged for a year before that. I should have had the sense to see I was making a mistake. You're a creep, Jeff. Now I'm going to name the baby after my mother for sure."

They both laughed, and Libby felt her own reserve fizzling. "Do I dare ask what your mother's name is?"

Aaron settled a hand on the back of her neck and brought his mouth close to her ear. "Wouldn't if I were you."

She raised her brows at him over her shoulder. "I've always had more guts than were good for me."

"Good," he said, his smile disappearing. "We'll both have to remember that."

"My mother's name is Petal."

A short silence followed before Aaron, sounding choked, repeated, "Petal? Petal…er, kind of delicate, I guess."

"Kind of sickening," Jeff said, not quite under his breath.

"Why Petal?" Libby asked.

"Just a minute, honey," Jeff said, his expression one of glee. He pulled forward a chair. "Sit. You'll need your strength for this."

Molly ignored the chair and pulled herself up to her full height of five feet. "You tell."

"Oh, no. I couldn't deprive you of your own story."

A bright flush whipped over her face. "It was my

grandfather's idea. When my mother was born and my grandmother nursed her… When my mother was nursed for the first time, she spread her hand on my grandmother's…breast.'' Molly raised her chin. ''Grandpa said her little fingers looked like flower petals, so they called her Petal. And what's wrong with that?'' She stared around, her eyes daring anyone to laugh.

''Not a thing,'' Libby said when she could find her voice. ''It's sweet.''

''Yeah,'' Jeff said. ''Sweet. Something any kid would enjoy explaining at school.''

''What if you have a boy?'' Aaron said. Libby jabbed an elbow into his solid midsection and enjoyed his audible grunt.

''If it's a boy,'' Molly began, ''his name will be—''

''We haven't decided,'' Jeff interrupted. To Libby he said, ''We'll continue this fascinating discussion later. I'm sure you have a few other things to do. Susan said she was sending a supply catalog in with you.''

''Yes. Here it is.'' She pulled it from the inside pocket of her parka and handed it over. ''Aaron and I are going out for lunch. It's sure good to see all of you.'' And to see how happy they were and that there were still people around who lived normal, relatively uncomplicated lives.

''I'm worried about Susan,'' Molly said softly. ''Sometimes I feel guilty because I'm so well while she's having all this trouble.''

''Don't, Molly,'' Jeff said, squeezing her arm. ''Libby's worried, too. She doesn't need—''

''Yes, I do.'' Libby gave Molly a quick hug. ''I need to know my sister has friends who care about her. But she's going to be all right, so don't worry. A couple of more months and her little boy will be in his crib and I'll be on my way back to Italy. You'll see.''

The stillness that fell was something she couldn't miss—and she pursed her lips, furious at what she'd said. A steady glance passed between Jeff and Aaron. Were they all plotting to keep her here?

Jeff shifted and looked away. "Yes, well..."

"Yes," Aaron said. "We'd better get on. Good to see all of you." His wave took in the entire salon.

"We'll see you again soon, won't we, Libby?" Molly said, sounding anxious.

"I...yes, I'll come in again. Take care of yourself. And you take care of her, Jeff."

His attention was already on his wife. "Oh, I will. I'm a lucky guy."

Once outside again, Libby made much of rezipping her rust-colored parka.

"It feels so good to be here," Aaron said, settling an arm across her shoulders as they clomped slowly down to the row of shops beneath the salon. "I should be frantic, but somehow—"

Libby stopped, drawing them both to a halt. "Frantic? About what? What's wrong? Do you know something about Susan you're not telling me?"

He smiled and urged her on. "No, of course not. I only meant I worry about snowfall at this time of year. We're still recovering from the last light year we had."

"There's plenty of snow, isn't there? I listened to the local ski news, and they said all areas are operating. Alpine Ridge has a base pack of—"

"Yeah, I know." He seemed to be rushing her along. "It's just me. You know how I am. Bit of a pessimist."

He reached the sandwich shop, and she tried to read his face as she passed him in the doorway. "You've never been a pessimist." Sometimes too quiet, frequently impossible to figure out, but never a pessimist.

"I've changed," he said, and a corner of his mouth twitched. "What are you going to have to eat?"

"You haven't changed. You're too old."

"Gee, thanks."

"I don't want you to change." She did want to know what was really on his mind, not that he'd tell her until he was ready, or made a slip.

Aaron paused, his eyes on hers. "None of us stays exactly the same, Libby. The world makes sure of that."

"Yes." She felt watched, and glanced at the woman behind the counter. "I guess I'll have tuna on rye. I used to like that."

As she stepped away, Aaron caught her arm. He bowed his head. "You and I will always be the same.... We'll always be the same for each other, won't we?"

She blinked rapidly and told him softly, "Yes."

"That's what matters, isn't it?"

"Yes."

STEAM COATED the panes of the kitchen's French doors. With two fingers Anne made squiggly lines, vertically on one piece of glass, horizontally on the next.

A pot, cracking against a stove burner, made her wince. Connie was mad. Connie had been mad almost from the minute Mimi Sedillot had walked through the front door for the first time.

"You're sure Susan likes these, er, what are these beans?"

Anne closed her eyes and waited for Connie's response to Mimi.

"Lima beans," Connie said, enunciating each word. "Susan likes them. Libby does, too."

"I doubt that. The smell is..."

Anne lifted her shoulders slightly, mimicking, without having to see, the Frenchwoman's way of shrugging.

"The smell is a good old-fashioned American smell," Connie said sharply. "Libby's too thin. A few more beans wouldn't go amiss there."

"Libby has always been very slim," Mimi said, sounding serene. "She eats adequately and well. I make sure of that."

A chair scraped. "I'm sure Susan and Libby know how lucky they are to have you two ladies."

Anne had forgotten her grandfather for a moment. Lester had a way of blending into his surroundings. Usually that made her feel good. Today she wished he'd go away. She wished they'd all go away—except Susan.

"Susan would be better for sleeping in her bed in the afternoons," Mimi said. "The chair doesn't support her back."

Again came the sharp smack of metal on metal. "Susan doesn't sleep in the afternoon. She rests quietly."

"She should sleep," Mimi said. "A darkened room where there would be no question of interruption would be preferable to the den."

Anne rested her forehead on the cold glass and stared outside. She wanted Libby to get back from Friday Harbor. When she was here, Mimi and Connie stayed out of each other's way.

"How was your school today, Anne?" Mimi asked.

"Fine." The fuchsia bushes that edged the patio were bare, like giant, multilegged gray spiders.

"Shouldn't you do your homework?"

"She'll do it when—"

"You don't have to worry about Anne, Mimi," Lester broke in on Connie.

"No," Connie said. "She likes to unwind a bit when she gets home from school."

Usually she did that unwinding with Susan, but today, when Anne went into the den, Susan had been drowsing and Connie said she wasn't to be disturbed.

"Would you like some more coffee, Lester?" Mimi asked.

"That would be great."

"Pour me some while you're at it, Lester." Connie, who regularly said that she'd worked "all her fifty-some years and it kept her young," never made any secret of her opinion that Lester shouldn't be "coddled."

"No, no," Mimi said. "Stay where you are, Lester."

The baby would be all right, Anne thought. And Susan. They'd all do things together again and stop being afraid. Her friend Brad had said his mom had had high blood pressure when she was pregnant with him and they were okay.

"Libby seems tired to me," Connie said. "When she was here after...after Georges died...then I made sure she ate plenty and got lots of sleep."

"Connie took wonderful care of Libby," Lester said.

"She was exhausted when she got back to Geneva," Mimi announced. "I was worried. But she improved with time."

"What she needs is to be here with family, not in another country with...well, you know."

Mimi said something Anne didn't understand.

Lester cleared his throat. "You've obviously done wonders with Libby, Mimi. She had a hard time, poor girl."

"She needs clothes," Connie commented.

Anne drew back her lips from her teeth, bracing herself for Mimi's response. Connie was sort of big, and she liked bright stuff with colored stones and fringes and things.

Mimi looked like a picture in one of Susan's magazines, a picture of some rich woman, dressed just right, posing in her big, expensive house somewhere.

"Libby hasn't had the need for an extensive wardrobe," Mimi said. "She isn't concerned with such things. Her interests are for others. The, er, less fortunate. They have become her work."

"Who's looking after that Italian cottage while you're here, then?" Connie asked.

"A woman from the village will check."

"Not the same as being there yourself, is it?"

They would fight on and on, Anne thought. In quiet voices—because Susan wasn't supposed to know and get upset—they'd argue about everything. And Lester would keep trying to make everyone happy, everyone all right.

"Oh, Anne," Connie said. "I forgot. Brad called just before you got home. He wants you to call him."

"Thanks," she muttered. Brad was perfect, the best boy she'd ever met, but she didn't want to talk to him now.

"There you all are."

At the sound of her father's voice, Anne turned. He was smiling and looked rumpled, the way he did most days when he got back from the yard. He brought his special smell of fresh air and wood shavings with him.

"Hi, son," Lester said. He got up. "We're holed up keeping things as quiet as we can."

Anne watched the smile leave her father's face. "I looked in on Susan. She's asleep. That'll do her good. How's she been today, Connie?"

"She's doing as well as we can expect." Connie sounded like a nurse.

Maybe she'd go and sit with Susan, anyway, Anne thought.

Mimi, a white apron over her dark blue dress, shook

her head. "She's lethargic, Mike. That isn't good." She folded clean towels into a precise pile on the kitchen table.

"Yes," Lester said, watching Mimi.

He watched Mimi a lot, as if he really liked her. Anne had noticed that. And he'd started dressing better.

"Mimi thinks Susan should rest in her bed instead of a chair," Lester added.

Anne looked at her grandfather. Lester was old, of course, seventy-one on his last birthday, but his white hair was thick and looked nice and you could still see why people said her father was like him.

Mike had begun to take off his parka. He pulled it back on as if he'd forgotten what he was doing. "The doctor said she should do what made her most comfortable as long as she was very quiet."

"Sometimes one has to guide the sick," Mimi said. She smoothed a towel against her chest. "She may not be thinking as clearly as she should."

"Susan knows what she wants," Connie said, and gave her bleached hair several ferocious pokes. As always, her bangs had frizzed in the heat from the stove and stood above her round face in a pale halo. "We've all got to keep level heads, is all."

Mimi pursed her lips. "She doesn't look well."

"I thought she did," Mike said. His throat moved sharply. "This morning—"

"Stop it!" Anne's heart beat very fast. She looked at Lester. He didn't get upset. "Grandpa, you tell them. Tell them to be quiet."

Mike came toward her. "Anne, sweetie—"

"No!" Her father was like the rest. He didn't understand. "Grandpa, Susan's okay, isn't she?"

He nodded, but his eyes looked worried.

"Then tell them." She evaded her father and reached the door to the hall. "I can take care of her and she's gonna be okay again…and the baby."

5

"Can Falk pull it off?"

Aaron took the glass of Scotch his father offered him. "If everything goes his way, he can. Not that I intend to sit back and watch him take over the Ridge."

"Sit down." Bill Conrad, slightly stooped, definitely gray, but still tall, rangy and handsome, waved toward his own wing chair. "It's been too long since we saw you. You don't take enough time for yourself, son."

"I had over a week off when I went to Italy," Aaron said. He settled back into faded blue velvet and planted his feet on a worn leather ottoman. "That was only three weeks ago."

"Do you any good, did it?" Dark eyes made fierce contact. "Wouldn't say so myself. Wait till your mother gets a good look at you."

Aaron knew better than to fence with his father in his present mood. He allowed his eyes to wander over the incredible view presented through a wall of glass in his parents' sitting room. Cantilevered on the second story and overhanging a hillside, this place wasn't the spot for those with a fear of heights. Incoming airline crews had similar outlooks. The harshly ragged peaks of the Olympic and Cascade mountain ranges—snowcapped against a dazzling blue sky today—formed a glittering ring around clusters of multicolored glass buildings in Seattle's and

Bellevue's business centers. And immediately below the Conrads' aerie, Lake Washington was spread out—cool blue, satiny and dotted with the craft of intrepid winter sailors.

Aaron smiled a little. His parents had bought their showplace retirement home in Seattle's eastside suburb of Bellevue three years earlier. Supposedly they had both been ready to reap the benefits of a successful life of hard work by shedding the old and acquiring new and "tasteful" everything.

The chair Aaron sat in, the smaller matching version that was his mother's, and many other mementos of a long marriage were crowded into this room where the senior Conrads spent most of their time: proof that they hadn't been able to let go of their past.

Bill Conrad sat in his wife's chair and picked up a pipe from an ashtray atop a table set with polished pebbles. Aaron remembered his father's rock collecting and polishing days and the many arguments his parents had had about what to do with the products. This table had been one effort.

"This Dennis Falk," his father said, tamping tobacco into the bowl of the pipe, "what sort of man is he?"

"Ambitious. Possibly unscrupulous."

"Hmm." He struck a match and puffed, watching the flame draw down while bursts of smoke issued from the stem. "Got a lot of resorts like yours, has he?"

"No. He's got a lot of other types of resorts. Hawaii, California, Florida, the south of France, Adriatic coast, Ibiza—on and on. No ski outfits. Evidently he thinks this is what he needs to round out his empire."

"Why yours?"

"Because it's the best." He laughed and caught his father's eye. "Isn't that what you and I know?" It had been Bill and Marjorie Conrad's unhesitating willingness to invest a staggering amount from the fortune they'd made in dry cleaning that had helped launch their only child's enterprise. Aaron had paid everything back, with interest, but he would never stop feeling his folks were partners in his business.

"Any idea what his holdings are so far?"

Aaron leaned his head back. "An idea. Nothing solid. But I do know he's making overtures to Roger. You know what it would mean if Falk could get his hands on Roger's block." Roger Chandler was Aaron's second-in-command and, next to Aaron, the biggest stockholder in Conrad Enterprises.

His father grunted. "If he needs Roger to pull it off, he can forget the whole deal. Roger's your man."

"I know. But I'm still worried. I've got someone checking out some of the biggest recent purchasers. If my hunch proves right, Dennis Falk could show up behind most of them. He's moving on me, Dad. And he isn't going to give up easily."

"Be honest, son. Are you shaky?"

"Not by most people's standards and not if I'm left alone for another couple of years."

"If you're nervous, why not start picking up more of your own paper yourself? Your mother and I—"

"No! No, Dad. Not this time. And it would take more capital than either of us could come up with easily. The new lifts and the lodge renovation were essential, but they were giant undertakings. I'm cut to the bone in a lot of areas. The shops are doing well, and my investment with Mike is beginning to pay off, but none of it's enough to make me totally comfortable."

"You're sure we can't help?" His father pulled sharply on his pipe and drew his brows together.

"Sure. Don't worry. The outlays I've made will pay off in two to three years. We'll make it." He'd like to feel as certain as he hoped he sounded.

Aaron's mother entered the room, pulling off her black woolen coat as she came. "Why didn't you call and say you were coming? I wouldn't have gone out." Her rounded cheeks were reddened by the sharp wind that bent the firs outside, and her short, silver-dusted brown curls were tousled.

"I didn't know I was coming until I drove off the freeway at Coal Creek Parkway and came up the hill. I was on my way from the Ridge to the Bellevue store."

Marjorie Conrad smiled, crossed the room and bent to hug him. "You look tired," she said quietly against his cheek.

When she released him, Aaron swallowed some Scotch and smiled at her. "I was in Friday Harbor again yesterday. Susan mentioned you'd been over to San Juan to visit last weekend."

She chewed her bottom lip before saying, "She isn't well, Aaron."

"I know. But she'll be her old self once the baby's born."

"There's a way to go before that." His mother perched on the ottoman and smiled at Bill. "We should go over to the island again. Take her some of that soup she liked the last time."

"Libby's there now, remember. And Mimi Sedillot. I think Susan's about on overload with caretakers and well-wishers." He didn't want to say that he thought all the attention could be becoming more of a hazard than a help.

"How is Libby really?" His mother wrapped her green plaid skirt around her legs. "She seems very quiet. When are you going to bring her here for a proper visit with us?''

Aaron immediately saw Libby's face, her golden eyes as they'd looked when she waved him off at the ferry yesterday afternoon. He'd only been able to get away from Seattle for a few hours. She'd agreed to meet him in Friday Harbor for lunch. They'd talked and laughed…and shared long silences when there had seemed no need to say or do anything. He'd enjoyed it. But he'd made zero progress with his plan because he couldn't seem to find the right words to broach the subject. ''Libby's…she's…I'm not sure.'' For a moment, just before they'd parted, he'd thought there was something she'd wanted to ask him. She'd drawn in a little breath, parted her lips and touched his arm where it had rested on the rim of the Peugeot's window. But then the touch had become a pat, and she'd smiled before turning away. And he'd driven aboard the ferry.

''What do you mean?'' Marjorie said. ''Not sure?''

''Oh, I don't know. Nothing, I guess. I'm glad I managed to persuade her to come back to the States.''

''I doubt if she'd have done it for anyone else,'' his mother remarked.

Aaron's parents had first met Libby when she'd been engaged to Georges, and since then had become fond of her.

''Libby responds to people she knows she can trust. I just had to be a bit firmer than usual with her.'' And devious, not that he intended to admit that aloud.

''It wasn't just anyone she trusted,'' Marjorie said. ''It was you. Libby knows what a special man you are.''

Aaron laughed. ''Could you be a little biased?''

''I know what I'm talking about.''

"What do you think of Roger Chandler?" Aaron suddenly asked.

"Huh?" His father stirred. "Why do you ask?"

Aaron set down his glass. "It was a simple question. What do you both think of him?"

"A good man," Marjorie said.

"Absolutely trustworthy," Bill added. "No question of his loyalty, if that's what you mean."

"I thought you'd say that. I wasn't thinking about business, though. Do you like him as a man?"

They both looked momentarily blank.

"Well, you've met him enough times," Aaron persisted. "You've met his girls." Roger, divorced for years, had custody of twelve-year-old twin daughters.

"He's done a good job as a father," Aaron's mother said at last. "Imagine that wife of his deciding she didn't want to be married anymore like that. Or be a mother."

"Doesn't seem to have slowed him down," Bill commented.

"He loves Sonja and Hilary," Aaron said. "But I do think it's about time he had a partner to share everything he's accomplished…and the girls could probably use some feminine influence at their age. Anne's certainly benefited from having Susan around."

"I'm sure you're right," Marjorie said. She got up and poured herself a Scotch and water. "Anyway, why don't you bring Libby over to see us?"

"As soon as I can pry her loose from Susan. I did such a good job… Um, she thinks she has to stay within shouting range at all times. But that'll pass if I have my way."

"Good," Bill said emphatically. "You make sure she gets out and about a bit more. If she spends more time with you, she'll soon see—"

"Yes," Marjorie said, walking between Aaron and Bill.

"You look after Libby, Aaron. She knows you have her best interests at heart. Bring her over. Maybe she could come for the weekend."

"I doubt it." Their warmth toward Libby encouraged him. "She is lovely, isn't she? I've never met anyone else like her."

"Exactly," Marjorie said. "I'm glad you've done something about it."

"She's so caring, Mom. The way she worries about needy children makes you feel you should be able to fix everything for all of them—for their sakes and to make Libby happy. I want her to be happy."

"Sure you do, son. And she will be." Bill held his pipe between his teeth while he talked.

"She will be if I have my way. I never knew exactly why she and Georges couldn't have children of their own, but whatever it was didn't seem to upset either of them too much. Seems to me Libby would take someone else's children and make them her own in no time. A ready-made family would be perfect…with the right man, of course."

He pulled his lower lip between his teeth and thought about what his next step should be. Care was the key. Care and careful overseeing on his part. He must be sure Libby wasn't hurt again.

His parents weren't saying anything. Aaron smiled at them. They stared back stolidly. When he'd been a kid, that had been their reaction to anything he did that didn't please them, which made no sense here and now. He broadened his smile. "Don't you think I'm on the right track?"

"I'm not sure what track you're on," Marjorie murmured.

"Yes, you are. Roger! He's a good man, Mom. And

the girls are sweeties. Libby would love them and be good for them." He puffed out his cheeks. "And she'd be good for Roger. He's getting too set in his ways."

"Men on their own tend to do that," his mother said. She looked...what? Irritated?

"Yeah, well, Libby deserves to be happy and I'm going to make sure it happens."

"What if she and Roger don't, er, click?" Bill asked.

Aaron glanced at his watch and leaped up. "Good grief. I'd better get going, or it'll be midnight before I get to my place. I've got to put in some hours at the office."

"Answer your father," his mother said quietly. "What if Libby and Roger don't hit it off?"

"Why wouldn't they? She's lovely—inside as well as out. And bright. She cares about people. I tell you, Libby is the most worthwhile woman I've ever met, the only one who ever made me feel I'd do anything to make sure she has the happiness she deserves."

"Really?" his father said, helping Marjorie to her feet. "We'll see you out."

At the front door, annoyed at their lack of enthusiasm for his project, Aaron faced them both. "Why wouldn't it work? Can you think of a single reason why any eligible man wouldn't rush to have a woman like Libby?"

Bill Conrad looked from Marjorie to Aaron. "She certainly is a prize, son," Bill said. "You're right. I can't imagine why any sane eligible man wouldn't jump at a chance to be with a woman like Libby. Of course, there could be the odd man around who'd have difficulty knowing what he'd be missing if he passed her up...until it was too late."

6

Mike broke into a run. Up the terraces in front of the house he raced, looking from side to side along the leafless hedges and rows of dormant rose bushes as he went. "Susan!" His stomach clenched. "Susan, where are you?"

He spun around, peering toward the house. The last thing she'd want was for the rest of the entourage to pour forth as a search party.

"Where are you?" he muttered under his breath. When he reached the road, he checked inside the garage and found the venerable yellow Volkswagen she refused to part with in place. His own truck was parked where he'd left it, close to the gate.

Suddenly needing to see Susan, to hold her, he'd left the boatyard just before noon, telling the girl who came in to answer phones that he'd decided to go home for lunch. He *needed* Susan. Where the hell was she?

Unnoticed, he'd gone into the house by the front door and straight to the den. She hadn't been there or in their bedroom, and when he'd stood in the hall, listening to conversation in the kitchen, he'd been able to tell that Libby, Mimi and Connie assumed she was resting upstairs.

"She sounded in a good mood, didn't she?" Libby had said.

"It's because she's more comfortable in bed," had been Mimi's answer.

"She wants some peace anywhere she can get it," Connie had retorted, producing a heavy silence and prompting Mike to slip out.

This wasn't the first time Susan had defied her doctor's orders and gone out, but it hadn't happened in the three weeks since Libby had arrived...until today.

He retraced his steps and loped rapidly down the fan-shape flights of white stone steps dividing the terraces, which held lush green lawns and brilliant flower beds in spring and summer. The flower beds, his occupational therapy in the years alone after his divorce from his first wife, had become an ongoing joy when he and Susan had worked outside together.

Without Susan there would be no point to any of this. He reached the side of the house. Thinking like that was wrong when he had Anne to consider, but he couldn't help it. He was scared, and there was no one he dared allow inside his fear. Even Anne had turned away from him since Susan had become pregnant, not that he would have burdened her with his doubts.

Lester's cottage. Mike's heart pounded. He hadn't heard Lester in the kitchen, which probably meant he was at his cottage—with Susan. Susan and Lester had become great friends. That was exactly where she'd go if she were desperate for a change of scene.

A shingle path edged by tall, waving grass wound down from the house to the guest cottage his father called home and on to the beach below the bluff. Running, Mike slid with every step as he bounded downhill. Fine mist buffeted him in gusts.

Out of sight of the rest of the property, with an unobstructed view of the ocean, the shake roof and dark siding of Lester's small domain complemented the architecture of the main house. Not bothering to knock, Mike reached the door and threw it open. "Hello! It's Mike. Where are you?"

There was only the ticking of the grandfather clock in an alcove beside the whitewashed stone fireplace...and silence.

Magazines cluttered the comfortable, gray damask-covered couch and well-worn maple coffee table. Papers and books scattered on the dining table by the window attested to the accounting work Lester, a chartered accountant until he retired, still did. Mike's decision, three years ago, to have his father continue working for him had been largely responsible for Lester pulling himself out of the worst crisis of his life. At that time a penchant for heavy gambling and writing bad checks had been revealed, and it had taken inventive footwork to keep Lester out of court.

All that was behind them, thank God. Mike rubbed his face. Susan must be somewhere in the main house, after all. In his hurry he must have missed her.

He shut Lester's door with the thought that it should be locked...and caught sight of a flash of red far below.

A pulse hammered in his throat. Slowly at first, gaining speed, he started down the track to the beach, squinting against the mist. For an instant he paused, raking back his hair. Wearing her old red parka, Susan sat on the massive, weathered wooden mast that had been their favorite spot since their first date.

"Idiot," he said. "Little idiot." He heard his voice break and skate upward.

By the time his feet hit damp sand, he could hardly breathe. Slowing down, he took in great gulps of air. He mustn't—*must not*—overreact.

Circling, trying not to surprise and shock her, he approached from an angle where she'd see him coming. Her face was averted. Her hair, longer than usual and blowing around her face, shielded her eyes.

He didn't have to get too close to see the dejected set of her shoulders.

A few feet away he stopped. Susan swept the hair from her face and saw him. Immediately she pushed herself to her feet.

"Sit down, damn it." Mike strode over, spread his hands on her shoulders and planted her back on the timber again. He pursed his lips, cursing his lack of control. "Just sit there, Susan. I'm going to have to get you back up in phases."

She smiled at him, but her mouth quivered and her too-bright eyes attested to tears already shed. "I needed some fresh air."

"So you walked all the way down here?" He clamped his fists on his hips and looked at the sky. No inspiration there. "The doctor said you might not be totally rational about this, but he didn't say you could become suicidal."

"I'm not suicidal."

"What would you call it when someone deliberately does something they know could help them to die?"

"It couldn't!" Her near-scream made him take a step backward. "I am resting. I rest all the time. Fresh air's good for anyone, and I feel calm down here."

He spread his hands helplessly. "Of course you do." Carrying her safely back up on his own wouldn't be simple, not with the steep grade and the shifting shingle underfoot. Aaron had been here yesterday and wouldn't be back for several days. Lester certainly couldn't help.

"Sit with me," Susan said in a small voice. "Hold my hand."

Mike did as she asked, slipping an arm around her shoulders and coaxing until she relented and leaned against him.

"Sorry I yelled," he said. "I decided to come home and have lunch with you. When I couldn't find you, I went nuts."

"How far could I go?"

"I'm just saying I couldn't find you. And you aren't supposed to go anywhere, Susan. You know that."

"I'm ruining things for everyone."

His stomach turned. "Don't say that. All that matters is getting you through this."

"And the baby."

"Of course, and the baby. I think of the two of you as a unit." He made himself laugh. "Anyway, Michael Georges is tough enough for both of you."

"I'm the one who was supposed to be tough enough for both of us."

Depression was another thing the doctor had warned about. "Okay, misery. I'm going to get you back into the warmth." He leaned to peer into her face, wrinkling his nose. "I don't suppose a piggyback appeals?"

She smiled and bowed her head. "*America's Funniest Home Videos* would probably buy a tape of that. Don't make me go in yet."

"It's cold out here. And wet."

"We're both dressed for it. Hair dries."

"But...okay, for a little while longer, then. Give me your hands."

Suppressing the temptation to say what he thought about her absence of gloves on such a day, he swung to sit astride the mast and rubbed her fingers briskly.

"I wish I was well enough to help Libby."

Susan's sudden announcement caught Mike off guard. "If you'd been well, she wouldn't have come."

"I know, but…"

"Sorry. I shouldn't have said that."

"But you're right." She pulled a hand free and rubbed his thigh.

Her touch brought a mixture of arousal and tenderness. And he'd once been afraid to love someone again? He almost laughed at his own stupidity. Even if he…even if he lost her, it would be preferable to never having had Susan in his life.

Negative thinking was destructive. "Don't worry about Libby. She finally seems to be relaxing a little."

"I'm not sure I agree with you." Susan glanced around. "I'm surprised she hasn't tracked me down yet."

They both laughed.

"I must admit—and don't think I don't love her—but I admit I occasionally get… It might be nice to spend a little time together without your sister hovering on the sidelines."

"She's only making sure I'm okay."

"I know. I think she's decided she can *will* you through this."

Susan's smile vanished. "I hope she's right. I wish she'd spend some time thinking about her own future. She mustn't go back to Italy and hibernate again, Mike."

"We may not be able to stop her." He glanced seaward and back at Susan again. "What do you think about Aaron lately?"

The smile resurfaced. "His behavior? Hopeless case, I'd say. He's really got the knight-in-shining-armor bit bad. He'll save the damsel in distress or else. Is that the message you get?"

"Yep." Mike agreed. "Sure is. Do you realize he's

made more trips over here in the past three weeks than he has in three years?''

"Close. And he still hasn't managed to whisk Libby away to meet Roger. I really thought he'd pull it off when he got her into Friday Harbor for lunch yesterday. Do you know how old Roger is, by the way?''

He inched closer. "Only thirty-five. He seems older, doesn't he?''

"Years. Pretty staid, I'd say.''

"Yeah. Not exactly a social trail burner.''

Susan wrinkled her nose. "He never seems to talk about anything but business.''

"Of course, some women prefer quiet, predictable men.'' He pulled up the collar on her parka and hitched the neck of her sweater higher. "So I'm told, anyway.''

"There's a difference between quiet and dull.''

He met her eyes. "I guess.'' They'd avoided deep discussion of Aaron's master plan for Libby.

Susan frowned and gazed into the distance. "Aaron's a quiet man.''

"Yes.'' He sat straighter.

"He sure isn't dull.''

"No way.''

"I'd say women would find Aaron mysterious. He's handsome and successful...and he's got that way of... He looks interesting.''

Mike crossed his arms. "Is that a fact?''

She colored slightly, in the special way that never failed to charm him. "I only meant that as a dispassionate observer, I've noticed that Aaron is very appealing. I suppose I'm saying I can't understand how he's managed to stay single.''

"More talented than most of us probably.'' He grinned.

Susan scowled at him. "I would have said less lucky.''

"True," he agreed hastily, but was still grinning. "Why did you bring up Aaron?"

She shrugged. "No reason, really. Probably because I've seen more of him lately and I've got too much thinking time on my hands."

"Probably." Her response had disappointed him, but obviously he'd better keep his notion that Aaron and Libby would be perfect for each other to himself. It was an impossible idea, anyway. Libby and Aaron would never see each other as anything but friends. A totally dumb idea.

A voice came to him on the wind. Looking toward the bank, he saw an unmistakable mass of red hair streaming behind a scrambling figure.

"It was nice while it lasted," he muttered. Susan had begun to look relaxed and, regardless of the rain and wind, he'd like to remain right where he was—alone with her.

"Hey, you two!" Libby hit the beach and broke into a run.

Susan tightened her grip on his hands. "Be nice. She's easily hurt and she means well."

"Of course I'll be nice." He smiled as Libby arrived beside them. "Hello, Libby. Out for a jog?"

Susan pinched his palm.

"No." Libby panted, planting her feet apart and bending over, audibly catching her breath. "What are you doing down here, Susan? You frightened me to death."

"I'm fine," Susan said gently. "I needed a walk, that's all."

Libby's head came up. She stared at Mike accusingly. "Why did you bring her down here without saying a word? You know she's not supposed to have any exertion. Not *any* the doctor said."

"I—"

"Don't you think you've done Susan enough harm?"

Several moments of shocked silence passed before they all spoke at once.

Mike overrode Susan and Libby. "We're all on edge. We'd better calm down, hadn't we?" He hadn't missed Libby's occasional oddly hostile glances. She'd just explained those. She didn't think Susan should be pregnant and blamed him. Well, so did he, but there was nothing to be done about it now.

"I'm sorry," Libby said. "That was out of line."

"Forget it." He thought about it day and night.

Susan looked stricken. "Libby, if you mean what I think you do, you're wrong. I was the one who was careless."

Mike got up. Somehow he had to take the explosive tension out of this encounter. "We're going to have to take this slowly. Libby, will you put your arm around Susan's waist?"

"And Mike didn't bring me down here," Susan said as if she hadn't heard a word he'd said. "I came because I'm sick of hearing all of you bicker over me in the house. Mike found me down here, just like you."

Libby wrung her hands and looked helplessly at him. "I'm sorry."

"You're sorry. I'm sorry." He shrugged and managed a smile. "We're all sorry. And now we're all going to forget it."

"I want you two to like each other. And—" Susan stopped, her lips parted "—is that Aaron?"

Gathering her banner of hair in one hand, Libby swung around. "Aaron," she called, and there was no mistaking the relief in her voice. "Hi!"

Mike chewed the inside of his lip thoughtfully. His sister-in-law was glad to see her friend. Very glad, indeed.

Of course, the fact that Aaron was breaking up a nightmare conversation might have something to do with the animation. But she was definitely glad to see him.

Aaron strode toward them, apparently unaware of the wind ripping into him through his gray business suit, making his jacket flap and his red tie stream over his shoulder. He waved at Mike and Susan, then concentrated on Libby.

"What are you doing here again?" Libby said.

"I shouldn't be." Aaron gave a wry grimace and gathered her into a quick hug. "To be honest, I need diversion, and you're about it as far as candidates go right now."

"Poor guy," Mike said. He looked at Susan, but she still appeared preoccupied.

Aaron laughed. "I didn't mean that the way it sounded. I was supposed to go back to the office and decided I couldn't face it. Anyway, don't you know I'd rather be with you than with some of the nicest people in the world?"

Mike snorted. Susan grinned, then laughed when Libby socked Aaron's vulnerable middle.

"Just for that," Susan said, "you don't get invited to dinner."

"Yes, he does." Libby held Aaron's arm. "We need him."

"We sure do," Mike agreed, and quickly added, "to help get Susan back to the house."

Aaron looked at the sand-coated tips of his obviously expensive black loafers. "Of course I will. But I can't stay."

Mike raised his brows.

"I'm begging," Aaron said to Libby. "Please save me, Lib. Come back to Seattle and be my date for dinner."

A beat passed before Libby gave her predictable shake

of the head. Mike met Susan's eyes, and their brows went up in unison.

"Please, Libby," Aaron said. His tan turned intriguingly ruddy. "I'm meeting a business associate and…and his, er, friend. I really ought to have someone with me."

"Why?" Libby's hands found her hips beneath the old rust-colored parka. "Did you say you had a date? Do you always escort someone? Doesn't the guy know you're single or what?"

Aaron appeared so miserable that Mike was tempted to try to bail him out. Only tempted. He cleared his throat.

"No. It's just that it makes it tough when you have to entertain some…well, woman you don't know. While you're having a business dinner, that is."

"Ah."

The amusement on Libby's face brought Mike a flash of pure glee.

"What you're asking me to do is to come along and entertain the dumb broad while *the men* talk." She dropped her voice.

"No, it's not like that." Aaron raised imploring eyes to Mike's, met an innocently blank stare and scowled. "Yes, that's exactly it. Why should I lie to my best friends. I'm in a jam and I need you, Libby."

Consternation immediately replaced amusement. "Oh, Aaron—" Libby turned up her palms "—I would if I could, but Susan…"

"Go," Susan said. "I'm fine."

"No."

"Yes," Mike heard himself say, far too emphatically. "You go, Libby. It'll do you good to get away for a few hours."

"But, Susan…"

"*I'll* stay with Susan. Okay? I won't go back to the yard today."

"But I don't have anything to wear and—"

"Something of mine will fit," Susan said. "Pre-pregnancy, that is."

Susan laughed, and Mike. Libby didn't laugh. Aaron waited, his attention solely on Libby.

"Well, I suppose so, then."

"Good!" Mike rubbed his hands together. "That's settled. Aaron, take Susan's other arm, would you, please?"

With Susan supported between Aaron and Mike, the four of them started toward the cliff.

Libby moved ahead.

"Who did you say this dinner was with?" Mike asked.

"How are you doing?" Aaron said, bending over Susan.

"Great."

Mike frowned. "Who's going to dinner with you, Aaron?"

Aaron scrunched his face into an unreadable message. "Uh, Roger Chandler. He's an associate of mine." When Susan raised her face, he shook his head and aimed an exaggerated nod at Libby's back.

"I see," Mike said, trying to sound neutral. The whole thing should seem funny, only, ridiculously, he was disappointed.

At the top of the slope Libby stopped and waited. "Let Susan catch her breath."

Susan smiled and paused dutifully. She looked better than Mike had seen her look in weeks. He checked his watch. "What time is this—What time is your dinner reservation?"

"Eight." Aaron appeared newly interested in the horizon.

"There won't be time to get back tonight," Mike remarked.

Libby frowned.

"I won't leave till you're here again tomorrow," Mike added hurriedly. "Don't worry about a thing here."

"Let's get to the house," Susan said, waving Aaron ahead until he fell in beside Libby and they all continued to walk. "Mike and I will do beautifully for a few hours, Libby."

"But I'll have to get a hotel room," Libby said over her shoulder.

"Don't be silly." Aaron took her elbow and urged her on. "You can bunk at my place."

"Perfect," Susan said. "I haven't been to Aaron's condo for a while, Lib. Report back on how messy it is."

"I will."

"Perfect," Mike said under his breath.

7

Roger Chandler looked more animated than Aaron ever remembered seeing him. Leaning toward Libby, smiling as he waited for her verdict on eggplant satay, the man appeared totally engrossed. He also appeared to have forgotten Aaron existed and hadn't mentioned business once in the hour since they'd all met and Roger had made his apologies for showing up alone. His date, he'd explained, wasn't feeling well. And he'd sounded convincingly sincere.

Libby worked a piece of vegetable from a skewer, expertly used chopsticks to put the food in her mouth and chewed. "Mmm. Good." She turned to Aaron. "Do you like it?"

"Yeah. I've been coming here regularly ever since the place opened. Great food and walking distance from my condo." He put brown rice on his plate. "Southeast Asian food is definitely—"

"Do you really like it, Libby?" Roger interrupted with no apparent qualms.

"Very much."

"You don't find it too spicy?"

She considered. "No." Her hair, pulled back from her face into a single French braid, fell forward over her shoulder in a long, glinting rope. Candlelight made her tawny eyes glow and cast shadows beneath her cheek-bones. She was so lovely.

Roger had paused, his chopsticks in midair as he stared at her. Definite case of infatuation at first sight, Aaron decided. And Libby showed signs of liking Roger, too. This was working beautifully. Aaron pushed food around his plate. He wasn't hungry.

"I'm sorry your friend's ill," Libby said to Roger. "I'd have enjoyed meeting her."

Aaron was instantly on alert. Roger had agreed to all this "to please" Aaron, and he'd played his part well, but one slip could ruin everything.

Roger cleared his throat. "She's er, well, to be honest, I think the illness was an excuse." His eyes downcast, he shrugged. "We've known each other a long time, and perhaps it's a case of getting too comfortable…or bored. She needs excitement and I always have to consider my daughters."

Realizing his mouth was open, Aaron closed it around the rim of his wineglass. He would never have guessed old Roger had it in him. Honest Rog was fibbing like a pro.

Sympathy radiated from Libby. She put a hand on Roger's wrist. "It's nice to meet a man who puts his children first. The world is full of people who become parents because it's the thing to do, then find they don't have any real interest in the responsibility parenting entails."

Aaron ran his tongue inside his cheek. What a routine. Roger was playing Libby's strings like a master musician who knew his instrument intimately.

"Sonja and Hilary keep me hopping." Roger's grin was genuine. That was no act. He did adore his kids. "Do you know what a Ralph Lauren shirt costs…for a twelve-year-old?"

"No," Libby admitted, smiling slightly. "I'm a bit out of those things. But I'm sure they're expensive. Do they have to have them?"

Roger, of medium height with slightly thinning blond hair, had pushed back his jacket and tucked his fingertips into his pant pockets. His white shirt fit well over a trim body. No fat around the middle, Aaron noted. "I can see you need education in the preadolescent girl department." Roger placed the back of a hand theatrically to his brow. "*Everyone* wears them, Dad. All our crowd." Animated, as he was now his blue eyes sparkled and he appeared young and... Aaron flared his nostrils. Some women might find Roger appealing, he supposed.

Libby laughed and leaned even closer. "I guess I really am a long way out of it. Heavy peer pressure even at twelve, huh?"

Aaron drummed his fingers on the table. Roger might not be Mr. Excitement, but he had the magic ingredient: motherless daughters.

"I understand you do a lot of work with homeless children," Roger said, serious once more. "Does that make you feel overwhelmed sometimes?"

Libby nodded. "Very. The needs only grow. But I don't let myself dwell on that. The one way to be useful is to keep working and telling yourself you'll do as much as you can."

"Very wise. I'd like to hear much more about it," Roger said.

"I'd be glad to tell you." Libby glanced around Wild Ginger's dimly lighted but charming main dining room. "Would you excuse me while I find the ladies' room?"

Roger leaped up and held her chair. Aaron half rose and quickly sat again as she walked away. Susan's black woolen sheath would be knee-length on her. On Libby the hem hit several inches higher. As she passed other tables, men's eyes flickered from the top of her shining red-gold head down to her long, long, shapely legs encased in black silk stockings. Susan had crowed over how wonderful it was that she and her sister had the same size feet. The plain black pumps Libby wore were very high, probably bringing her close to six feet, and every inch was delicately sexy. Aaron frowned. Obviously he was going to have to take very good care of her, because she didn't seem to realize the effect she had on men.

"She's something," Roger whispered. "Beautiful and sexy."

Aaron scowled. "She's a very nice woman."

"Oh, yes. Certainly." Roger rearranged his napkin. "I noticed how nice she was immediately. It'll certainly be a pleasure to be her friend…if things work out. How's it going so far, d'you think? Am I doing okay?"

"Great." He shouldn't feel morose. "She's fragile, Roger. What she needs are some friends to draw her out."

"She's very gentle." Roger's eyes took on a dreamy quality. "Ethereal."

Aaron stared. *Ethereal?* Coming from Roger's lips? "That was quite a job of improvisation you did? Neat footwork."

"Well—" Roger grinned "—I thought it might be easier if Libby believed there wasn't anyone else in the picture now. Not that there is, but…"

"I know," Aaron said shortly. "But play it cool, huh? Don't get carried away."

Roger turned pink. "This was your idea."

"I know." Aaron let his muscles relax and smiled. "And I'm glad you two like each other. I guess I'm just a bit nervous. Libby's been through a lot and she's very important to me."

"Would it be appropriate to bring up her, um, tragedy?"

"No!" He bowed his head. "Sorry, Roger. Overreaction. Libby's still very scarred, and that's one area we should continue to avoid—until she's ready to talk about it." Which showed no sign of happening.

"Do you think she'd accept an invitation to do something else?"

"I'm not sure. We could engineer another meeting and see how it goes."

So far Aaron had only revealed the tip of his great idea to Roger. His friend might need to be held back from pursuing Libby rather than encouraged. This must be taken in slow, careful steps. It might be wise to look for an alternate candidate in case Roger didn't work out.

"Here she comes," Roger said softly. "Are you sure I shouldn't just ask her out?"

"Quite sure." Aaron watched her approach. She walked with slow grace, her hips swaying. "If we rush her, she'll dig in her heels and retreat."

Libby sat down. "I must apologize for the way I look," she said to Roger. "This is my sister's dress, and she's much smaller than me. I didn't expect to be going out while I'm here, so I only brought casual clothes."

"The dress fits you." Roger made an airy gesture. "It looks as if it were made especially for you. It does great—"

"I like it on you," Aaron cut in.

"It's too short," Libby said. She'd reddened. "I didn't realize how short until just now."

"You've got spectacular legs," Roger said blithely. "Why not show them off?"

"I'm sure Roger doesn't mean—"

"Thank you, Roger." Libby touched his hand. "You say all the right things for the ego."

Aaron slumped against his chair.

"I'm a man in an all-female household," Roger said, managing to sound both resigned and satisfied with his lot. "I've learned how fragile you women can be."

Libby wrinkled her nose. "We can also be very strong. But you're right. We do respond to a male who makes an effort to understand."

"The right woman makes a man want to understand," Roger said, patting Libby's arm. She smiled at him.

"Want to understand," Aaron mimicked under his breath.

Libby turned to him. "What did you say, Aaron?"

"Er, it's an art, learning to understand."

Two puzzled pairs of eyes regarded him until he signaled the waiter for more wine.

"I'm going to have to do something with this hair," Libby remarked. "I didn't realize how long it had gotten."

"Long hair is wonderful," Roger said. "I'll bet it's really something when you wear it loose."

Aaron looked at the ceiling. He couldn't believe it. And he couldn't take much more. And he was out of line. This was what he'd hoped for and everything was working perfectly.

"My girls are growing their hair," Roger said. "They're both dark with brown eyes...like their mother."

In the small silence that followed, Libby's gaze slid to Aaron. She bit her lip. "I'd love to meet them sometime."

Roger nodded, not looking at anything in particular. "I'd like you to, but not if it's an imposition."

"Oh, it won't be."

Aaron chewed a knuckle.

"I love children," Libby continued. "Not that I've spent much time with any. I'll have Aaron talk to you about a good time."

"Speaking of time," Aaron said. "You'll want to catch an early ferry in the morning, Libby. We'd better get you set with a bed for the night."

"That's right." Roger slapped his brow. "I'd forgotten you weren't staying in town. Look, there's plenty of room at my place. The girls are sleeping over with friends."

Aaron knew he hadn't misheard. Either Roger truly was gullible, or he thought Aaron was. "I was talking figuratively about finding the bed," he said smoothly. "Libby's staying with me. That way I can drive her to the ferry in Anacortes in the morning and look in on the Everett store on the way back."

"Oh, of course." The hint of disappointment in Roger's eyes wasn't something Aaron imagined. "But remember, Libby. Anytime you need a place to stay when you're in Seattle, my house is yours."

"Thank you," Libby said, smiling warmly.

Roger held her chair while she stood. "I'll look forward to seeing you again."

"Yes."

This matchmaking thing was one of his talents, Aaron decided. Watching Roger help Libby with her coat, he found himself picturing them together—alone. He turned away.

"What a lovely night," Libby said as they waved Roger Chandler off in his sleek black Jaguar. She turned up her face to the sky. "It must be just for me."

Snow fell softly, and she stuck out her tongue to catch a flake.

Aaron laughed. "You baby. Come on. Home to the fire before we both freeze."

"You're the baby," she grumbled, allowing him to bundle her along Western Avenue. "You're always complaining that you're cold."

"No, I'm not. I spend half my life in the snow."

"And you moan about it."

"I love it." He leaned down to peer into her face. "I make my living out of it."

She put her arm around his waist but didn't say she was grateful for his warmth. Susan's coat really was too small, and too thin for this weather.

Cars splashed by, throwing up sprays of slush. To the right, along the waterfront, the lights of more vehicles shone in an elevated stream along the viaduct.

They broke into a trot until Libby fell over her heels and they slowed down, giggling.

"I didn't realize Roger was going to be someone who worked for you."

"For years. I guess I never thought to mention him."

She didn't, Libby realized, know much at all about the makeup of Aaron's extensive organization.

"Do you two have dinner often?"

"Watch where you step." Aaron pulled her closer to shop windows. "Umm, it's nice to have a chance to talk business in totally neutral surroundings sometimes."

"Mmm." She thought back over the evening. "You didn't talk much business, did you? Was that my fault?"

"Oh—no, no. Not at all. It must have been a good time for Roger and me to relax. You made that possible. Here we go."

They ran across the slippery street, and Aaron let them into the foyer of the building where he lived.

"Evening, Mr. Conrad."

"Evening, Jim." Aaron greeted a security guard stationed discreetly behind a rosewood desk in a corner. "I'll take the bag now." They'd dropped off Libby's overnight case on the way to dinner because there had been no time to stop.

A gilt-lined elevator whisked them to the courtyard outside Aaron's penthouse condo.

"You still like this place?" Libby asked, as Aaron unlocked his front door and ushered her inside. He'd already bought the condo the last time she'd been in the States, but there had never been an opportunity to visit.

Aaron closed the door and slipped her coat from her shoulders. "I like it fine. I don't spend enough time here, particularly in winter."

"Always on the move between the Ridge and the Seattle office?"

"And the stores." He hung his own coat in a closet, then appeared to dither.

"Well, show me."

Aaron grimaced. "I get a bit careless around here."

She tugged off the shoes that had been hurting her feet all night and sighed. "That feels so good. Are you telling me you're a messy housekeeper?"

"I'm telling you I can't remember what the place looked like when I left this morning."

Anticipating the worst, and looking forward to giving him a bad time, Libby walked across short-piled gray carpet to a big L-shaped living room.

Low-slung black leather couches and chairs, glass-topped tables, two walls covered with white lacquered bookshelves, the facing white stone fireplace flanked by walls of glass overlooking Elliott Bay—all were expensively masculine and not a thing was out of place.

"Aaron, you're a fraud."

When he didn't respond, she turned and discovered he hadn't followed her. He still stood in the small hall, a hand over his eyes.

Libby pulled the hand away. "I said you're a fraud. You know this place is immaculate."

A grin transformed his face. "Of course, Friday, the cleaners came."

She hauled him along behind her. "I'm disappointed, Aaron. I was looking forward to telling Susan you live like a slob."

He took off his jacket and tossed it over a stool. "Sit here." Without waiting for a response he deposited her in a chair by the fireplace and bent to light logs already arranged atop kindling.

"That's better." He rubbed his hands together, went to a drinks cart and poured brandy into two glasses. "This'll warm us up on the inside."

For Aaron this was too much light chatter and too much keeping busy with small tasks. "Sit down," she said, eyeing him covertly. "You must be tired."

"No, I'm not." But there was a tightness about his mouth and a watchfulness in his eyes. "What do you think of Roger?"

Poor Aaron. He thought he was so subtle. "A nice man, a wonderful father. I imagine he's good at his job, too." And not Libby's type…if she had a type anymore, which she didn't.

"He's as solid as a rock," Aaron said. He rested an elbow on the mantel, crossed one foot over the other and swirled his brandy. "His wife left him to bring up the girls on his own. I've never heard him complain once."

"You don't complain about something you love," Libby said quietly. "Even if it gets a bit much sometimes, which it probably does for Roger."

"It may, but he doesn't talk about it."

"You really like him, don't you?"

Aaron drank some brandy before saying, "Yes. He's one of the most solid men I've ever met."

This was becoming repetitive. Libby decided "s*t*olid" might be equally appropriate but wouldn't dream of saying so.

"You liked him, too, didn't you?" Aaron said.

Libby stifled a sigh. It was all so clear. Aaron wanted her to meet people, to do things. He'd decided she needed someone who would entertain her...and share his self-imposed responsibility for making sure she was happy.

"Libby?"

"Yes, I do like Roger. He's a very nice man." If this was what Aaron wanted, she'd go along—not that she intended to be easily lured away from San Juan again.

As if he'd read her thoughts, Aaron said, "I think it would do you good to get away at least a couple of times a week."

"Away?" she repeated innocently.

"From the island. You're obviously doing Susan a lot of good, and I know she needs you there, but she seems to be doing much better and you don't have to be... Well, as long as you're close by in case she needs you, it would be nice for you to get out and about a bit."

Libby had already decided Aaron didn't fully comprehend the seriousness of Susan's condition. Which meant that he'd exaggerated his concerns ever so slightly to make sure he got what he wanted—Libby back in the States.

"Do you have a balcony?"

He took an instant to register her question. "I—yes. But it's too cold out there now."

"I just want to look quickly." Her job must be to take

care of Susan and to convince Aaron that he wasn't responsible for anyone but himself.

She got up and set down her glass. Aaron didn't try to stop her from locating the sliding doors and opening one. When she stepped outside, a bone-raking wind ripped through her woolen dress. Libby crossed her arms tightly and tucked herself into a corner beside the chimney where she could see lights over the water and along the viaduct.

"You're nuts." Aaron came through the door and closed it behind him. He carried two parkas. One he wrapped around Libby, the other he put on before drawing her close. "Now you've seen. Can we go in again?"

"In a minute." Her stockinged feet made themselves felt, and she turned to Aaron, stood on his shoes and held on.

He rocked, then steadied them both and laughed. "What are you doing?"

"Forgot my shoes."

"What?" He tried to move, but her feet hampered him. "You'll get pneumonia. In, immediately."

"I'm used to the cold, Aaron," she said softly. "I live in it, remember. And you aren't my mother."

He became very still, his arms rigid. "I'm sorry if I sound like an overbearing parent."

Libby slipped her arms around him inside his parka. "And I'm sorry if I sometimes behave like a not very smart kid. Humor me, okay?"

He didn't answer, but his embrace relaxed and he stroked her back rhythmically. "There are a few things I do want to say to you, Libby. And I don't want you to get mad."

She was growing warmer. Aaron could always make her feel good, then better. He was a rock, the only person she really trusted never to change.

Libby rested her cheek on his shoulder. "Let's have the lecture. All I can promise is that I'll try not to stomp on your toes if you annoy me."

"I don't think my feet can take it. I'd better shut up."

She pinched his side. "Tell me now."

"Ouch," Aaron muttered. "You've got a really mean streak."

"So why bother with me?"

He searched for and found her braid, using it to pull her head back. Peering down into her face, he smiled. "I bother with you because it's a habit. How does that make you feel?"

"A nuisance," she said without thinking.

"Well, you're not," Aaron said. "But now I'm going to tell you what's on my mind. Do you know what a beautiful woman you are?"

Libby was startled. "What a funny thing to say."

"Only funny because I'm a friend, right?"

"My best friend."

He released her braid and held her head against him. An overhang sheltered them from snow, which was beginning to fall heavily. A thin layer painted the bare branches of a potted tree in one corner. The softly falling snow, the subdued whisper of tires on the raised road below, lights turned to laserlike prisms on the nearby dome of the sports stadium—Libby felt surrounded by magic.

"Do you know you're very sexy?"

Narrowing her eyes, she kept her face where it was.

"You do know, don't you?"

"No!" She straightened to see his face. "I'm not sexy, because that's something that comes from the inside as well as the outside. You have to *feel* sexy, and I don't. I don't want to. Why would you say such a thing?"

A great sigh lifted Aaron's chest. "I knew it. Do you think you somehow got ugly, just because you aren't interested in men anymore?"

"No, I don't. That's stupid. But men don't find me…"

"Don't find you what?" he prompted.

"They can tell I'm not interested in any of that anymore." She felt like telling him that the only comfort she ever expected to get from any man in future was from him. And she knew this physical closeness they were able to enjoy would always be strictly rationed and never sexual.

"Come inside." He opened the door, swept her into his arms and carried her into the warmth where he could set her down on the carpet.

"We should get some sleep." Libby was pretty sure she didn't want to continue this conversation.

"True. Listen, friend, no matter how hard you try to put me off, I'm going to say one or two things. And you do have some idea that men might pursue you. If you didn't, you wouldn't have run away from me on the mountain."

That was an event she'd like to forget. "I was jumpy, that's all. It never happened before."

He took the parka from her shoulders and threw it with his onto a chair. "Hear me out. Then we'll get you settled. You're the kind of woman men can't keep their eyes off. When you walked across the room at Wild Ginger tonight, you got yourself mentally undressed by about a dozen males."

"Aaron!"

He shrugged. "Might as well give it to you straight. I just want you to bear in mind that not all men are as decent as Roger. If anyone tries to put the make on you, turn the problem over to me."

A laugh bubbled in her throat. Libby coughed it away, but her eyes began watering. "I do love you, Aaron. You're the sweetest, most naive man I've ever met."

He turned away.

"Hey." She tiptoed around to look up into his face. "That was a compliment, not an insult. Thank you, my dear friend. You've been one of the few reasons I'm able to keep on believing there's good in this world."

"Thanks. That goes both ways." He wasn't smiling. "Come on. I'll get you squared away and collect a few of my things."

"You're angry with me." Her stomach turned over slowly.

"Not at all." There was no change in his somber expression as he strode into the hall and came back with her bag. "The cleaners changed the sheets, so everything's set."

When he passed her, she wanted to touch him but decided he wouldn't appreciate the gesture. Slowly she followed him into a bedroom almost as large as the living room. The same gray carpet had been used on the floor. Mirrored closet doors covered two walls. The third wall, behind the bed, was massed with black-and-white photos, enlarged and framed in black. The fourth wall was all window and, as Libby stood on the threshold, Aaron pulled a cord to close heavy kelly-green-and-navy-blue striped drapes that matched the enormously thick comforter on a king-size platform bed.

Aaron, his face still shuttered, put her bag on the bed and went into the bathroom. With her hands behind her back Libby walked to look at the photos—and had to blink back tears. They were all there: Aaron's parents alone, another of them with Aaron, Susan and Mike on their wedding day with Anne making a face, a very young

Aaron with a huge many-variety dog, Aaron skiing—alone and with Georges, and with Georges and Libby. She put one knee on the bed and stared at a shot of the three of them. Georges, tall, his dark wavy hair ruffled, stood with one arm around Aaron's shoulders, one around Libby's. They were all smiling. Without planning to she placed a finger on each of their faces in turn. Georges's smile, even in a picture, made her smile back through blurred eyes.

"Everything's set in there. Oh." Aaron came to stand behind her. "I forgot about that."

"They're wonderful. Wasn't he something, Aaron?"

"He sure was. I miss him."

Libby drew in a breath and blinked rapidly. "I do, too, but it gets better as time goes by. He left me a lot of good memories."

"Me, too. If the photos make you unhappy, I'll take them down."

"No." She turned to him. "Don't you dare. I love them. I'm going to do a wall like this in the cottage."

He looked away. "I think I've put out everything you'll need. Shout if there's something else." In his arms he carried a pile of miscellaneous possessions.

"This is a pretty spectacular guest room, Aaron. To-morrow you must show me the rest of the condo."

"There aren't any more bedrooms."

Libby glanced around. "Just one bedroom in a place this size?"

"It was laid out according to my specs." He appeared uncomfortable with the discussion.

"I see." She couldn't help adding, "Where will the children sleep?"

He looked blank.

"Your children, Aaron. When you get married and

have children, they'll have to sleep somewhere. Or you'll have to move."

"I never thought about it. I like kids, but I guess I'd just as soon spend time with other people's and give 'em back when I've got something else I want to do."

Saddened by what she saw ahead for him but not deterred, Libby pressed on. "You'll change your mind."

"Doubt it. I'm never going to have time. I'll make a fantastic grandfather, though. Spoil 'em and then send 'em home to make their parents miserable."

"Haven't you forgotten something?"

He shrugged. "I don't think so."

"If you don't have children, it's going to be tough to become a grandfather."

"I'll borrow some kids if I feel the need. Right now I feel the need to sleep."

"Where?" Suddenly it registered. She was supposed to sleep in his room, and there wasn't another bed in the place.

"On the couch. It's great. I'll have to use this shower in the morning, but I'll worry about that then." He headed for the door.

"I'll sleep on the great couch. I'm the intruder." She started to gather her things.

"You could never be an intruder to me, kid. And you're here because I… You came over to do me a favor. Get to bed and get to sleep. See you in the morning."

Two hours later, still very much awake, Libby rolled over in Aaron's sumptuously comfortable bed and stared at the red numerals on his digital clock. Two in the morning. She was tired, but her eyes felt stretched wide open.

She turned on her back once more and listened to night sounds. A creak, the subtle shifting of darkness around the room. Aaron slept here. A good thought. In future she'd be able to visualize him in this bed...or anywhere else in his home.

Carefully, afraid to make a noise that might awaken him, she pushed back the covers and swung her feet to the floor. Hot milk, much as she hated it, usually helped her through sleepless nights.

No noise came from beyond the bedroom. Aaron must be asleep, thank goodness. Despite his protests he'd looked so tired.

Libby got up to glide noiselessly over the carpet. She turned the doorknob with both hands and pulled slowly inward until she could slip out. Where was the kitchen? It had to be at the far end of the living room, somewhere beyond the area where she'd seen one side of a dining table.

She made it to the couch before noticing a tall silhouette at the window. Her hand went to her throat. "Aaron?" she whispered.

The shape turned. "No sleep for you, either?"

"No. You're probably uncomfortable on the couch. Change places with me."

"It's not the couch."

Libby hesitated, then went to stand beside him. He'd drawn back the sheer drapes. The snow had stopped falling, but the shape of the world outside was blurred under an undulating blanket of white.

"Can you tell me why you're not sleeping?" Libby asked tentatively.

"No."

He wished she wasn't here. She could feel it. "I'm sorry, Aaron. I didn't mean to intrude."

"For the second time, you're not intruding. Just stand here with me."

She looked at him. He looked straight ahead. Subtle

light from beyond the windows touched his face, glinted in his dark eyes and caught his teeth where he held his bottom lip. The light also gleamed over the muscles in his crossed arms—and his chest. He wore only pajama bottoms. Those were probably in her honor, Libby realized.

Aaron glanced at the sky, stirred and put an arm around her shoulders. Libby slipped her hand across his smooth back. The satin nightgown Mimi had packed was cool on Libby's skin. When her body touched Aaron's, his solid flesh warmed the slippery fabric, then warmed Libby.

He shouldn't be alone so often. "Aaron, have you started seeing anyone?" She cringed, waiting.

Aaron looked down at her. "No."

Libby smiled and turned to wrap him close. "It's time you did. Work shouldn't be everything in anyone's life."

He closed his eyes, and she expected him to tell her to back off. Instead, he embraced her so hard, with such shaky vehemence, that she trembled. Something was wrong, but he wouldn't say as much because he was always guarding her.

As abruptly as he'd pulled her against him, he set her away and turned his back.

"Aaron, what is it?"

"Nothing. Everything's fine."

She touched his shoulder and felt him start, but didn't remove her hand. "Please, I'm a very strong woman, Aaron. Honestly I am. And I'm your friend. Trust me and tell me what's bothering you."

When he didn't answer, she moved closer and began to massage his tense muscles. His wide shoulders didn't relax, even under her ministrations, and the muscles at his sides and along his spine, down to the hair-roughened dip at his waist, only sprang harder. She felt panicky.

"Susan's going to be all right, Aaron. I'm going to make sure of that."

"I'm sure you will. And then you'll rush back to Italy."

She grimaced in the darkness. "Only a few hours away from all of you, remember?"

"But you still intend to leave."

"I—" Why couldn't he understand how torn she was?

Aaron turned and held her face in his hands. "I love you, do you know that?"

Libby nodded. "Yes. I love you, too. I wish… This is childish, but I wish you were always there where I could see you. I wouldn't intrude on your life, just take you out and make you give me a hug from time to time." She laughed.

The rise and fall of Aaron's chest was something she felt as well as saw. She glanced at the dark hair that fanned across his chest, then narrowed to a line at the waist of his pajama pants. An odd, almost uncomfortable ripple passed through her. This was the first time she'd ever seen Aaron less than fully dressed. There had never even been an occasion to see him in a swimsuit.

She should forget the milk and go back to bed. "I feel calmer now," she lied. "Thanks for never giving up on me."

Smiling gently, he bent to kiss her cheek. "No thanks necessary. I couldn't if I wanted to." He dropped his hands. "Like it or not, we're stuck with each other. Somehow or other we signed an invisible pact to care."

Libby could still feel his hands on her face. And she could smell his clean skin, almost taste it…

"We're stuck," she said, and laughed.

"Off you go," Aaron said. "You'll be happy again, kid. Trust me."

"I'm happy now. Here, with you…and often at other times."

"Go, Libby. Please. We both need to sleep or we'll be useless tomorrow."

Impulsively she rose on her toes, braced herself on his shoulders and planted a firm kiss on the corner of his mouth. "You're absolutely right. See you in the morning."

Aaron didn't answer.

Back in the bedroom, with Aaron's sheets pulled up to her chin, Libby closed her eyes. And opened them again. Why did her insides feel like a Mexican jumping bean factory? What was the matter with her?

8

"This is great," Mike said. "You have wonderful ideas, Mimi."

"She sure does," Lester agreed, smiling fatuously in Mimi's direction as she busied herself around the table.

"Routine is imperative," Mimi announced while she served eggs Benedict to Lester. "A correct breakfast where people can start the day peacefully and well fed. This is the civilized way. Not the quick eating without even sitting down." She looked hard at Mike, then Anne.

Libby watched, unsure whether to be amused, apprehensive or irritated by Mimi's take-charge attitude.

"I haven't salted your eggs, Susan," Mimi said, putting down another plate. "It would be best if you ate them so."

An impish grin made Susan look almost her old self. "Would I do anything else?"

Mimi's new master plan was that they all, including Susan, eat breakfast together each morning. She'd decided it would start the day well for Susan and ensure that she didn't sleep too long, which would enable her to nap in the afternoon. All this had been announced the previous night.

When everyone was served, Mimi took a chair beside Lester, and Libby didn't miss the companionable glance that passed between them. It was nice for Mimi to have made such a good friend here, particularly since she had no specific function in the household. Not that she hesitated a moment before saying what she did and didn't approve of.

"You don't like your eggs, Anne?" Mimi asked.

"They're fine." The girl gave her plate a dubious stare.

"Would something different please you more?"

Libby tensed. "The eggs are great, Mimi. Thanks for doing all this."

"I like the eggs," Anne said. She sat between Mike and Susan at one side of the long walnut dining table. "You wanna play rummy this morning, Susan?"

"Sure, sweetie."

"This is the third no-school day in a month," Mike remarked, obviously enjoying his breakfast. "Maybe I should have become a teacher."

"The teachers are at school today, Dad," Anne said sharply. "It's an in-service day for them."

"Sure, pumpkin." Mike poured more coffee. "You're quiet this morning, Libby."

"Dad, I'm too old for the pumpkin bit."

"I'm always quiet in the morning," Libby said.

"Dad, I don't like you—"

"I heard what you don't like," Mike said, setting down his fork. "Sorry about that. I'll do my best not to make the mistake again."

"Mike." Susan reached past Anne to touch his arm. "Try to remember how you felt about these things when you were Anne's age."

"Sometimes I think I never was her age. I certainly didn't get to tell my father what he should and shouldn't call me."

Libby's stomach clenched. Her appetite fled.

"I always called you Mike," Lester said, looking peeved.

Mike drank coffee before looking at his father. "You called me one or two other things that weren't my favorites. And they weren't terms of endearment like pumpkin."

Lester concentrated on his plate. "I wasn't a perfect father, just did the best I could with the resources I had."

"I'm sorry, Dad." Mike set down his cup and rested his jaw on a fist. "Sure you did the best you could. We had a lot of good times."

"Yeah. That's right, son." Lester sounded anything but mollified.

"I'm sure Lester was very good to you," Mimi said. "Being the single parent can be very difficult."

"How right you are," Mike said.

Susan got as close to the table as her belly would allow and smiled at Libby. "We didn't have much trouble dealing with what our parents called us, did we, Lib?"

Libby let her eyes wander over white wainscotting that met rose-colored grass cloth halfway up the dining room walls. "No," she said, considering. "They didn't go in for 'mush' as Dad called it. But they were good parents."

"They called from Florida last month," Susan said. "Said they'd call again closer… They'll check in around the time the baby's due."

Looking at Susan, seeing that she was more emotional than normal and more needy, made Libby sad. What they weren't saying was that they'd long ago come to the conclusion that, to their parents, having children had been one of those things people did. Then came the bringing-up phase, then the letting go. And their folks had managed the last step admirably.

"I don't want to be called pumpkin," Anne said loudly. "Does that have to be a big thing?"

After a short silence, Mike shoved his plate aside. "That's it. Enough. If you behave like a baby—fussing and whining—you deserve to be treated like one."

The door swung open and Connie entered. Windblown, her bleached hair standing on end around her plump face, she planted her hands on her hips and surveyed the room. One side of a brilliantly flowered blouse had wriggled free from the waistband of her jeans.

"Hi, Connie." Susan smiled, but her knuckles showed white in clenched hands. "Come and have some coffee with us."

"What are you doing?" Connie demanded. "I stopped and got a cantaloupe. You like cantaloupe. I was going to bring some up with your toast."

"We've decided it would be good for Susan to do a few things to make her tired." Mimi wrinkled her nose, and Libby knew she was searching for more words. "Not strenuous things. The healthy tiredness is what we want. Too much lying down isn't a good thing."

Libby breathed in slowly. "We can go over this later. This is just an experiment today, Connie."

"Not at all. In future—"

"Sit down, Connie," Libby repeated, cutting Mimi off.

"And if I do, who's going to be the one who cleans up the mess I didn't make in the kitchen?"

"I'll be glad to do it," Libby said.

Connie sniffed. "No, you won't. You aren't up to it. You should still be in your bed, too. Look at you. Thinner by the day. It's time someone took you in hand and gave you some healthy looking after."

"This wasn't supposed to cause an argument," Libby said.

"No," Susan murmured faintly.

"Everything's okay," Mike said. "Let's eat our food."

It was too late. Libby saw the sheen of perspiration on Susan's brow and upper lip. Her hands shook.

"I've got an idea," Mike told Anne. "You've got a whole day on your hands. Come to the yard with me."

"Great idea," Susan said.

"I'm playing rummy this morning."

Libby pressed her hands together between her knees. "I'll be with Susan, Anne."

"Thanks." Mike smiled at her. "Anne's always enjoyed poking around the yard. I've missed her lately."

"I'm too old for that now. I don't want to leave Susan. Anyway, I don't have the whole day, so it wouldn't work out. I've got a drill team practice at school this afternoon."

Nobody moved. Then Connie slipped a plastic carryall bag from her wrist, took up the coffeepot and began to pour without asking who did or didn't want more.

Mike gripped the edge of the table and looked at his daughter. Anger was there, but so was something else—hurt. He got up and left the room without saying another word.

"Anne." Connie stood opposite the girl. "Look what you've done."

"I haven't done anything," Anne declared. "Susan needs me."

Libby winced.

"There are plenty of us to look after Susan, *chérie*." Mimi's voice was consoling, but her bright brown eyes were loaded with worry.

"That's right." Connie smiled at Mimi...a rare event. "You listen to Mimi, Anne."

"I'm staying here," Anne said defiantly. "Let's go and get the cards."

Susan bowed her head. "I'm making such a mess of this. Such a mess for everyone." Her shoulders lifted and shook, and Libby knew she was crying.

AN UNASSUMING BRASS PLAQUE bearing Aaron's name confirmed that Libby had found the right location. She'd phoned from her room at Mike and Susan's house and been told that Aaron had been at Alpine Ridge overnight but would return to his office by 12:30.

Somehow the explosive tension building around Susan must be eliminated. A week ago, on the morning after their dinner with Roger Chandler, Libby had said goodbye to Aaron at the ferry terminal in Anacortes and promised herself to try to show him that he didn't have to worry about her. But today she needed his help, or at least his sympathetic ear while she tried to work through what had happened at breakfast.

There was still time before he would arrive. The red brick building was one of a group that had been renovated in Seattle's historic Pioneer Square district. The same shade of red brick, worn smooth by many feet, had been used to pave the square. Naked trees poked through planting areas. The glass and wrought iron domes of an intricate pergola sheltered a scattering of tattered street people from light rain.

Aaron would help figure out what she should do next.

"Got a quarter, lady?"

Libby hadn't noticed the shuffling approach of a hunched man in ragged clothes, wearing a purple woolen cap tipped low over an equally purple face.

Shaking her head, Libby stepped backward. He reeked of cheap liquor.

"Where d'you come from, then?" the man asked, swaying. He stood between her and the door to Aaron's offices.

She locked her knees against a sudden, violent trembling. "Excuse me, please."

He didn't budge. Libby wanted to run, but couldn't make her legs move.

A blond man in his twenties, exuding the energy of the young and flamboyantly determined, hurried from the square to the door of a small shop nearby. He glanced at Libby, passed an artist's folio from one hand to the other and stopped. "You heckling the lady, Fred?"

"Nah," the wino said. "You know me."

"Sure do." He smiled at her. Kind brown eyes. "You don't have a quarter, right?"

She shrugged. She'd already started fumbling in her pocket for money.

"That's what I thought. The lady'll pray for you, Fred. How's that? I will, too."

"Pray?" Snorting, mumbling, the man hitched his filthy jeans over his skinny hips and ambled away.

"Thanks," Libby said.

"Anytime." He rushed on to disappear into the shop that appeared to be a designer sportswear salesroom. Before Libby could move he popped his head out the door. "Telling them you'll pray works every time. And not letting 'em see you're intimidated. Motto for life: never mind the turkeys. Don't let the homo sapiens get you down."

This time he disappeared for good. Libby pressed a fist over her heart. Since she couldn't seem to get over being afraid of almost everything, she'd try to put his advice to good use. The sign over the shop read Exit West Designs. She'd go in and take a look some time.

Dodging a strutting crowd of pigeons, she went through the door leading to Aaron's offices, found the suite number on a board and gratefully closed herself into an elevator lined with green marble and trimmed with mahogany moldings.

Aaron's business took up the entire third floor. Libby walked down a long hall, her shoes clipping sharply on gleaming wood. There was a vague scent of lemon in the air.

"Mrs. Duclaux?" A tall woman with sleek shoulder-length dark hair and brilliant blue eyes got up from a desk as Libby walked around a corner. "I'm Aaron's secretary, Selena Walker. Aaron called. I told him you were coming and he said to make you comfortable."

Settled in a bright yellow leather chair with a cup of freshly brewed coffee in her hands, Libby divided her attention between watching for Aaron and watching his secretary. The latter frequently got up and went through double doors into a room Libby couldn't see. Aaron's office, she decided.

"Libby!" Roger, his jacket discarded, the sleeves of his shirt rolled up, came from the hall. "I didn't know you were coming in. This is terrific. Selena, when's Aaron due?"

"Probably another twenty minutes or so."

Libby's eyes dropped to the woman's hand. No wedding ring. And she was pretty in a wholesome way, with a hint of a tan that suggested she spent time outdoors. Aaron's type, although he probably hadn't noticed.

"Let me take that." Roger removed the cup and saucer and waved Libby ahead of him. "Come and see a photo of my girls."

She swallowed a sigh and did as he asked, walking until he dropped a hand on her shoulder and steered her into a big office carpeted in a rich plum color and furnished with darkly gleaming mahogany. Conrad Enterprises must be doing very well.

Roger indicated a brass-studded wing chair and gave back the coffee. With a flourish he presented Libby with a silver-framed photograph of two smiling, dark-haired girls wearing identical sets of braces.

She smiled and looked closer. "Are they as spirited as they look?"

"And how." Roger let out a soundless whistle.

"They're lovely. You must be very proud of them."

"I am, when I'm not gnashing my teeth."

"I'm sure they keep you on your toes." Libby had a sudden thought. "How do you manage on your own?"

Roger looked at his hands. "Very well—most of the time. We have a woman, Nonnie, as the girls call her, who's a gem. She's been with me ever since... Since Joan left. Eight years."

"Eight years?" Libby frowned. "Roger, you've been alone for eight years? The girls were only four. Why haven't you remarried?"

He looked awkward and Libby felt more so. A raging blush suffused her face. "I'm sorry. That was unforgivable. It's just that, well...you're an attractive man with a lot to offer and I would have thought..."

His smile did delightful things to bright blue eyes in an otherwise unremarkable face. "Don't stop. I like it."

Libby shook her head, unable not to laugh. "I flunked tact and the noble art of diplomatic conversation. But I do congratulate you on your daughters. They'll always be able to say they had a great dad."

To her horror, she thought a sheen appeared in Roger's eyes. His Adam's apple moved sharply.

"Look," she said hastily, "this is another of my out-of-line subjects to raise, but what's she like?"

Roger looked bemused.

"Aaron's secretary? Selena Walker?"

"Nice." He puffed out his cheeks and frowned. "Certainly efficient."

"She doesn't wear a wedding ring."

"No. She's not married." His brows jerked upward. "You're not suggesting... I...really...Selena's a nice person. Good at her job. Reliable."

"Do you like her?" Libby couldn't resist asking. This felt like an instant replay of a recent conversation she was unlikely to forget.

"Well, yes, I suppose so."

"Does Aaron?"

"She's his secretary."

"Have they ever dated?"

Roger's expression cleared and he grinned. "Ah, I see. Now that's an interesting thought. No, to my knowledge they never have."

"Who are *they*? And what have they never done?"

At the sound of Aaron's voice, Libby jumped so violently that she slopped coffee on the leg of the only pair of good wool pants she had packed.

While Roger produced a handkerchief and dabbed at the drips, Libby looked over her shoulder at Aaron, who lounged in the doorway. "Roger and I were having a private discussion," she said, deliberately pompous. "He's been kind enough to entertain me while I waited for you, and he's a busy man, so I'm very grateful."

"So am I," Aaron said, but his set features showed anything but pleasure. "Actually, I'm only blowing through. So if you two have already decided to go for lunch, my feelings won't be hurt."

But hers would. Libby began to simmer. What was with Aaron? Last week, on the drive to Anacortes, he'd been distant, only speaking when she asked a direct question. Then he'd walked away from her at the ferry landing without a backward glance.

"That's a great idea," Roger said, beaming. "Umbertos is close and wonderful. Great atmosphere. Do you like Italian food?"

Did she like this, did she like that…did she like Roger? Damn Aaron and his manipulating. She turned her best, if rusty, brilliant smile on Roger. "I'm already disappointed, but I've got a couple of business nuisances to talk over with Aaron, and then I've got to get back to Anacortes for the ferry as soon as possible." And in time to do what she intended to do by the end of the afternoon…unless Aaron disapproved.

Roger's smile disappeared. "Another time?"

"Yes," she said, and meant it. Roger was one of the world's decent people, and he deserved decent treatment. "I'll give you a call when I can get into Seattle again."

He nodded, and the expression in his eyes clearly said he'd translated her messages as, "Don't call me. I'll call you." She couldn't help that now.

"Bye, Roger. I'll be talking to you." She passed Aaron. "This won't take much of your time, I hope."

Assuming she'd been right in picking out his office, she made her way to the double doors near Selena's desk and walked into a room that was smaller than Roger's, and considerably less impressive.

The doors closed behind her, but she didn't turn around.

"I heard more than you think I did, y'know."

Libby rolled her eyes. "You know what they say about people who listen at doors."

"Yes. And it's true. Forget any matchmaking plans,

please. I'm very capable of taking care of myself in that area.''

His tone brought her head sharply around. "I didn't intend to attack your male pride. It was just a silly romantic idea. You know, thinking every single person should be matched up with a partner in order to find eternal bliss?''

He didn't even have the grace to appear uncomfortable, which meant he really did think he could hoodwink her with his own diversionary tactics.

"I was surprised when Selena said you were coming.''

"I could have waited to talk on the phone, but I wanted to see you.'' Libby was almost surprised herself at being here. Even driving Susan's Volkswagen had taken courage after not being behind a wheel in several years. She still felt edgy from the experience.

"Is something wrong? Or can I hope you've got cabin fever?''

She prowled between the broad, scarred expanse of his cluttered desk, overcrowded bookshelves spilling their contents, and an obviously very much used ski exercise machine. Blunt-tipped poles lay on the floor.

"Your cleaners don't come here,'' she remarked.

"Ouch.'' Aaron hitched himself onto the corner of his desk. "That had an acid ring. I didn't say I was tidy. We do manage to afford a janitorial service. I like my office the way it is.''

"Mmm. Lived-in. But I like it, too,'' she added hastily. "I'm not here because I've got cabin fever.''

"Too bad. You got my hopes up.''

"Concentrate, Aaron. I'm worried and out of my depth.'' She leaned against the wall. "So what else is new, huh? You must think I only come to you with problems.''

"You don't usually come to me at all. You never complain. I'm the one who has to dig you out, remember?"

They weren't going to get into that subject if she could help it. "I promised myself I wasn't going to do this anymore."

He swung his leg but made no effort to respond. Evidently he'd been into his office before finding her with Roger. A black parka hung on an antique coatrack. He was dressed for the slopes in a black turtleneck sweater over black ski pants. Libby found herself making a thorough physical check of Aaron Conrad. He was worth the effort, and she refused to believe there wasn't a row of women out there who also thought so.

She picked up the poles and stepped on the exerciser. "You aren't going to help me, are you?"

"When you tell me what's up, I'm sure I will."

"I'm sorry to come and take up more of your time."

"You aren't…I'm glad you're here. How long ago did you arrive?"

"Half an hour, maybe a bit longer." She experimented, dropping her knees, shifting her weight to simulate balance and edging on the rocking bar.

"Roger took good care of you?"

"Very good care," she told him, resigned.

"It wouldn't have hurt you to have lunch with him."

"This is great for balance and rhythm."

He got up and stood in front of her. "I know. I sell them."

"Aaron, could we not talk about Roger for a while. He's a great guy. I will have lunch with him as soon as I can. That won't be very soon because, after today, I don't intend to budge from Susan's side."

"I see."

"No, you don't. I haven't told you. Aaron, even if Susan were the healthiest pregnant woman in the world, living in the kind of zoo that house is becoming would make her sick.''

''Not so far forward.'' Moving beside her, he flattened a hand at her waist. ''Keep your weight trimmed over your knees.''

Libby hopped off and dropped the poles. ''You really don't want to know, do you? I'm sorry. I shouldn't have come.''

He stood virtually toe-to-toe with her. ''I'm not going to argue with you. Let's have it.''

''Susan's buried in people telling her what to do. And every one of them tells her something different. Then they bicker with each other…in front of her.''

Aaron frowned. ''You're kidding.''

''Oh, yes. I'm known as a great kidder, right?''

''Mike wouldn't stand for that.''

Libby pulled her mouth into a straight line and wandered to look out the window. The rain was heavier. That would make driving rougher. ''I'm worried about Mike, too. I didn't think I'd get to that point over all this, but I have. He's so in love with Susan.''

''I know.''

''I was angry with him, Aaron. I blamed him for this pregnancy. That was wrong. He's so worried about Susan, and with Anne behaving the way she is… It's truly hell there at times.''

''Come here. Tell me about Anne.'' The irritation had fled his voice.

Libby went to him, and he took her hand. ''Oh, I shouldn't be here. What right do I have to come running to you every time I'm out of my depth?''

He dropped her hand. ''Just tell me.''

It was there again, irritation. Libby inclined her head.

"Okay, here goes." She explained everything that had happened at breakfast, and several other skirmishes she'd witnessed. "So you see, Mike's upset because Anne seems to be trying to shut him out of her life. And Susan's getting more and more upset because Mike's unhappy, but she doesn't want to alienate Anne and risk jeopardizing the relationship they've formed. Anne idolizes her. I think I know what's happening and why, but I'm not sure I've got the right to interfere."

"Whew! I wouldn't begin to know what to do."

Libby straightened her shoulders and felt in her pocket for the car keys. "Aaron…I really was wrong to bother you with this. I'm a big girl and I'll work it out. Look, don't give it another thought."

The bunching of muscle in his jaw made her feel sick and desperate to leave. "Soon this will be over," she told him. "Safely, I'm sure. Then I'll get out of your hair again."

"Libby—"

"No. Really. It's okay. You're right to be fed up with my family's problems. I've taken advantage of you." If she didn't get out immediately, she'd cry in front of him. "Bye for now then. And again, I'm sorry I wasn't strong enough to know I shouldn't come."

"Damn it!" He took her by the shoulders and gave one firm shake. "What the hell are you babbling on about? You shouldn't have come? You take advantage of me? And as soon as you can, you'll get out of my hair?" His fingers tightened. "As in run away and hide in Italy? You can't hide anywhere from reality. When are you going to figure that out? Do you think like a cat with closed eyes? What I can't see, can't see me? Which you translate into, What I don't know can't have happened? When are you going to face up to the games you're playing?"

Libby tried to speak but could only make a dry sound with her throat. *No tears,* she willed. "I'm sorry I've upset you," she finally mumbled.

"Well, you have." His dark stare went on and on, and then he pulled her close and held her in a hard embrace. "I'm sorry. God, I'm sorry, Libby. Don't take me seriously. You shocked me, that's all. I had no idea things were so bad."

The rotten tears were determined to come. They ran down her cheeks, but she managed to make no noise.

Aaron looked down at her. "Oh, sweetheart, I'm sorry. Lately I've been uptight. Some business worries. Nothing big, but they set me on edge. Will you forgive me?"

She nodded, giving him a watery smile. She'd forgive him anything. And she couldn't bear having him angry with her. "I was going to ask you something."

"Ask." Gently he pushed her hair behind her shoulders.

"I can handle Mimi and Connie. And I can get Lester to help me. But I'm not sure about Anne. What would you think if I suggested meeting her at the school this afternoon, after drill team practice, and trying to talk to her?"

"With me, you mean?"

"She adores you. I think if you were there, she'd hear me out."

"Sounds logical to me. But we'd better be prepared to come away as a couple of walking wounded. That girl has quite a mouth."

"So do I if I have to."

"Sure you do." He released her and walked around his desk. "Should we let Mike know what we're doing?"

"Yes. You always think so clearly."

"Not always." He picked up the phone and punched in numbers.

9

Anne saw them as soon as she came from the gym. Aaron waved, but several moments passed before she responded and broke into a run. When she was close enough for him to see her face, he swore under his breath.

"Aaron?" Libby shot him a quick glance.

"Look at her," he whispered. "She thinks we're here to tell her something awful's happened."

"Geez. You're right. Anne! Hi, pum—Hi, Anne." The girl arrived, panting loudly, her face splotchy. "I tricked Aaron into coming over for a visit, and we decided to pick you up on the way."

The girl dropped her bag and held her sides. In white shorts and a baggy green sweatshirt, with a jacket tied around her waist by its sleeves, she looked vibrant and pretty. "I thought Connie was coming for me."

"We said we'd pull the duty since we were driving past," Aaron said. Lying wasn't his forte, but this was a justified effort.

The Volkswagen was in a parking lot near the harbor, so they'd brought the Peugeot. Aaron slung Anne's bag over his shoulder, and the three of them walked to the car.

"Bye, Anne." A boy almost as tall as Aaron grinned at Anne as he passed. "See ya tomorrow."

"Yeah."

Aaron eyed the boy's broad back, the leg muscles that flexed inside his jeans with every stride he took. "Is he on the drill team?" he asked.

"Nope. That's Brad. He's a trainer."

"Coach, you mean?" Libby asked.

"Nope. He straps the girls' ankles or whatever. He's real good at it."

"I'll bet," Aaron muttered, glaring at what he knew to be one oversize bundle of hormones.

Anne laughed. "I know what you're thinking. It's no big deal like it was when you were a kid—guys and girls and all that stuff."

"All what stuff?"

"Isn't Brad your boyfriend?" Libby broke in.

"Sort of. We hang out sometimes. He's perfect. His mom had what Susan's got when she was pregnant with him."

Times had definitely changed. Aaron felt suddenly ancient. "When I was his age, I wouldn't have been caught dead talking to a girl about what happened when my mother was pregnant."

"Exactly," Anne said, lifting her palms. "Point made. Finally we kids are getting it all together. The mystery's gone."

Aaron was formulating his response when he saw that Libby's hand covered her mouth and she was losing a battle with laughter—at him.

"We'd better get home," Anne said.

They got into the car and drove, not home, but to a small restaurant on Spring Street. "We'd like to talk to you," Libby told Anne before she could fire questions. "We thought we'd do it over coffee or whatever."

By the time they were seated near the window at a table

covered with a red-and-white checked cloth, Anne's back was ramrod straight, her face white.

"We're not going to drop bad news on you," Aaron said, more sharply than he'd intended. "Relax, will you?"

The waitress arrived, and he ordered coffee for all of them, while Anne kept her face averted toward the window.

"I fibbed when I said this was a spur-of-the-moment thing." Libby, sitting beside Anne, rested her elbows on the table. "This morning, after breakfast, I made an excuse to go to Seattle. Then I persuaded Aaron to come back with me."

"No persuasion was necessary. I wanted to come."

The coffee was served, but Anne continued to look out the window.

He realized he hadn't asked what she wanted. "Would you have preferred a soft drink?"

Anne shook her head. "Everyone made a big deal out of the breakfast thing."

Aaron turned sideways in his chair and hitched up a knee. This was one time when he'd have to let Libby take the lead because he had no idea what to say.

"You're afraid Susan might die, aren't you?" Libby asked.

Aaron froze, his concentration on Anne.

She lifted her chin. "She's not going to."

"No, she's not. But don't you worry that she might?"

Anne turned to Libby. "Is she? Are you just trying to make me feel better for a while?"

"No." Libby glanced at Aaron, her face drawn tight. "Tell her, Aaron. Susan's ill. The situation's tough now, but this isn't an unusual condition, so she'll get through it."

"That's right." If only he could think Libby really believed her own words.

"I feel rotten." Suddenly Anne dropped her forehead to rest on her crossed hands. "All the time I'm thinking about it."

Libby gathered her hair into one hand and tugged. She was paler now, Aaron noted, her mountain tan faded. He began to remember the night she'd spent at his condo and tried to shut out the sensations he'd already found impossible to control.

"Do you hear anything from your mother?"

Libby's question startled Aaron, and he frowned.

"Sometimes," Anne said, her voice too toneless to be natural. "My mom's in Vegas again. She called last week. This singing job's going to be the one that puts her into the big time. Then she'll come and see me." The girl's hard laugh made him look away. No kid should sound that cynical. "And then hell's gonna freeze over," she added.

"It was tough having your mom walk away," Libby said. "Did you used to get afraid your dad might go, too?"

Anne stiffened, then nodded. "Susan wouldn't let me keep on thinking that. She told me he loved me too much to go away. It was hard to believe her because my mom used to love me and she went. Being a singer and doing stuff with flashy people was more important than Dad and I. But Susan was right."

"And now you're afraid Susan will go away, too."

The girl hesitated. "I don't want to think about it."

"I know. But that's it, Anne. You finally got the mother you wanted, the one who loves you no matter what and is always interested and understanding and on your side, and you're scared she's going to drop out, too."

Aaron stared at the beautiful, serious face of the woman across the table. She honestly didn't know that she was describing virtually the same thought processes responsible for keeping her hidden away halfway around the world from the people she loved.

"Is that what it is?" Anne tilted her face, and tears glittered in her blue eyes.

"Yes. And while you're so busy trying to make sure it doesn't happen, you're shutting out your dad and making him even more miserable than he already is."

"I don't mean to."

"But you are. He's worried about Susan and the baby and he needs your love and support. But it isn't there."

"Just because I wouldn't go to the yard today?"

"You're shutting him out, Anne."

Aaron sighed quietly. Would Libby eventually see that her own fear of loss was hurting people who loved her? If she didn't, he wasn't sure he had what it took to enlighten her. He certainly hadn't done so well with his efforts so far.

"Will you at least think about it?" Libby persisted.

"Yes," Anne said softly. "I love Dad." She twisted to hug Libby.

"Then tell him," Libby told her. "Tell him tonight and ask if you can help each other."

Aaron watched and waited...and remembered how Libby had felt in his arms that night. Slim and small-boned in the demure satin gown, her body had been soft...and his body had reacted as any man's would react to the knowledge that almost nothing separated his skin from full breasts, gently curving hips and long, fantastic legs. And the whole package belonged to a trusting woman whose late husband had made Aaron promise to look after her should the need arise. That night had taught

him a lesson. For the sake of his mental health there must
be no repeat performance. If Libby ever guessed he'd
wanted to tear off that slip of satin and carry her back to
share his big, inviting bed, he'd lose the most worthwhile
friend he had.

"I'll try," Anne said finally.

"And I'll help you." Libby smiled. "Will you help me
with Mimi, and Connie and Lester? They're even getting
on my nerves."

"Mine, too." Anne grimaced and took a first sip of her
coffee. "Mimi and Connie fight over Susan and me and
you, too."

"Me?"

"Yeah. Connie says you're too thin and you need
new—" She coughed and turned red. "She says you need
looking after. And Lester's in love with Mimi."

Aaron, his mouth full of coffee, coughed and grabbed
a napkin.

Libby grinned at him. "I'm afraid she may be right.
But that's not our problem."

AT LEAST THE RAIN had stopped. Libby sat beside Aaron
in the Peugeot as he drove back from Mike and Susan's
toward Friday Harbor. They'd dropped off Anne and used
the facts that Aaron had a ferry to catch and Libby needed
to go back for the Volkswagen as excuses to leave almost
immediately.

"You're never going to make the next ferry." Libby
glanced worriedly at the dashboard clock.

"I don't intend to." With that, Aaron turned from Har-
rison Street onto a small road that ended at a barricade.
He switched off the engine. Below lay the channel between San Juan and Brown Island, a tiny lump of land
plunked down in the entrance to Friday Harbor.

"Does this mean I'm in for some sort of lecture?" She hoped he wasn't going to use the chance to sing the praises of Roger Chandler again.

"No lecture. Accolades. You handled Anne absolutely beautifully. You certainly didn't need me."

Libby thought a moment. "Not to help say what needed to be said maybe, but just because I needed you, period. You give me confidence."

He wrapped his arms around the steering wheel and stared over the dusk-darkened water. Libby followed the direction of his attention. Brown Island. Once she'd thought there could never be a time when she'd be able to look at the place where Susan had once lived and not cry for the loss of Georges and the times they'd spent there together.

"Does that make you think of Georges?" Aaron nodded ahead.

"I wish you wouldn't do that."

"What?"

"Read my mind." She pressed a palm to his back and massaged slowly. "That's exactly what I was thinking. But I can look now, and think, without feeling as if I'm going to choke and die. It almost surprises me."

"Good. I want you to come skiing with me next week."

She stopped rubbing, caught off guard by the swift change of topics. "That's so sweet of you, but—"

"Nope. Stop right there." He switched on the dome light, reached behind his seat and produced a large, shiny black box. "Open this first."

"What is it?"

"Typical woman. Questions, questions. *Open* it."

Wriggling to make room on her lap, she slipped off the

lid, peeled back sheets of beige tissue and unfolded the most fantastic ski suit she'd ever seen.

"Well?"

Her heart began to thud. "I've never seen anything like it."

"That's because it's the only one. One of the French reps had it made for me."

"How did you know my size?" Maybe it wasn't her size.

"I have my sources."

"Mimi?"

"I said I have my sources, that's all."

Libby pulled the outfit farther out of the box. Solid black and finished with an outer shell of fabric that resembled silk, the sleeves were cut wide and tapered to tight silver cuffs. Silver hand embroidery and mirrored disks covered the top above a narrow silver belt and tight pants.

"You'll come with me next week?"

She shook her head and began to cry.

"Now what?"

How could she explain that he didn't have to give her beautiful gifts to let her know he cared? Her hand went to her throat, to the necklace she always wore. Georges had given it to her, and within days he was dead. Gifts weren't worth anything. Only people mattered.

"Thank you." She turned and flung her arms around him. "You shouldn't have spent all that money."

"Why not? I don't have anyone else to spend it on."

"You should have someone else. Stop worrying about me and find someone, Aaron."

"Damn it, Libby. I gave you a little gift, that's all. I want you to ski with me. You used to enjoy that."

"I still would enjoy it. You know that. But you didn't have to get me something so expensive."

"I wanted to."

"You didn't have to get me anything at all."

"I know," he said against her neck. "Will you come?"

"I can't leave Susan anymore."

"This is nuts." He sounded furious, but he continued to hold her in a crushing embrace.

"It's the way it is. Oh, Aaron, the suit's beautiful. I'm going to look at it every day."

He sat up and rested his head against the back of the seat. "Wonderful. Just what I bought it for—to be looked at. I should have found a picture that would make you cry."

"You shouldn't have bought me anything."

"So you've already said." He started the car and put it in reverse. "Next time I feel the urge to give you a gift, I'll grab a few dandelions on the way down Mike's driveway."

"Now you're mad at me."

"You bet I am, and you're not off the hook, lady."

She clutched the suit to her chest. "Don't be angry. We're all uptight. That's all it is. But everything's going to be—"

"Okay?" he said explosively. "Yes, I know, everyone around here tells me that several times an hour and you know what? They're right."

Libby laughed shakily. "Of course we are." The pall began to lift.

"And everything includes you, my friend. I know what you need and I intend to make sure you get it."

He understood after all. Libby bowed her head and breathed more easily. Aaron knew that the best thing that could happen would be for her to return to her home as

soon as possible. "You understand how I feel. I knew
you would eventually."

"You were right. And all we're going to need to make
you happy is a little cooperation in the right places."

10

"Well?" Libby askedas she went into Susan and Mike's bedroom. "What did the doctor say?"

"More of the same." Susan lay on the bed, her dark hair a sharp contrast to pale pillows. A high, almost feverish flush splotched her face and neck. "Did you see Mike?"

"Yes. He said he was running over to pick Anne up at school."

Susan rolled her head away. "He must wish he'd never met me."

Dread turned Libby's palms clammy. "You know that's not true. Mike adores you."

"I think he does adore me. All the more reason for him to wish the two of us had never gotten together. I hate seeing him as worried as he is."

Mike and Susan had just returned from her checkup with the obstetrician in Seattle. There had been bad news. Libby was convinced of it.

A soft sound let Libby know Susan was crying. She cried more and more often. "I don't want to leave him to bring up two children on his own...if the baby survives. I'm worried about how he'll manage and what'll happen if he doesn't snap back as quickly as he's going to need to. You won't forget your promise—?"

"Don't!" Libby put her hands over her ears. She felt

deeply, mortally sick. ''You aren't going to die because I won't let you.''

Susan was quiet for a long time before she said, ''You're right. You won't let me and I won't allow it, either. I'm sorry, Lib, I seem to feel so sorry for myself these days. Then I get maudlin. Remember how I used to do that when we were kids in Portland? You'd invent those pretend games and give me the rotten part to be. Then I'd cry and be so sad for myself.''

Libby sat on the edge of the bed and stroked Susan's flaccid hand. ''I thought I was the one who did the crying. You were always stoic. I expected you to look out for me. And you usually did.'' Swallowing became painful. ''Maybe that's what's wrong with me. I spent a long time pretending to be brave while I really wasn't. There was always someone to look after me, so I could seem brave without ever having to prove it.''

''Maybe.'' Susan turned her deep blue eyes on Libby. ''But you are strong, Lib. If you weren't, you wouldn't be here with me now. You didn't have to come.''

Libby laughed. ''Yes, I did. Maybe you've never been exposed to Aaron at his persuasive best. He's an awesome operator.''

''I'll bet.'' Susan smiled. The redness had begun to fade from her skin. ''You two have a wonderful friendship. It makes me feel better to know he'll be here, too, if—''

''Please, don't!'' A desire to run almost overwhelmed Libby. The inside of her head felt tight and stretched by fear. ''The doctor said something. Don't hide things from me. I want to know why you're saying these things.''

Susan plucked absently at red piping that trimmed the boxed midnight-blue bedspread. ''It's nothing much. Just that my blood pressure has gone up more. Or it had this afternoon.''

"How much more?" Not that the figures meant much to her. She had to force herself not to jump up and pace.

"I don't know."

Libby did get up then. She walked a track around the big bed, picking up a photo of Mike and Susan from a table draped in the same midnight-blue as the spread and went to the window. Vertical blinds were slanted almost closed beneath a draped valance, more of the beautiful blue Susan loved, this time sporting random red stripes.

The photo had been taken in the yard, in summer. Susan and Mike both wore shorts and T-shirts and held trowels. "In a few months you two will be out there digging again," Libby said. She returned the photo to its appointed spot. "You do know how high your blood pressure is. You're just not telling me."

Susan sighed. "Okay. It's very high. It must come down, or they'll try to hospitalize me. Does that satisfy you?"

"No, it doesn't." Libby paced some more. "And it's going to stop, you understand? It's going to go down."

"I hope so."

"It will. You've been worrying about everyone but yourself. Do you worry about me?" She turned sharply to face her sister. "Do you?"

"Um, sometimes."

"Well, stop it. I'm absolutely fine, and so is everyone else around here. They're feeding on one another's anxiety over you. Only there's nothing to be anxious about. Do you have a blood pressure cuff?"

"No."

"We'll get one, and I'll check your pressure three times a day."

"I don't think—"

"As soon as Mike gets back and I can leave you, I'll

run into Friday Harbor and get one." She went to the bed and felt Susan's ankles. "They're swollen."

"I know. Very."

She made up her mind. "The doctor would like you on total bed rest, wouldn't he?"

"Yes, but—"

"That's what you're going to get. If you don't cooperate with me, Susan, I'm going to make Mike cart you off to the hospital and keep you there till the baby's born. And I'll volunteer to sit by your bed to make sure you don't move."

A tap on the door broke her concentration. "What?"

The door opened slowly, and Mimi poked her head inside. She nodded at Susan and immediately studied Libby closely. "You didn't have your lunch."

Hadn't she? "I don't remember. I'm not hungry."

"Please come down and eat."

"Mimi, you're used to driving the Volkswagen now?"

"Yes." Her voice was devoid of enthusiasm.

"Good. I want you to drive into Friday Harbor and buy a blood pressure cuff. Get the best one you can. And on your way out, make sure anyone else in the house knows Susan is sleeping. From now until she delivers she'll stay in this room, and no one gets to come in unless they tell me why they want to."

"You're upsetting yourself," Mimi said quietly. "I'd like you to come and eat."

"I am not upset. Please do what I ask." She wished Aaron were here. He listened and understood, and he didn't question every decision she made. But he hadn't contacted her for two days, and she didn't blame him. Aaron was a busy man, and even if he weren't, he could be forgiven for growing tired of the complications she threw his way. "Please, Mimi," she added.

With an elegant incline of her head Mimi withdrew.

"There," Libby said. "You don't have to worry about a thing because I'm taking over. I should have done it the minute I arrived." She glanced toward the window. "Did you hear Mike's truck just then? I need to talk to him."

"We're too far from the road to hear," Susan said.

Libby glanced at her watch. "How long does it usually take him to get to the school and back?"

"It varies. Sometimes they stop and do errands on the way."

"They've been gone a long time, haven't they?"

"I don't think so. Lib, why don't you do as Mimi suggested and eat something?"

"When Mimi gets back, I'll have her bring something up. You shouldn't be on your own."

"Umm, you know, I'm thirsty. Would you mind going down and getting us some tea? That would be so nice."

"Herbal tea." Libby frowned. "I'm going to set up your menus for each day."

"Herbal tea would be wonderful."

Susan should drink a lot. "Let me get you some water, then I'll go for the tea." She filled a tall glass in the bathroom and put it into Susan's hands. "Drink it all before I get back."

She sped down to the kitchen where Lester was poring over papers at the table while Connie worked at the island chopping vegetables.

There wouldn't be a better time to say what must be said. Libby filled a kettle and plunked it on the stove. "Do you always bring your work up to the house, Lester?"

He raised his face and pushed rimless glasses up his nose. "I often do. I like to know I'm close if I'm needed."

"By Susan, you mean?"

"Primarily."

"Would either of you like some tea?" Libby arranged mugs on a tray and selected tea bags.

"No, thank you," Lester said.

Connie glanced up. "Not for me, thanks. Susan doesn't like that nut-and-spice stuff. Good cup of Darjeeling's her favorite."

"Not anymore." Libby pursed her lips. "No caffeine. And in future, until all this is over, I don't want Susan to eat or drink anything I don't okay first."

Connie blinked and set down her knife.

"What are you making there?" Libby indicated a pot on the stove.

"Soup. Susan's favorite. And your sandwich is covered in the refrigerator if you want it."

"I don't. Did you salt the stock for the soup?"

"No more than necessary." A defensive tightening pinched Connie's face. "If you ate your meals, you wouldn't be so thin."

"We're not talking about me. I'm as healthy as a horse. I'll get Susan's dinner myself, and in future I'll be deciding what she should have for each meal."

"Well!" With a flounce Connie swept the chopped vegetables into the soup pot.

"What point were you making about my working here?" Lester asked.

"There's altogether too much bickering going on in this house." A twinge of discomfort hit, but she plowed on. "Susan's aware of it and it isn't helping her blood pressure."

"And I'm adding to this bickering you're talking about?"

"Not necessarily, but we have to do everything we can to ensure a completely quiet and calm atmosphere. In future no one goes near Susan without talking to me first.

I'm not trying to be unpleasant, but it's clear that someone has to take total charge of my sister's well-being for a while. I'm the obvious choice.''

"You don't suppose Mike might think otherwise?" Lester said, so gently that Libby faltered. "He is her husband."

"Well...he can't be here all the time and I can."

"I see. Would you prefer me not to come to the house for a while?"

Libby thought. "Not necessarily. No. In fact, I'd like you to help me make sure the others take this step seriously. Will you do that?"

"I'd do anything to help Mike and Susan."

"Good. That's settled then. I'm also turning the phone off in her room. She gets calls from the salon and she shouldn't be trying to make decisions now. If they try to reach her, I'll deal with any valid questions. Don't forget what I said about the food, Connie." With the mugs balanced on a tray, she opened the door and left the room.

A thunderous crash reverberated behind her, almost as if something heavy had been thrown. Libby gritted her teeth. A noise like that would be heard all the way upstairs. Connie must have dropped a pot again. That would have to stop, too.

ANNE CLOSED the den door firmly behind her. "Dad, we've got to talk."

Her father, seated in his favorite chair by the stove, looked up from a sheaf of papers. "Why are you whispering?"

"In case *she* comes." Anne turned her eyes upward in the direction of the bedrooms.

"Ah." He dropped the papers onto the floor, took his

feet from an ottoman and waved her there to sit. "Speak to me, please. I feel like a stranger in my own house."

"I know. She makes me ask permission to be with Susan and sometimes she says no! Just like that. No!"

"Don't feel like the only one. Your grandfather's taking the line of least resistance and making appointments. And Connie, well." He laughed without mirth.

"Yeah, I know. Poor Connie's mad and sad at the same time, and it doesn't help that Mimi's making a big fuss about how Libby's making herself ill with worry."

Mike leaned forward and rested his chin on his hands. "I'm honestly not sure what to do for the best, but it's going to have to be something. Libby's glued to Susan. Mimi's backing her up because that's all she knows how to do. That means my wife's shadow has a shadow. Double fortifications against us right there. And we're only into the second day of what could be weeks of siege."

Anne hunched over. It felt good to be talking to her father like this. That had been one great thing Libby had done—showing how her father needed her and how she was shutting him out because she was so worried about Susan. Only now Libby was doing the same thing to all of them. "I wish Aaron would come over. He hasn't come for at least a week."

Her father patted her shoulder. "Aaron's been coming far more often than he has time for. He'll be here as soon as he can."

"You know what Mimi's worried about, don't you, Dad?" As soon as she'd said it, she wished she hadn't.

"I think I do. What's your version?"

She shrugged. "Nothing."

"Come on. No covering up with each other anymore, remember? We promised that."

Anne looked up at him. Her father was big and strong

looking and he always helped work things out. "Okay. I think Mimi's getting uptight because she remembers how Libby was after Uncle Georges was murdered. I think she's losing her cool because she's expecting the same thing..." Her eyes filled with tears. She swallowed and swallowed again. She never cried.

"Susan isn't going to die," Mike said. "But I know what you're trying to say."

"It makes me feel weird and horrible when I think that's what's in her mind all the time." A creepy choking noise came from her throat. "They're keeping us away from Susan when she needs us. We're good for her."

"Yes, I know. And Susan and I have talked about it. As soon as we can come up with a way to work it out, we will." He smiled. "I suppose you're too grown up to give your poor old dad a hug?"

Anne launched herself from the ottoman, and her father caught her tightly against him. She tried to sniff back the tears, but they came, anyway, and she clutched at his shirt.

"I need you, Anne," he said in a funny voice.

"Me, too." She turned her face to his neck and smelled her favorite wood shavings scent. "And I kind of like the pumpkin bit when I'm not being a pill."

MIKE HEARD FOOTSTEPS on the stairs to his loft office and swung his chair around. The top of Aaron's curly head was rapidly followed by the rest of his rangy body. He seemed out of breath, an unusual condition for Aaron the jock.

"Hey, buddy," Mike said, tossing his pencil onto the desk, "come to view your investments?"

"Come to find help before I go out of my mind."

Mike raised his brows and got up in time to watch

Aaron drop onto one of the matching leather love seats in the area Mike used when talking to customers.

"Make yourself at home."

"I am." Turning sideways, he propped his head on one arm of the seat and draped his long legs over the other. "Anne called me."

Mike sat on the edge of the facing couch. "Anne? Why?"

"To come and save the two of you, she said. And Lester and Connie."

"She shouldn't have done that without consulting me."

"Sure she should. You wouldn't have, and I need to know what's going on over here."

"Why?"

"Because…"

Aaron's puzzled frown interested Mike, but he had other things on his mind than the complexities of Aaron Conrad.

"You people are important to me. If you're having bad times, I want to help."

Mike looked over his shoulder toward a pale blue winter sky. The sound of hammering and sawing came from the workshop below his office. "Things have never been better in this part of my life," he remarked. "I used to think boats were the most important things in the world—and getting people to let me work on them. Listen." He cocked his head. "Hear that. Four crews working flat out, Aaron. Not one like it used to be, but four."

"You must be a very happy man." Aaron's voice was neutral.

"Yeah, only we both know I'm not. How much did my headstrong daughter spill on the phone?"

"I've got the whole picture, I think. Libby's turned into a martinet, and she's ordering the rest of you around."

Crossing his arms over his chest, he closed his eyes. "Geez, I'm tired."

"Not sleeping?" Mike was glad of a chance to change topics, even if only for a few moments.

"I sleep when I get to lie down. Sleeping vertically is something I can't seem to get the hang of. We're having a hell of a year with avalanches."

"Cascades always have held the record there, I thought." Skiing again might be fun. He wasn't great, but he could enjoy it with Susan. Damn, but he wished the baby had been already born and installed safely at the house with Susan back to her old, wonderful self.

Aaron stirred and jerked as if he'd almost dozed. "Steep slopes are great when you don't have changeable weather. We always do. I've got a guy holed up in a cabin up there. His job is to watch conditions and tell us if we're getting into trouble. For the last few weeks he's been telling us exactly that at about five every morning. Avalanche crews are working ten- and twelve-hour days. Those people are toting enough dynamite on their backs to blow up a city. We had a big down this morning. Climax, full-depth slab."

"Down to bare rock, huh?"

"You've got it. Anyway, that's why I'm bushed. I feel on alert all the time. There's always one fool hotdogger who thinks he's immortal and wanders off the tracks. We've never had a death, and I want to keep it that way."

"Yeah." Mike got up. "Why don't you sack out here for a few hours? You look bushed." He hadn't spent the night at the office since he'd married Susan, but the bed was still in the corner.

"No." Scrubbing at his face, Aaron swung his feet to the floor. "No time. I want to ask your help with something. Then I'm going on to the house to see Libby and beg an audience with Susan. Then I've got to get back.''

"Anne did tell all.''

Aaron nodded. "Every detail. I was afraid of something like this.''

It was Mike's turn to feel puzzled. "You'll have to spell out what you mean.''

"I'm going to. But I don't want you getting upset about some of what I say or laughing at the rest of it. Got that?''

"I'm listening.'' And he wasn't about to give guarantees about his reactions.

"Susan's condition is obviously precarious. Neither of us can brush that under the mat.''

"No.'' His stomach made an unpleasant roll.

"You and I know she'll come through okay. And so do all the others involved. But Libby doesn't believe that.''

"I know.'' He sat down again, slid to the back of the couch and stretched out his legs. "Even Anne had it figured that Libby can't face even the suggestion of losing someone she cares about. This thing she's doing is keeping panic from ripping her apart.''

"And while she's behaving like a lunatic, she's wearing herself out.'' Aaron sounded distant. "It's got to stop, for all of you and for Libby. In the past few days I've tried to persuade myself that I should keep out of it all, but I can't. I can't keep her out of my mind.''

Mike fidgeted. "Susan?''

"Libby,'' Aaron said. Then he hastily added, "And Susan, of course.''

"Mmm. Well, I can't tell you I've got some fantastic master plan because I haven't.''

"I have.''

Mike sat up, every nerve on alert. "Why didn't you say so when you walked through the door?"

"I was getting to it."

"Do it! Tell me how we convince Libby that all she's doing is making a wreck out of us all and we'd like to be her friends still when she goes back to Italy."

Aaron bowed his head and buried both hands in his hair. "She's not going back to Italy. What does it take to get someone else on my side in this?"

"I'm always on your side, but you know she'll hotfoot it away from the States the minute Susan and the baby are safe. She hates it here."

"She hates it everywhere. It's not the place that's the problem. It's what's going on inside her head. Fear of losing the people she loves. Fear of getting too close to anyone else she might come to love, then lose. Denial of reality. Contempt for anything worldly because it usually represents ambition and she's found out, firsthand, that ambition can kill. I won't let her shut herself away again."

Mike watched Aaron through narrowed lids. Aaron was a quiet one, people said, a thinker, a dark horse. Susan had once called him mysterious. Today there was no sign of the old reticence. On the subject of Libby Duclaux, Aaron Conrad was positively garrulous and, now that Mike thought about it, that was usually the case. Even climax full-depth slab avalanches and men and women hauling backpacks full of dynamite over icy slopes in the near dark of early morning didn't keep Aaron's mind off Libby. Interesting.

"This is what I intend to do and you've got to help me," Aaron said. He punched a fist into the other palm with every word. "I may be way off base, but nothing will happen if it's not supposed to."

"What?"

"Let me finish." Aaron avoided Mike's eyes. "Some people would say it's pretty wild and that I'm playing God. That's a risk a man should be able to take for someone important."

"Probably." Unease slunk into Mike's brain.

"Definitely," Aaron retorted. "Now don't forget that Georges trusted me to look after Libby if anything happened to him, and it did. So I'm going to look after her."

"Would you like a drink?" He certainly would. The tension in the room was flaying his nerves.

"No thanks. I need a clear head for this. You do agree that I've got a responsibility to carry out Georges's wishes?"

"You already do that, Aaron. No one could do more."

"Yes, they could. And I'm going to."

So tell me about it, Mike longed to yell. "I'm glad."

"Everything's in place. I've done the groundwork and this is going to be a winner. You just watch me, friend. I'm going to pull it off."

"Yeah. So what exactly is this plan?" Surely he wasn't persisting with the husband theory.

"All I'm going to do is set up the opportunities, that's all. But I've got to have help."

Mike had had enough. "*What* are you talking about?"

"Can I rely on you?" Aaron's dark eyes flashed. His hair stood on end. "Can I?"

"Can you rely on me to do what?"

"If you believe in me, you'll say yes. I've never led you astray."

"Yes… I mean no. I'll help you Aaron, but if you don't tell me what I'm supposed to do…" He spread his hands.

Aaron smiled. The lines around his eyes and mouth relaxed. "Okay, good."

Mike nodded slowly. "Yes. Good. So what is it?"

"Give me time." Clasping his knees, Aaron leaned forward. "We're going to have to be very careful how we proceed."

"Aaron!"

"Okay, okay. Here goes. I'll explain everything."

11

Mike walked from the bathroom to the bed without turning on the light. Susan had been asleep when he came upstairs. Very carefully he climbed between the covers and lay on his side where he could see her profile.

After a while he began to relax. Her breathing was regular. He looked down at the mound of her belly and smiled. Please God let them both come through alive and well.

His glance returned to her face—and the glint that gave her away. Her eyes had opened, and she didn't close them quickly enough.

"Are you avoiding me?" He rose onto an elbow and propped up his head.

"Uh-uh. You've had a long day. You need your sleep. I know you feel you have to entertain me if I'm awake."

"No, I don't. I'm glad if you're awake. I hardly ever get you to myself otherwise."

"I know." She sighed hugely and turned her face toward him. "I'm trying to see the funny side. It almost works some of the time."

With the side of his hand he stroked her hair back and bent to kiss her soft mouth. Susan rolled toward him and the kiss deepened. He closed his eyes and tasted her, a sweet, familiar taste. Edging closer, he ran his hand down over her shoulder and down her back. And then another presence made himself felt.

"Ouch." He laughed against Susan's neck. "Michael Georges is really getting feisty."

"You should be in here with him."

"Sometimes I think I'd like to be. But the urge passes."

She giggled. "Aaron said he'd been to see you this afternoon. He wangled an audience with me."

"Talented guy."

"Libby sat in the corner like a prison guard."

"Oh, God."

"He said you invited him for dinner on Friday."

Absently Mike made contact with Susan's full breasts, and she drew in a sharp breath.

He withdrew his hand quickly. "Sorry. Are you sore there again?"

This time her giggle was silvery. "Men can be remarkably obtuse. Not sore, just sensitive. You aren't the only one who misses...well, you know."

Mike smiled. "Good. I don't want to do all the suffering on my own around here."

"Well, we could..."

"No, we couldn't. The doctor said it wasn't a good idea."

"Mike—"

"Libby would probably let herself in with a skeleton key and banish me to the attic." He laughed.

Susan stroked his shoulder. "You may be right. Make sure I get to see Aaron again on Friday. He makes me feel calm."

Mike gave a snorting laugh. "He didn't make me feel calm today."

"Why?"

''He's got a master plan. I was going to wait till the morning to tell you, but this is as good a time as any. He wants our help. All of us. And he invited himself to dinner on Friday just to make sure we've all carried out our missions.''

Susan shifted and wriggled. ''What are we supposed to do?''

''Do you want a pillow under your knee?''

''No. And don't stall.''

''I wasn't. Evidently Aaron didn't mention to you that he's going to spend the night on Friday. We're supposed to work it so that Libby agrees to go with Aaron when he returns to Seattle on Saturday.''

''Oh, Michael. This sounds great.'' With effort she hauled herself up to sit against the pillows. ''He couldn't say much in front of Libby. What's he going to do? Did he say…do you think… Well, what did he say?''

''He said that Libby really likes Roger Chandler.''

''Oh.''

She sounded as flat as Mike felt about the subject. ''He said he thinks she could come to enjoy his company.''

''So?'' Irritation entered her voice. ''What's that supposed to accomplish around here? I want Libby to relax and I want her to decide to make her permanent home back in this country. I don't see what liking Roger's going to do about that.''

''Everything according to Aaron. But he needs our help. He's got all the details worked out—providing the opportunities, as he puts it. All we have to do is make Libby feel free to leave your side quite frequently.''

Susan ran her fingers through his hair. ''Why don't you tell me exactly what Aaron has in mind? All of it?''

''Okay. But I don't think it's going to thrill you.'' The

hand he splayed on her stomach located one rolling motion after another. "This kid's a night owl."

"I've noticed."

"Aaron's determined that if Libby were to marry Roger Chandler and become mother-in-residence to his daughters, the result would be total bliss that would wipe all thoughts of Italian mountains from your sister's mind."

Susan's hand stilled. She was quiet for so long that he peered up to be sure she hadn't fallen asleep.

"Aaron was Georges's best friend," she remarked.

"I know. And Aaron believes he's doing exactly what Georges would want for Libby."

"But Georges was an exciting, stimulating man." She looked down at him. "What makes Aaron think Libby's going to fall for someone like Roger?"

"I asked the same question. All I got back was that Libby definitely likes him."

"*Like* is a nauseating word. Like nice. Blah. Nothing."

Mike put his ear on Susan's tummy and pretended to listen.

"What are you doing?"

"Shush." He replaced his ear with his mouth. "Your mom's in a snit, kid. Better lie low till she gets over it. We men have to stick together on these things."

Susan laughed and pinched him. "I kind of thought you might be going to say something else."

"Like what?" Mike almost stopped breathing. If Susan thought what he thought about Aaron, maybe they could try to do something about it.

"Nothing. Just a silly notion. This is all academic, anyway, because Libby won't leave on Saturday."

Disappointment weighed on Mike. "Oh, I think she will if we all play our parts, and Aaron has every one of those worked out down to the last detail."

"Then he'll take her to meet Roger on Saturday," Susan said sounding morose. "What happens next?"

"He's not taking her to meet Roger on Saturday. This weekend Aaron intends to spend the time with her himself. Helping make sure her guard is down was the way he put it."

"Aaron's inviting Libby to spend the weekend with him?"

Mike sighed. "Sort of. But the idea is to set the pattern for getting her to go with him again and eventually to go with Roger."

"Damn, damn, damn." Susan wriggled down into the bed once more. "Sometimes people can be so stupid."

"What makes you say that?"

"I don't know."

"But we will help Aaron with this? After all, it'll help us, too. We may even get to talk in daylight."

"We'll help. What are we supposed to do?"

"Set a trap for Libby."

SUSAN COULD hardly believe her luck. Her ploy had worked perfectly. Libby had gone into Friday Harbor to talk to Jeff about salon matters that Susan insisted were upsetting her. Mike had left that morning ready to call and warn Jeff of Libby's visit and to make sure he delayed her as long as possible. Meanwhile, as expected, Libby's handpicked relief guard was Mimi Sedillot.

"We'd better take your blood pressure," Mimi said as Susan came from the bathroom, freshly showered, her hair wrapped in a towel.

Glancing at the clock, Susan slipped off her robe, sat on the edge of the bed and presented her arm. There was no time to waste on argument.

"How are you feeling?" Mimi asked, frowning over the gauge.

"Impatient," Susan admitted. "But I suspect all pregnant women feel that way by this stage."

Mimi inclined her head. "It was so for me."

"Mimi, can we talk about Libby, please?"

The Frenchwoman was immediately attentive. She took the stethoscope from her ears and unwound the cuff from Susan's arm. "What about Libby?"

"Do you feel the way she's behaving is normal? This guard she's keeping over me?"

Mimi's dark eyes moved away.

"Please. I know you're devoted to my sister. But so am I, and I want the best for her."

"I'm also worried," Mimi said simply. "But I have been for a long time. I'd hoped that coming here and being with all of you would be enough. It hasn't been."

"Aaron seems to be the only one who can get her to relax." Susan almost held her breath.

Mimi set the cuff on the bedside table. "Libby trusts Aaron. He is very good for her."

When it became obvious that Mimi wouldn't continue on the subject, Susan let out a long, frustrated sigh. Was she an incurable romantic, or was she the only one who could see the obvious? Aaron and Libby would be perfect for each other, but she didn't dare make such a suggestion as long as the rest of the world—including the two subjects—seemed to view them as brother and sister in everything but blood.

"Mike and I set Libby up this morning," she said matter-of-factly as she pulled the towel from her hair and ran a comb through the curls that would spring into place of their own accord as they dried.

"Set up?" Mimi said, as if trying the words for taste or form.

"Yes. We made sure she'd leave so I could have a chance to talk to you. We need your help."

At Mimi's distracted gesture Susan dutifully sat on the bed, swung her feet up and allowed the Frenchwoman to pull up the covers.

"Do you believe Libby should go back to Italy after the baby's born? If you do, there's nothing more we have to talk about and all I'd ask is that you never tell Libby what I've just told you."

Mimi straightened, her face slightly flushed from exertion. Her brilliant eyes were thoughtfully veiled. She pulled a chair close to the bed and sat down, arranging the draped skirt of a soft butter-yellow woolen dress.

"I don't believe Libby should return to the kind of life she's been living for the past three years," Mimi announced. "But I haven't seen anything happen here that gives me hope that she won't."

"Aaron's decided that he'll make sure she doesn't."

The other woman's deep breath was audible. "I was waiting for this."

"You mean he told you what he intends to do?"

"Not in words. But there was something…it seemed possible."

Susan glanced at the clock. How long did she have? "Aaron thinks, and Mike and I agree, that Libby won't be herself again until she can truly put what happened to Georges behind her."

"I think it's unreasonable to expect her to forget that her husband's nephew, a man who was like a son, used Georges's love as a way to try to take all that was his."

"That would be unreasonable. But it shouldn't be allowed to stop Libby from loving again without being afraid that she might have to go through the same kind of horror she went through then.''

Mimi spread her hands. ''I agree. But, as I've told Aaron, love is the only thing that can save her, while it's also what she fears most. On the night when Jean-Claude Duclaux lured Georges aboard that yacht in Hawaii, he began luring away the Libby we all knew. With the blow to Georges's head he delivered a blow to Libby, and part of her died with Georges.''

''I'd prefer to say that it was stunned.'' This conversation made Susan squirm. She wasn't likely to forget the details, but she hated every one of them.

''So would I,'' Mimi agreed. ''And I believe that may be so. But I've watched her withdraw. She doesn't want to be a part of the world anymore, because the world may hurt her again as it did before. And then she thinks— although she doesn't say so or even realize as much I believe—that at some level she'll die, too.''

Aaron's plot began to sound better. ''Will you help us try something?''

''If it seems that it'll be of use.''

As briefly as possible, Susan outlined Aaron's idea as Mike had explained it. ''So, in effect, we'd make it almost impossible for her to refuse to go,'' she finished.

Mimi was quiet before she said, ''This Roger Chandler, do you think he's a good man?''

Susan shrugged. ''Yes, a good man.''

''He isn't someone who appears... He wouldn't be interested in Libby because of her money?''

Shocked at the question, Susan shook her head. ''No, of course not. He's already well off, and Aaron says he's obviously smitten with Libby.''

''I ask because, although Libby doesn't say this she's wary of avaricious people. It would be disastrous to expose her to a, er, a fortune hunter? Someone who sees her as a source of wealth. She's constantly appealed to by funds and organizations with extensive administration networks. The money wasted on those networks angers her because she says those who need help get so little once the overheads have been paid.''

"I don't know Roger well, but Aaron does. He wouldn't be going to such elaborate lengths if he wasn't sure it would work." She wished she was sure it would work. And she wished she knew Roger Chandler well enough to judge him for herself. "Of course, he also thinks Roger's daughters would be good for Libby."

Mimi stood. "I don't believe it's possible to manipulate the lives of others. The head must always be followed, but without the heart there is great danger for a woman like Libby."

"So you don't think we should do this?" A burst of relief surprised Susan.

"I didn't say so. This weekend, if Libby agrees to go, she'll be with Aaron only?"

"Yes."

"Then what can happen that wouldn't be good?"

Susan frowned, trying to read the other woman's face. "Nothing."

"So, of course, we should do what Aaron suggests. Did Libby show you the ski suit he bought for her?"

"No."

"She didn't show me, either. But I saw her bring in the box after she went with him to the ferry the last time he was here. The box has the name of his company on it."

What was Mimi telling her? "So you know he gave her the box?"

"The ski suit in the box, yes. The suit is beautiful, but Libby no longer cares for those things."

"I know."

"But she looks at it often. I have seen her touch it."

Susan nodded slowly.

"Yes," Mimi said. She straightened nonexistent wrinkles in the spread. "Yes, we must be sure that we give Aaron whatever help he needs."

ANNE CLOSED Susan's door behind her. "Mimi told me to come," she said, glancing at her father. "She said Libby's taking a shower and to be quick."

"That's right. Listen carefully and save the questions."

"Whew." She felt jumpy all the time, and this wasn't helping.

"Aaron's coming to dinner on Friday night," Susan said. "Then he'll stay over."

"Great!"

"Just listen," Mike said in a low voice. "You've got a date on Saturday night."

Her mouth fell open. "No, I don't. I'm not allowed to date till I'm sixteen."

"Not a real date." He sounded exasperated. "You don't even have to go out."

She nodded, then shook her head. "I don't get it."

"What's the name of that boy you like? The one you talk to on the phone for hours."

"Dad!"

"Gimme. What's his name?"

"Brad. And we don't talk for hours."

"Brad's going to pick you up and take you to a dance at school on Saturday."

Anne rubbed her hands on her jeans. "Are you okay, Dad?"

"Anne." Susan smiled and held a finger to her mouth to quiet Mike. "Your father isn't a natural at this sort of thing. Men often aren't. We're trying to work out a way to get Libby to start going out and having fun."

"A way to get her off our backs, you mean," Anne said enthusiastically.

"If you like. All you have to do is start talking about the date you've got on Saturday night."

Anne screwed up her eyes and thought for a moment. "Why Brad? Why not one of my girlfriends?"

"Because none of them can drive," her father almost shouted. Lowering his voice, he crossed the room and put an arm around her shoulders. "We've got to convince Libby that if she goes away with Aaron on Saturday and doesn't get back until late that night or even the following morning, Susan will be kept as quiet as she is when Libby's here. Do you understand?"

"I think so. What about the others?" This was really weird, she thought.

"Leave the others to us. Everything's in hand—almost."

"Okay." Anne smiled to herself. And adults thought kids' minds needed help?

"All you have to do for now is start talking about the dance. Can you do that?"

"I—" She stopped as the door opened behind her and Libby came in. "Hi, Libby."

"What are you doing here, Anne? You know Susan has to be kept very quiet."

"Yes. I'm sorry." She looked guiltily at the floor. "I just had to come and ask if I could do something special."

Libby held the door open. "I hope you haven't upset Susan."

"I haven't, have I?"

Susan and Mike shook their heads in unison.

Anne smiled broadly. "Dad and Susan have decided I'm old enough not to wait until I'm sixteen to start dating. I'm going to a dance with Brad on Saturday night."

"LIBBY DOESN'T HAVE a thing to wear," Connie said.

This was going to be difficult, Mike decided. He glanced at his father in mute appeal, and Lester ducked his head.

Connie went into the pantry and returned with several cans of food. "But that doesn't matter, I guess, because she won't go, anyway."

Mike ground his back teeth together. "She will if we all play our cards right. I need your help, Connie. Do I have it?"

"It's not me you have to worry about. It's Mimi. What do you intend to do about her?"

He looked at the ceiling. When had his happy home become a boxing ring? "Don't worry about Mimi."

"No," Lester said, finding his voice for the first time during this impossible conversation. "Mimi's no problem. I'll take care of that."

Mike opened his mouth to say that Mimi was already on their side, but thought better of it. If Connie thought she hadn't been approached before her rival, she might decide to make things difficult. "That would be nice, Dad," he said.

"So what am I supposed to do?" Connie asked. "Tell Libby I'll be here to look after anything Susan needs? I'd be glad to, you know that, but it won't work." She tucked her chin into a cushion of fat and turned her back.

"What I want you to do," Mike said, trying to sound patient, "is to cook a lovely dinner on Friday and then work with Mimi and the rest of us to give Libby the impression that everything's very calm and peaceful around here. Can you do that?''

"I always give the impression things are calm. They are.''

Mike rolled in his lips and willed himself not to say what he thought. "Of course. But on Friday we're all going to try especially hard. And then I want you to mention—very casually—that you won't be in on Saturday or Sunday because you're visiting relatives.''

"The only relatives I've got are in Oklahoma.''

Lester's grin was quickly covered by the newspaper he raised.

"Libby doesn't know that.'' His patience was slipping.

"Who's going to do everything around here?'' She turned on him, suspicion alight in pale blue eyes. "Where will Mimi be?''

"Not here,'' Lester said from behind his paper.

"All we're trying to do is give Libby the impression that there'll be perfect peace in her absence. I'll be the one who'll take care of Susan.'' He closed his eyes envisioning the bliss of having his wife to himself. "All I need from the rest of you is the assurance, as far as Libby's concerned, that there's no chance of your being here to—as she so frequently puts it—overtax Susan. Will you help me?''

"I want to.'' Connie gave him her full attention. Clasping her hands under her considerable bosom, she assumed a mournful expression. "I'm just not sure you'll be able to convince Mimi. She can be such a...so difficult.''

Lester folded his paper and smoothed it over his knees. "I wouldn't worry about that, Connie.''

"Why? You've seen how she is.''

"Oh, I certainly have. But you can leave Mimi to me.'' He got up. "All of you can leave Mimi to me.''

Mike watched his father put on his jacket and open the French doors. He stepped outside and closed them again. Before he walked away he smiled at Mike through the glass and waved at Connie.

"Well," Connie said, "what's all that about?"

Mike stuffed his hands into his pockets. "I'm not sure I'm ready to know."

LIBBY SMILED at Aaron across the table. "You were hungry." He'd devoured two servings of Connie's beef Wellington, a masterpiece that had surprised Libby. Now the last morsel of his second helping of grasshopper pie was disappearing into his mouth.

"Umm." He swallowed and nodded, grinning. "Who wouldn't be hungry with food like this?" His winning smile flashed upon Connie whom Mike had insisted upon inviting to eat with them.

"Mimi gave me the recipe for the beef," Connie said, and Libby winked at her, knowing how difficult it was for Connie to share any praise with Mimi. "Grasshopper pie is all mine. I adapted it from a recipe I found... My cousin who lives in Vancouver gave it to me. That's the cousin I'm going to visit tomorrow and Sunday."

No one seemed to notice what Connie had said. Aaron's attention had returned to Susan who, against Libby's wishes, had come down to dinner.

Libby toyed with her pie. "I didn't know you had a cousin in Vancouver. I thought you told me your only relatives were in Oklahoma."

"Did I?" Connie's round eyes became rounder, and her skin turned bright pink. "Poor Doris. We all tend to forget her. She's, er, she's the black sheep, as it were. But I believe in letting bygones be bygones. When she called yesterday and said she wasn't feeling too chipper, I prom-

ised I'd go up tomorrow and stay overnight. It's a sin
really—me not going up there for so long.''

"Your cousin lives in Canada?"

"Um, oh, yes. Vancouver. I'll be leaving first thing in
the morning, and I definitely won't get back before late
afternoon on Sunday, so don't expect to see me at all for
those two days because I won't be here."

Libby chewed the inside of her lip. Connie looked...
funny.

"I'm glad to hear you're going somewhere," Mike said
in a huge and hearty voice. "About time. We take you
for granted. You'll make us appreciate you more."

"Don't worry about us, Connie," Susan said. "Have a
good time."

Libby looked from one to the other and then at her pie,
which was melting.

Connie got up and began taking dishes from the table.
"I'll make coffee. Would you like it in here?"

"In the den, please," Mike said.

"What do you think of my dress, Libby?" Anne asked.
"Isn't that the most awesome blue you ever saw?"

"What dress?" She set down her fork and gave her
whole attention to Anne.

"Didn't I show you? Oh—" she clapped a hand to her
mouth "—I forgot. You were with Susan when I got back
yesterday. I thought you were in the kitchen with everyone else. When Dad picked me up from school, I stopped
to get my dress for the dance."

"Dance?"

"Libby!" Anne frowned at her. "Don't pretend you've
forgotten I'm going to a dance with Brad tomorrow
night."

Libby studied the greenish ice cream soup spreading
across her plate. "I've been upstairs so much I must have

lost track." That or she was losing her mind. "You'll have to show me the dress."

"I will. Tomorrow, when I get dressed. Dad says it's all right if I stay out till one in the morning." She squealed.

Libby winced, considered questioning the wisdom of allowing a fifteen-year-old to stay out half the night, but changed her mind. "You must be careful, Anne. People can get wild at those events."

"Oh, Libby. Chill out, will you? There are chaperons and no booze or anything."

"We're not worried," Mike said. "It'll be nice to have a quiet evening around here."

Everyone laughed.

Libby didn't. "Don't go anywhere in the dark on your own, Anne."

"Relax, Libby," Aaron said. He smiled at her, reached and touched her hand. "Anne will be perfectly safe. Mike and Susan wouldn't let her go if they didn't think she would be."

His fingers slipped between hers and tightened. Her tummy flipped, and she felt oddly warmer and less worried. Aaron's smile always had that effect on her.

"Looks as if we're all deserting tomorrow," Lester said. Libby hadn't failed to note that he and Mimi had been lost in each other throughout the meal. He turned to her now and said, "Mimi and I are going over to Anacortes tomorrow. Then we're going to drive to a little inn near LaConnor for dinner."

"That's wonderful." Susan nudged Libby's arm and turned her head so that neither Mimi nor Lester could see her face. She raised her brows. "Isn't that great, Libby?"

"Great."

"Looks as if it's going to be real quiet around here,"

Mike said, and Libby noticed the way he stroked Susan's wrist on the table. Maybe it would be a good idea for the house to be really quiet for a while. Cooking would be no trouble. Libby had done plenty of that in her time.

"You know, I do believe I'm tired." Susan rested her cheek on Mike's shoulder. "Will you all forgive me if I go to bed? This was my first time downstairs in over a week."

Immediately Libby stood and moved behind Susan. "You should have said you were getting tired. I told you this wasn't a good idea."

"I just did say it." Susan got up.

"I'll come with you," Mike said.

"Oh, no. Libby will help me. You stay here and play host. See you all tomorrow."

Half an hour later Libby left Susan comfortably tucked in bed and made her way back downstairs. The dining room was silent. She wandered into the den and found Mike and Aaron sitting companionably, one on each side of the stove.

As soon as Aaron saw her, he got up. "Sit here. I'll pull up another chair."

Libby didn't argue. She was tired herself, but happy. Susan seemed quiet tonight, accepting the need to allow herself to be cared for. "Her blood pressure was down a bit tonight."

Mike's grin made her smile broadly. This man's love for her sister made her like him more every day.

"Everyone else decided to call it a night too," he said.

Aaron brought her a cup of coffee and set a small glass of clear liqueur on a table beside her chair. "Cointreau. Do you still like it?"

She nodded and leaned her head back. "Thank you."

He settled in a chair, and they sat quietly, looking into the fire.

"My parents want you to come and see their new house," Aaron said. "I told them I'd suggest we make it tomorrow, if you don't have anything else you have to do."

The Cointreau burned her throat and she coughed. "Tomorrow?"

"Mmm. I thought we could go on to the Ridge afterward and ski, then have dinner before I bring you back."

Libby swallowed. "That's so sweet of you, but I can't go. I really do have to make sure Susan stays quiet, and I've promised myself I'll do that until the baby's born."

"Surely that doesn't mean you can't leave for a few hours?"

She looked at Mike, but he continued to stare into the fire. "You don't understand. Everyone...they all mean well, but they crowd in if I'm not here. There's only one way to cope with what needs to be done for Susan now, and it's my way. I keep her away from anything that might upset her. If I'm not here, one or the other of them will go to her with a question and then everything I've accomplished will be wasted."

"Am I included with 'them'?" Mike asked.

"Of course not."

"Well, then?" Mike turned his steady green gaze on her. "There's nothing to worry about, is there?"

"Not from you. But the others."

He squinted. "I see what you mean."

"We're going to make it, Mike," she said gently. He'd suffered too much and the strain was beginning to show. "She's at thirty-one weeks. Only a few more to go."

"My folks will be disappointed," Aaron said, his nose in his coffee cup.

"Wait a minute." Mike sat straighter. "Surely the rest of them will all be gone tomorrow, except Anne. And she'll be off in the evening."

"What does that have to do with anything?" Aaron put down his cup and took up a brandy snifter. The disappointed droop of his shoulders troubled Libby.

"It has everything to do with everything." Mike spread his arms. "With only Susan and me here there won't be any fuss at all. I'll make sure she stays quiet. It'll probably be very good for her."

"Oh," Aaron said. He frowned at Libby. "What do you think?"

"I don't know."

"Good, then you'll go." Mike's chest rose with the big breath he took. "Can I be absolutely honest with you two?"

"If you can't, you don't have a real friend in the world," Aaron said.

Libby smiled. "Aaron's right."

"Okay, here goes." He bit his lip and averted his face. "I'd like to spend some time completely alone with Susan. I miss our times together."

Libby was in the act of reaching for his hand when Aaron leaped up and went to the window. He stared out into darkness, and her heart felt suddenly too tight. These were such special men. Mike, big, successful Mike, could show his need for his wife's company without any trace of embarrassment. And Aaron, despite his supposed self-sufficiency, was as moved as she was. Only he wasn't comfortable letting them see his emotional reaction to Mike's plea.

She made her mind. "Thanks for inviting me to go with you, Aaron. I'll enjoy it."

12

"Aaron loves having you here."

Libby smiled at Marjorie Conrad. "I can't imagine why. I'm sure I must be an added complication in his busy life." This morning she wished she'd made an opportunity to buy a few new clothes. Her jeans and sweater really were quite worn—worn-out would be more accurate.

Marjorie watched her steadily before saying, "Surely you know you could never be a complication to Aaron? He's, um, well, he's very fond of you. And I think you're good for him."

"You're all so kind to me." She sat forward in her chair and looked down on the swaying, snow-covered crowns of pines growing from the sheer hillside below. "You and Bill chose a beautiful spot for your home."

Marjorie grunted, and Libby glanced at her sharply. "You do like it here?"

"Oh, yes. It's just that I sometimes miss the old neighborhood and being close to our friends." They had lived most of their married life on Queen Anne Hill close to downtown Seattle.

Libby nodded. From time to time clumps of snow slipped from branches to fall in cascades of sparkling powder. "I love it here." She was instantly surprised at what she'd said.

"Mmm. Not so surprising. The northwest is your home."

"My home is—" Libby bit off the rest of what she'd automatically almost said. "Surely you get to see your friends regularly."

"Oh, yes. And I shouldn't complain. You won't ever tell Aaron or Bill, will you? Bill would be so upset with me."

"I wouldn't say a word." She smiled at Marjorie again—a good-looking woman who seemed much younger than what had to be her almost seventy years. Aaron had said he'd been a surprise arrival when his mother was already in her early thirties. "Where did they go, anyway?"

Marjorie made an airy gesture. "Oh, Bill had some project in the workroom that he wanted Aaron's opinion on." Her short, curly gray hair framed a face that bore feminine similarities to Aaron's strong features.

"What kind of project?" Libby didn't see Aaron as the handyman type.

"We've decided to build in bookshelves at one end of the dining room."

"And Aaron knows about things like that?" If it had been Mike, she'd have understood.

"Aaron's always been good with his hands—and at working things out. He used to come quite often on weekends to work with his father. Lately he's been too busy."

Libby bowed her head. "Too busy running around worrying about Susan and me."

"Not a bit of it," Marjorie protested. "He seems happier since… This is always a hectic time of year with his business."

"Naturally."

The sound of approaching voices grew louder, and Marjorie put a finger to her lips. "Not a word?"

"Not a word."

"Are you two still gossiping?" Bill asked, pushing open the door, a laden tray in his hands.

"Absolutely," Marjorie said serenely. "Women don't know how to do anything else."

With a bottle of wine in one hand and four glasses hanging by their stems between the fingers of the other, Aaron followed Bill into the room.

"What's this?" Marjorie stood up, but Bill waved her back into her chair.

"We decided to surprise you with an early lunch."

Libby pressed her hands between her knees. "I thought you were making bookshelves or something." The sight of Aaron's fierce concentration as he helped his father set out plates of sandwiches made her feel ridiculously happy.

"That's all under control," Bill said. "These days it's not often I get an opportunity to have my son's advice on a project, then eat something he's made."

"I didn't know Aaron was a cook." Evidently there were a number of things she didn't know about him.

"A very good one," Marjorie said. "He's enjoyed puttering around the kitchen since he was a little boy."

"I helped Dad make sandwiches," Aaron said, and Libby noticed his ears had reddened. "Hardly a gourmet effort."

"No." Marjorie turned to Libby. "But he really can turn out wonderful meals when he wants to. Remember Aaron's Stroganoff, Bill?"

"Great." Bill handed Libby a plate and offered sandwiches.

Libby took half a roast beef sandwich and, when Bill didn't move away, sighed and took the other half.

"And then there's that spinach quiche," Marjorie added.

"The quiche with the soggy crust," Aaron said in a distinctly dark tone.

Other than Mike and Susan with Anne, proud parents were a novelty to Libby. She grinned. "I'll bet your quiche is spectacular."

"It—"

"It is," Marjorie carried on happily. "A man who can turn out a good meal is a rarity these days."

"Always was," Aaron said, sinking his teeth into a wedge of apple while he poured wine.

Bill thumped his son's back. "That's what your mother means. You've got a lot of special qualities, Aaron. You don't give yourself enough credit."

Aaron's evident discomfort made Libby want to giggle. He caught her eye and scowled.

"And he can do absolutely anything around the house," Marjorie said. "Can't he, Bill?"

"Absolutely."

"What is all this?" Aaron said. "The Aaron Conrad Appreciation Banquet? I'd have done something a bit more spectacular than roast beef sandwiches if I'd known."

"Don't sneer," Marjorie said, sounding huffy. "Your dad and I must both have been thinking along the same lines. We take you for granted, and it's time we let you know how much you mean to us."

Libby choked on a piece of beef and blinked back tears. She wasn't sure if she should agree with the Conrads or keep very quiet. Judging from the expression on Aaron's face, keeping quiet might be wiser.

"Thanks," he said finally. He gave wine to his mother and Libby.

"I envy you," she said without intending to. "Being so close, I mean. That's a gift."

Aaron came and sat on the arm of her chair. "You aren't very close to your parents, are you?"

"You shouldn't say things like—"

"It's all right," Libby said, cutting Marjorie off. "Aaron's right. I guess that's why I envy what you three have."

"I'm sure your mom and dad love you very much." Marjorie appeared uncomfortable.

"I'm sure they do."

"Aaron was an unexpected gift," Marjorie said, gazing up at him. "Maybe that's why we've never stopped being so grateful for him."

Libby glanced at Aaron in time to see him rolling his eyes. "Could we change the subject, Mother?"

"We didn't mean to embarrass you."

"We just wanted you to know that we're grateful we were blessed with you, son," Bill said. "But enough said."

Aaron sighed, and Libby took a deep swallow of wine.

Marjorie leaned toward Libby. "Do you think it's wrong to tell your children how important they are to you?"

"Ah, no. I think it's very nice." The thought came and quickly fled that she'd never have children of her own to receive her affection.

"I don't know anyone with as good a son as we have," Marjorie commented, a dreamy look in her eyes.

Aaron made a strangled noise.

Libby rested a hand on his knee. "There probably isn't anyone. He's a pretty special guy."

"There!" Marjorie plumped up visibly and beamed.

"You see, Aaron? Libby agrees with us that good men are rare and you're a good man."

Libby squeezed his very solid leg reassuringly. "He's certainly been good to me. Sometimes it's only been Aaron who made…well, he's helped me through some sticky times."

After a short silence, Bill busied himself offering sandwiches again. Libby, her plate still full, shook her head. Aaron had covered her hand on his leg. Their eyes met, and he smiled, biting into his bottom lip. He was good, and she wouldn't want to think of a world without him in it, or where she couldn't be sure that she'd see him again and again.

"So," Bill said, "the two of you are going skiing this afternoon?"

Libby couldn't take her eyes from Aaron's. He kept on smiling and said, "Yes, Dad, I'm finally getting her up there with me. Libby on skis is like a bird in flight, y'know. Doing what comes naturally and doing it perfectly."

She grinned and withdrew her hand. "He says things like that to flatter me. I can't imagine why."

"Can't you?" Marjorie asked. She cleared her throat. "I'm sure he says them because he knows we all like to hear nice things about ourselves. Aaron's always thoughtful."

"That he is," Bill agreed. His nose had taken on a reddish hue, and Libby noticed he'd drunk his wine rapidly and refilled the glass. "A better son no man ever had. Anyone would be lucky to have a man like Aaron Conrad care about them."

Libby frowned. From her previous experiences with Bill, she knew he drank very little. "I'm sure you're right.

Aaron, maybe we should get on the road and leave your folks in peace.''

"Good idea." He got up so quickly that he had to steady his own glass. "We're going to ski and have dinner."

"That'll be lovely." Marjorie stood, her brows arched expectantly.

Libby hesitated, unsure what was expected of her. "Thank you very much for lunch."

"My dear," Bill said. "Our home is your home. Always will be. In fact, Marjorie and I hope you'll let Aaron bring you often."

"Thank you."

Marjorie led the way into the hall. "We're glad you like the house."

"Oh, I do," she said truthfully.

"Good. I'll call Aaron to find out when he's bringing you again."

"Ah—"

"Get along with you both now." Marjorie shoed them ahead of her. "It's a wonderful day for skiing. Don't waste any more of it."

Bill and Marjorie stood, side by side, in the front doorway while Aaron ushered Libby to the car.

As they drove down the steep driveway, Libby looked back and waved. "They're so proud of you."

Aaron's eyes were firmly trained ahead. "They aren't usually so voluble on the subject."

"Oh, Aaron. You weren't really embarrassed, were you?"

"What do you think?"

"That they're right. You are a special man. Certainly the most special man I know."

He took his eyes from the road for an instant and

glanced at her. His eyes were cast in shadow, almost black, and impossible to read.

"GOOD TO SEE YOU, Mr. Conrad."

Aaron pulled the door to the lodge closed behind Libby. "You, too, Bill." He nodded at the man who paused in front of him and blessed his total recall for names. "Keeping those lots in shape?"

"You betcha. Only towed three abandoned wrecks with tires down to the cords so far today."

"Some people never learn." Aaron laughed and noted that Bill, who was in charge of the Ridge's parking lots, was looking at Libby with frank admiration.

"Libby, this is Bill. He's worked for me for...how many years is it now, Bill? Ten?"

"Right on. I don't know how you do it."

"I don't forget those things," Aaron said honestly. "This is Libby Duclaux. A very old friend of mine."

Bill smiled widely, creasing his weathered face and showing a gap in his front teeth. "More good than old I should say, Mr. Conrad."

"You're right." He grinned as the man went on his way. "I should bring you up here more often. All this forelock tugging is only because everyone wants to get a closer look at a beautiful woman."

She wrinkled her nose, her very appealing uptilted nose. And her golden eyes shone in a face whipped to a peachy glow by three hours of the kind of skiing he rarely took time to enjoy these days. "Something tells me you're the kind of boss who attracts loyal employees. I haven't met one person who works here who doesn't also look at you with adoration."

"Don't you start."

Libby giggled. "Ooh, I thought you liked being told how wonderful you are."

"Don't get going on that again," he warned. "I can't imagine what got into them. Are you hungry yet?"

"Ravenous." Stamping snow from her boots, she pushed up the silver cuff on the suit he would always be glad he'd ordered for her. "But I should probably think about getting back."

"Why?" A cold little knot of disappointment made itself felt in his belly.

Libby tugged off the black hat he'd helped her select from the shop in the lodge basement. "Don't you think it would be better if I was there to help Mike?" Her hair, pulled back severely into a rubber band, was damp around her face where snow had seeped under the hat.

"Nope, I don't. I think he's desperate to have some time alone with Susan. Will you listen to what I'd like you to do?"

She tucked a piece of hair into the band and winced when it broke, sending a tumble of red-gold over her shoulders. "I've got to get some of this mess cut."

"It's not a mess. It's beautiful. Now, will you listen?"

"Yes. But I don't promise to agree."

"When we left this morning, I could tell Mike and Susan could hardly wait to get rid of us."

She frowned. "You think so?"

"Don't you?"

"Maybe."

"Definitely. Right now they're enjoying each other and looking forward to a quiet evening with no interruptions. Mike knows exactly how to reach you here, and you heard him promise that he wouldn't hesitate to do so if anything happens that you need to know about."

Uncertainty lingered in the downturn of her full mouth.

"They did seem to be happy. And Susan was very calm. Her blood pressure hasn't gone up in several days."

"There you are, then. They're happy. And you'll make me happy if you'll agree to keep a lonely man company at dinner."

She glanced down. "I'm not really..."

"Not really dressed for it? You'll need a different excuse, my love. You look fantastic, and you know it." How true. Not one pair of passing male eyes failed to linger, and those women who didn't cast an admiring glance in Libby's direction spared her a look of envy.

"Good grief. We've turned into a mutual admiration society. Yes, I'll have dinner. And it had better be soon because I'm starving. Let me tidy up first."

"It's casual, remember. So you don't need to. You can take your boots off and warm your feet by the fire."

"You're impossible. I'm a wreck."

"You're the one who had to have that last run down Screamer, and *I'm* impossible?" He took her arm and started for the stairs and the loft restaurant.

"That little run?" She laughed. "Where I come from we'd call it a bunny hill." He stopped climbing behind her, and she looked down. "What is it, Aaron?"

"This is where you come from, Libby. You're home."

She lowered her eyes and continued up.

At the top, in the flickering light of candles on round oak tables, the crowd was loud and cheerful. Two men working a bar at one end of the room tossed bottles and banter at each other and ran to keep pace with orders.

More friendly voices greeted Aaron by name. He'd always believed in being visible in every aspect of his business and, although it had become harder as the enterprise grew, he never intended to give up personal involvement.

"I'd almost forgotten how much I liked this place." Libby shook her hair and combed it with her fingers.

Again Aaron was aware of attention turned in their direction. He looked at Libby who was unzipping the top of her suit to reveal the tight silver turtleneck beneath.

"Let's sit down." He held her elbow firmly and steered her across bare wooden boards toward the huge fireplace. "Give me a foot," he said when they were seated at the table always reserved for him.

Libby dropped her head back and slid down in her chair. He had an urge to zip up the suit again. She was breathtaking. "Your foot," he said, and lifted her unresisting ankle onto his knee to pull off her boot. He repeated the process with the other foot.

She sighed, smiled and closed her eyes. "My favorite atmosphere. Woodsmoke, wet wool, steam and happy people. And the smell of beer, of course…and moody music."

He felt a surge of pleasure. Just being with her made him feel good. And he was beginning to allow the hope that she was unfurling, letting go.

"Will you have beer?"

Her eyes snapped open. "You know I won't. I hate the stuff. But I will have wine. Mulled maybe?"

"You've got it." At his high sign a hovering waitress was instantly present. He ordered wine for both of them, and the meat pies the restaurant optimistically referred to as their famous specialty.

"Is this a private party or can anyone join?"

The muscles in Aaron's jaw jerked, but he managed to relax his face before looking up at Dennis Falk. "Hello, Falk." He'd recognize those New England vowels and the silky voice anywhere. "What a great surprise."

Falk, not quite tall enough to be called tall, but with

the massive shoulders, tense torso and slightly spread stance that hours of conditioning bought, slid eyes the color of blue steel from Aaron to Libby.

"I hope you had a good day's skiing," Aaron said hastily. The bastard was too damn good-looking, and his mind was moving in easily readable patterns. "See you again, I'm sure." He was aware of Libby shifting in her chair. Undoubtedly she was wondering why he didn't introduce her.

"Don't we know each other?" Falk snapped his fingers at Libby, turned a chair around and sat astride the seat. "Don't tell me. I never forget a face. Not that one could forget a face like yours."

Aaron gritted his teeth. "This is Libby Duclaux," he said tightly. "Libby, Dennis Falk."

"Oh, Aaron. You always could be a pain in the ass. Sorry." Falk pushed his fingers through curly blond hair and gave Libby a boyishly apologetic smile. "Libby. Of course I remember."

That she clearly didn't remember Falk gave Aaron some pleasure—but not enough.

"Georges was one hell of a man."

Aaron frowned, then remembered. Of course, Falk had a place at Aspen, and he'd been at a party given there by one of Georges's clients. Georges and Libby had only been married a year at the time, and Aaron had flown to Colorado to ski for a few days with them.

"You probably don't remember," he told her, trying to hide his satisfaction. "When we were all in Aspen, Dennis came to that party for you and Georges."

Apparently unconcerned, Falk wrapped his arms along the chair back and propped his chin. His undivided attention was on Libby. "I've still got my place there. The Denvers are almost my neighbors. Ring a bell now?"

"Of course." She flipped back her hair. Maybe cutting it wouldn't be such a bad idea.

"There's no right way to say this." Dennis dropped his voice, and his eyes. "What happened to Georges was unthinkable. I really admired that man. Everyone who knew him did."

"Thank you."

Aaron felt vaguely sick. Falk sounded sincere, but his timing was lousy.

"I'd love to have you come to Aspen. The house is huge. Plenty of room." He laughed. "Of course we'd have to have a chaperone for you. My housekeeper lives in."

If he hadn't heard it, Aaron wouldn't have believed even Falk would have that kind of nerve—and in front of the man whose business he was doing his best to steal.

"I don't live in America now." Libby's voice was low, with a hint of something that made Aaron regard her anxiously.

"But you'll be visiting for a while?" Falk continued to smile.

She shrugged and looked into the fire. "I'm staying until my sister has her baby."

Aaron sat straighter. Thanks to Falk, Libby showed signs of retreating into her too-available shell. She was clearly reacting predictably to Falk's undisguised attraction to her.

"Isn't your sister married to Kinnear, the boat refurbisher up on San Juan?"

Libby nodded.

"Dennis," Aaron began, "perhaps—"

"Is it painful for you to talk about Georges?" Falk asked.

Libby shook her head.

"He really was an idol of mine." The sincerity in the man's voice threatened to choke Aaron. "I used to tell Penny about him. You know I lost...no, you probably don't know my wife died."

"Oh, I'm so sorry." Libby roused herself. "When?"

"Two years ago. An accident. It's hard to talk about those things, isn't it?"

"Yes." Libby's smile was soft and sympathetic.

Aaron seethed. It must be particularly hard to talk about a pointless accident on a mountain road that was caused by driving at high speed while drunk.

"It might do us good to talk." Falk shrugged. "Of course, I understand better than anyone how hard that is. But we might be able to help each other."

"Of course," Libby said.

"I regarded Georges as a good friend," Falk said. "Let's get together."

"That might be nice. I'll call you."

Falk looked at the grandfather clock beside the fireplace. "I've got to go." He stood. "Look, I can't stop now, but I can get the Kinnears' number. I'll call you." He brushed the backs of his fingers across Libby's cheek. "Seeing you is really wonderful." Without a backward glance at Aaron, he left.

"Poor man," Libby said, smiling her thanks as the waitress brought their wine. "Such a hard thing to live with."

The *poor man* was a gambler who knew his game. He was counting on Aaron being hesitant to accuse him of underhanded business practices for fear Libby might think he acted out of jealousy. And Falk was right. Aaron couldn't take that chance.

"Drink your wine," he said. "It'll warm you inside." He'd promised himself not to mention Roger today for fear of tipping his hand. But if Dennis Falk was about to start prowling around Libby, Aaron was going to have to speed up his plans.

The pies came and they were as good as billed. Libby ate little, and her smiles became more and more distant. Damn Dennis Falk, anyway.

When the table had been cleared and more wine brought, she fell into a total silence, which Aaron felt incapable of penetrating.

"I think about it a lot," she said abruptly, lifting her chin. "Not the way people think I do. It's different."

Aaron's breath jammed in his throat. He watched her and waited, certain there was nothing he ought to say.

Without looking at him she reached across the table. He scooted his chair closer and held her slim hand. Music swelled around them. Moody music as she called it, with a strong beat. A few couples danced on the tiny floor.

"It can't be possible to be prepared for the death of someone you love, can it?"

He swallowed. "I don't see how."

"Murder's different." She looked directly at him, and he caught his breath at the puzzled horror there. "It's different from an accidental death."

Instinct told him he was witnessing a breakthrough, and he prayed he'd know the right things to say.

"It was so violent and it didn't have to be."

"Murderers aren't sane, Libby. Georges was helpless."

"Yes. It's hard to trust again. Jean-Claude…" She opened her mouth to breathe. "He never got over the fact that his father squandered a fortune and killed himself. Jean-Claude made himself believe that somehow Georges had no right to be successful when his brother wasn't. And even though he would always have been a wealthy man, he wanted it all and he wanted it then. So he had to get rid of Georges…and me.''

Aaron closed his eyes. ''Thank God he didn't. At least he didn't pull the whole thing off.''

''No. Sudden death doesn't let you prepare.'' Her mouth trembled. ''It overwhelms you and stuns you. You're thrown into mourning without going through the steps of starting to let go.''

''I know.'' He felt so helpless.

''But that's not all, Aaron. Murder is completely evil, and that's what makes the whole thing so hard to reconcile—that good people can be victims of evil.''

He pulled her fingers to his mouth and pressed his lips to her whitened knuckles. ''It's out of our hands, isn't it? We can't control what other people do. Are you starting to accept that? You'll have to if you're going to heal.''

She smiled, a sweet, sad smile. ''I've already accepted it. And maybe I'm healing. When I'm with you, I feel as if I am.''

His lungs expanded and his heart pounded. He wanted to sweep her into his arms and hold on to her forever. ''This is your moody music,'' he said, cocking his head. ''Would you like to dance?''

''I don't think I remember how.''

''Let's find out.'' He pulled her to her feet and onto the floor. The number wasn't too slow or too fast, but the beat made him want to move…with her.

She hadn't forgotten how. Her features relaxed and she looked up at him. ''I didn't know you could dance, Aaron.''

''Most people can.'' He swung her around. They moved well together, as if this were a hundredth rather than a first effort.

''But you can *really* dance.''

"Mmm." He slipped her hands around his neck and wrapped her closer. "The partner makes the difference." He guided her with his body, with his thighs against her hips. Libby rested her face on his shoulder, and he felt her warm breath, soft on his neck. Concentration became a feat.

"Can Serena dance—I mean, ski?"

He frowned and missed half a beat. "Serena?"

"How many Serena's do you know?"

The music mustn't stop. "Do you mean Selena?"

"You know I do."

"Selena's my secretary. I believe she's probably got lots of friends, but I know absolutely nothing about her private life, and I'm not interested."

"Why haven't you ever married, Aaron?"

He sighed and rested his cheek on her temple. "The truth?"

"Is there anything else between friends?"

"I hope not." Somewhere in the past few seconds they'd stopped dancing and simply swayed together. He liked that. "I never thought I'd make a good husband. And although I enjoy kids, I wasn't sure that if I had my own I'd give them the kind of time they deserve."

The music stopped and they stood a little apart, holding hands. "You could change your mind," Libby said. "Do you sometimes think you'd like to now?"

"Maybe. If I ever met the right woman at the right time."

13

Wind drove the rain like horizontal ice spicules. Aaron leaned into the blast and forged ahead down Fourth Avenue with Roger mumbling something incoherent at his side.

"What's the matter?" Aaron asked.

"Madness," Roger said. "We can get coffee in the square or in the office, for that matter. But you have to drag me halfway across Seattle in a hurricane."

"I needed to clear my head. And so do you." They paused at a curb to wait for lights to change before crossing to the triangular espresso bar in front of Westlake Center, Seattle's most-touted new multistoried shopping center.

Roger put on a sudden spurt of speed and pushed open the door to the bar. Once inside they were surrounded by swarms of the young and apparently idle, all dressed to be "different" in outfits that ensured them of safe similarity. Animal prints abounded, and manes of bleached hair—on males as well as females.

Aaron saw Roger's disdainfully curled lip and grinned. "Chill out, Rog," he said. "You've got to get used to being where it's at."

"*Chill out?* Good God, Aaron. Get me some coffee before I go into shock. And for your information, as far as I'm concerned I'm not sure what 'it' is, nor do I care *where* it's at.''

Aaron fought his way between artfully posed bodies to reach the counter and returned with two cups of cappuccino. Roger was already perched on a stool where he could look moodily through the window.

''I had a reason for getting out of the office.''

''Okay. But I didn't, so this had better be good.''

''I didn't want to risk being interrupted and I wanted your undivided attention.''

''So you brought me to the zoo?'' Roger smirked at his little joke. ''This must be the antifur group. The branch going through withdrawal.''

''Yeah. Right. Can you concentrate, or shall I find somewhere else? I'm sure another bracing walk will find us surroundings more to your taste.''

''I'm not going back out there.''

''Good. I brought Libby over from San Juan on Saturday. She visited my parents, then we went skiing and had dinner.''

Roger raised his eyebrows. ''How did you pull off that coup?''

''With a lot of help. The point is that now she's done it once I think we can get her to do it again.''

''She had a good time?''

Aaron's chest tightened. ''I think so. She seemed to relax.'' He'd had a good time, the best he remembered in years. The rest of this had to be over soon, because he wasn't sure how much more he could stand. There was no point in denying the truth to himself anymore. He wanted what he couldn't have. He wanted Libby.

''What's this all about?''

The sharpness of Roger's question snapped Aaron's head around. ''You sound uptight.''

"Maybe I am. I would like to have called and invited her out myself."

It couldn't be that Roger felt jealous of Aaron spending time with Libby? "I told you we couldn't go too quickly. And she decided she was going to stick to Susan's side like glue. Prying her loose wasn't easy."

"But you managed."

Definitely a hard little edge there. "Yes. And now I think it'll be easier to persuade her to leave again. I was going to ask what you've got on for next Saturday."

Roger turned to regard him steadily. "Are you sure you're going about this the right way? Don't you worry that Libby might figure out how you're manipulating her?"

Aaron bristled. "Manipulating's a bit harsh, isn't it? She needs help, and I understand her well enough to give her that. I thought you enjoyed her company."

"Oh, I enjoyed it all right. I enjoyed it very much." His mouth thinned. "What have you got in mind?"

"Why don't you and the girls go skiing at the Ridge next Saturday?"

"We could." The look became speculative. "I thought we were taking things very slowly. Why the sudden rush?"

"Dennis Falk," Aaron said simply.

Roger set down his glass cup with a smack. "What the hell does Falk have to do with this?"

"Libby and I were having dinner on Saturday night and he showed up."

"You're kidding."

"I wish I were. The guy sat down and turned on his charm, if that's what you'd call it, on Libby. Sad widower with so much in common, admirer of Georges, terrible tragedy, we should console each other—the whole works. I thought I was going to throw up, or punch him.''

"My...good Lord, Aaron. What's his angle?"

"Obviously he was at the Ridge to look over what he hopes to make another jewel in his crown. But as far as why he made a play for Libby—'' he turned up his palms "—who knows? Could have been no more than a chance to annoy me. Or he could suddenly have remembered how wealthy Libby is and entertained some wild notion of a different kind of financial merger. It's no secret that he worships at the altar of the dollar. He probably has a picture of Donald Trump in a niche somewhere.''

Roger pushed his cup away, then pulled it back. He picked it up and took a distracted swallow. "We've got to act fast. That piranha's reputation with women isn't built on speculation. Libby's too gentle to understand what he's like. She'd be an easy mark for a pro like that. Do you think he really intends to make a move on her?''

Aaron had to hide a smile. "He said he was going to call and arrange to meet her.''

"Hell! Aaron, he's, well, he's...women find him very attractive I'm told.''

"Libby likes you.'' Aaron watched people passing, leaning into the wind. "She's already told me so.''

"She has?''

"Yes. Will you go to the Ridge on Saturday and let me take it from there? I'll let you know how I intend to work things.''

"I could. The girls have been nagging to go.''

Aaron relaxed a little. "They ski alone now, don't they?''

"Alone?'' Roger snorted. "You bet they do. I can't keep up with them.''

"Good.''

Roger smoothed his hair. "I'm not sure about this."

"I know." Aaron punched the man's shoulder. "You're unsure and so is Libby. But she's unsure about everything and, as I keep telling you, she definitely thinks you're a nice guy, which gives you a head start."

Roger mumbled something.

"What did you say?" Aaron moved closer.

"Nothing. I'll do it."

"Great. What is there to lose?"

Roger stood. "Maybe more than either of us realizes."

14

Libby ran downstairs. She felt in a wonderful mood this morning. Susan looked positively glowing and seemed more relaxed than she had since Libby arrived.

"Libby?" Mike called from the den. "Phone call for you."

Maybe it was Aaron. He hadn't called in two days, not since Monday when he managed to get her to agree to go skiing again on Saturday.

Mike stood in the den, holding the telephone receiver. She took it, smiled at him and said, "Hello. This is Libby Duclaux."

"Hello, Libby Duclaux." The deep male voice was familiar.

She frowned and caught Mike's eye as he sat down and adjusted a pile of papers on his lap. He raised his eyebrows in query, and she shrugged.

"Are you there, Libby?"

"Yes. Who is this?"

"I'm wounded you don't know. It's Dennis Falk."

"Oh." Libby wound the telephone cord between her fingers and perched on the edge of a table.

"Mmm. That doesn't sound too promising. I did say I'd call."

"Yes."

"And you did say you thought it would be a good idea for us to get together."

She bit her lip. Mike had set his papers aside again and moved to the front of his chair as if he intended to leave the room. She covered the receiver. "Don't go. Please."

He stood, looking concerned. "Problems?"

Libby shook her head. "Yes," she said into the phone, "I did say that. Sorry. You caught me off guard. How are you?"

"Better now that you don't sound as if you've received a call from Jack the Ripper. Or as if you'd hoped I was someone else."

She laughed uncomfortably. "Sorry." She *had* hoped he was someone else.

"You already said that. Don't be. When can I see you?"

Her mind blanked. "Umm."

"I'm the one who should be apologizing, aren't I? I've caught you at a bad time."

Mike was frowning deeply. A panicky feeling thrust upward in her throat. "No, it's not a bad time. You surprised me, that's all."

"I think you already said that, too." Dennis paused, then said, "Should I call back, or would you rather I didn't call at all?"

He sounded…sad? Libby rubbed a hand across her eyes. "It was lovely to see you again on Saturday." She must learn to cope well in social situations again.

"Was it? I'm flattered."

"I've made you angry."

He laughed. "You haven't made me angry. Bruised my ego a little perhaps, which is probably good for me, but not made me angry."

Libby smiled. "In other words, you're used to women falling at your feet?"

"Something like that."

"I've always been a pushover for humble men."

"Ouch. Maybe I'd better go cool my heels in my room."

"Only if you think it'll help." She began to feel less tense.

"It'll help if that's what it takes to get you to see me."

A small shaft of warning insinuated itself and widened. What exactly did Dennis Falk want from her? "Dennis, my sister's in the final stages of a very difficult pregnancy."

After a short silence, he said, "I'm sorry. I didn't realize. She's going to be okay, isn't she?"

Libby stood and turned her back on Mike. "Yes."

"Did I say something wrong...again?"

"No."

"Did Aaron say something to make you change your mind about us getting together?"

"Aaron? Of course not." She was making too much of a simple invitation. "I guess I'm a little preoccupied. What I was going to tell you is that until my sister's baby is born I'll be spending most of my time with her."

"That sounds like something you'd do."

"You don't really know me."

"I know you're special. That doesn't take great insight."

She tipped her head back. "Thanks." He was nice... and very attractive. Her own smile was a surprise. Libby Duclaux hadn't entirely forgotten how to notice a good-looking man, after all.

"Most of the time doesn't mean all of the time, does it?" His voice had a low, smooth quality—mesmerizing.

"What?"

"You said you'd be spending most of the time with your sister. Could I put in a bid for some of what's left over? I still think it would do us both good to compare notes. I'll come and get you and deliver you back safely. I promise."

She couldn't help laughing. "I'd like that. But I'm not sure when it'll be possible."

"How about Saturday?"

"Saturday? Well…oh, not Saturday. I'm skiing."

"Aaron again?" The change in tone was almost imperceptible, but there nevertheless.

"Aaron's a very dear friend."

"Lucky man. I didn't realize you were that close. Look, I won't be a pest. Could I call, say, on Monday? We could work something out then."

There was a plea in his voice.

"Do that, Dennis."

After she hung up, she turned to find Mike standing behind her, puzzlement in his frank green eyes. "What was all that about?"

"Someone who was a friend of Georges. I forgot to mention that Aaron and I ran into him at the Ridge on Saturday. His wife died a couple of years ago."

Mike nodded. "Rough."

While he said it, she knew his mind was flitting past his own worries, unable, or unwilling to face the possibility of being in the same position as Dennis Falk.

"I told him we could spend a few hours together. He's going to call me next week."

"You've known him a long time?" He flexed big shoulders inside one of the gray sweatshirts that were almost a uniform.

"Georges and I met him in Aspen." Now that she considered it, she really didn't know the man well at all.

"Sounds like a good idea, then."

"Mmm."

"Tell Susan about it. She'll be pleased." Mike always thought about Susan and ways to distract and entertain her. Libby hadn't failed to notice that there were more and more days when he found excuses to work at home.

"I'm getting her some tea. I'll tell her when I take it up."

Mike returned to his chair. "Does Aaron know this guy?"

"Oh, yes. They've obviously been friends for years."

He smiled. "Good. I guess I feel a bit like an anxious father where you're concerned, huh? Now you can tell me to mind my own business."

"Now I can thank you for caring, you mean. I know I'm not always easy to get along with."

"You only want what we all want—for Susan to be well and stay well. Who did you say he was?"

"I don't think I did. Dennis Falk. He's really very nice."

Mike blinked and his eyes narrowed.

"Is something wrong?"

"Wrong? No, no, nothing." He gathered his papers into an untidy stack and stuffed them under his arm. "Tell Susan I had to go out. I just remembered something I've got to do at the office."

WHY DID SHE HAVE to cry because Aaron gave her something? She sniffed and tried to laugh. "They're absolutely beautiful. But you've got to stop spending money on me." The box on her lap contained short black leather après-ski boots. "How do you know my size?"

"Have you forgotten that I was the guy who was with you when we fixed you up with equipment last week?"

Libby looked through the car windshield at the slopes ahead. Pristine from an overnight snowfall and glittering in pale sunlight, they were already dotted with the morning's first rush of brightly garbed skiers. Aaron had arranged for Mike to drive her to the ferry in Friday Harbor so that they could make an early start on their day at the Ridge.

"You shouldn't spend money on me," she repeated.

"They're just a pair of boots. And who else am I going to spend my money on?" Aaron had departed from his usual black and wore a purple-and-navy-blue racing suit, its bold pattern winding about his body like a second skin. "Anyway, it's my business what I do with my money."

"Not if it makes me cry." She hiccuped and began to laugh.

"You look cute when you cry, but I did anticipate this particular emergency and I've got it covered." Reaching behind his seat for a second time, he produced a flat parcel wrapped in newspaper and tied with string. "Here we go. This'll fix you up."

"What is it?"

He shoved it into her hands.

Libby pulled off the string and paper and stared down at an acrylic painting in a lime-green frame. "A little girl," she said, afraid to look at him. "A little girl holding a bunch of yellow flowers?"

"What do you think?"

She looked at the sickeningly cutesy, oval-faced urchin with huge, doleful blue eyes and wispy brown hair, holding a bunch of pathetic yellow and totally unrecognizable somethings. "It's…interesting." She peered closely.

Jiggling made her glance up. Aaron, a hand over his face, laughed silently.

"What's funny?"

"You. I'd have brought you real dandelions only they aren't in bloom right now. That picture was the answer to my prayers until I can get the live thing." He held up a hand. "Honestly, I got the picture at Pike Place Market for a song. A true steal. You'd have been proud of how little I paid for that masterpiece."

"Thank you," she said gravely. "Aaron, why do you feel you have to give me things?"

He regarded her steadily, all traces of mirth gone. "And why can't you just accept something at face value? You don't buy the things you need for yourself, so someone has to."

The swift change of mood, the anger in his voice, made her feel wobbly. "You don't have to shout."

"Georges used to buy you things." He hooked his finger under her necklace.

Libby flinched. "Don't."

"That's it, isn't it? You associate getting gifts with Georges. You can't let go of the past and move on."

"Maybe. I don't know. Maybe it's because somehow I'm afraid of... Things do remind me of how it felt to lose him. I couldn't bear to lose you."

She felt suspended, cold and removed as if she were outside looking in at herself and at Aaron. Her own words echoed in her brain.

"Oh, Libby. Forgive me." He gathered her in his arms and held her tightly, crushing the awful picture, pressing the boots in their box into her stomach, and she hardly noticed anything but his warmth, the clean scent of him— the pressure of his jaw on her brow.

"It's my fault," she told him. He was broad, and strong

and reassuring. "Anyway—" she tipped her head back to see his face "—I like dandelions, so your mean little joke didn't work."

Aaron studied her carefully, smiling while he massaged the back of her neck beneath her hair. "I suppose you're ready to go conquer the hills?"

At the moment she'd just as soon stay where she was. "I guess so."

He released her and took the picture and box from her lap. "Put on the boots and let's get going."

Her heart beat erratically. Learning not to need him so much was another obstacle that loomed ahead. For now, she was aware of still feeling his arms around her and of wanting them there again. Bending over and hiding her face while she pulled on the boots was a relief. "They're perfect." She'd known they would be.

An hour or so later she skied in Aaron's wake down the most treacherous run Alpine Ridge provided. Narrow, almost vertical, "Screamer" as it was known by regulars, offered the ultimate thrill for experts.

Aaron's falsetto yodel wafted back, and she laughed. He moved as only a man who had been a world-class skier could move, his supple body and powerful legs flexing and in total harmony with the terrain. Libby hit a mogul she hadn't anticipated, and her arms flailed. Regaining control, she chided herself for carelessness and blessed her luck that Aaron wasn't behind instead of in front of her. However—and the next thought brought wry discomfort—if he hadn't been in front of her, she wouldn't have missed the mogul. No woman could fail to be distracted by that most spectacular male in a suit that demolished the need for imagination.

He reached the bottom of the run and carved up a spray

of snow when he stopped. Libby tucked and swooped to catch up.

"Ha!" Shoving his visor on top of his head, he grabbed her around the waist, and she scrabbled, clinging to him while her skis threaded between his. "Gotcha!"

"Aaron!" She slid farther, laughing helplessly. "Let go! You'll kill us both!"

He didn't let go.

"Aaron!" Losing her balance completely, she slithered to her back between his legs. A blur of black and purple cartwheeled past her head and she squealed. Flying clumps of snow sprayed her face.

"Argh!" Aaron let out a mock groan. "I think I did kill something."

Flat on her back, arms outstretched, Libby looked sideways. Spreadeagle himself, Aaron stared back.

"Will you look at us?" she said, completely winded. "Like a couple of kids making snow angels."

Aaron was silent.

She passed her tongue over dry lips.

"Libby…" He stretched out his arm until their gloved fingers touched. "Libby, I…"

She held her breath. Something had changed in his eyes. Hadn't it? "What, Aaron?"

"I…nothing." He smiled and sat up. "I was just remembering that we did this before."

Libby made herself smile back. "You're right. In Italy. Only this time I wasn't running away." What was wrong with her? What had she thought he might say—wanted him to say? She shouldn't feel disappointed.

Swinging his skis, Aaron found his edge and pushed upright. "Give me your hand, Angel. We'd better work on our form." He hauled her up. "Are you okay?"

"Terrific. Don't I look terrific?" She wiped melting snow from her eyelashes.

"Yes, you do." Aaron kissed her cold face soundly. "You're something, Libby. I love skiing with you."

"Me, too—skiing with you, I mean." Everything was all right between them. Nothing had changed. "Let's go again."

The grin was there, the white teeth catching at his lower lip. And Libby's heart seemed to stop.

"Hey! Aaron!"

At the shout they both turned.

"Isn't that Roger?" Libby strained to see the features of a man plodding toward them.

"Looks like it."

"Tried to reach you by phone." It was Roger. Dressed in a red hat, red parka and navy blue windpants, he wore ski boots and used poles to speed his passage over the snow. "I'd promised the girls I'd bring them up for the day, so I decided I'd come and find you. Hi, Libby. How's the skiing? Is he wearing you out?"

It wasn't fair on Roger to be irritated by the sight of him, but she couldn't help her own reactions. "The skiing's great."

"She's the one who does the wearing out around here," Aaron said, but he wasn't smiling. "Why were you trying to reach me?"

"It's complicated," Roger said. "Mind if we go back to the lodge? The girls are hopping around waiting to get going. They don't want me along, but I do like to set down a few rules before they start. Even if they don't remember them for more than two minutes. Anyway, you'll need to make a call."

Aaron didn't ask any more questions before setting off in the direction of the lodge.

Even in ski gear Roger's daughters were easily identifiable.

"Hot chocolate for anyone?" Roger asked. He appeared awkward.

"No thanks." Libby smiled at him. "We're planning a couple more runs before lunch. The piste's getting pretty torn up already."

"I've skied in Italy," Roger said. "Beautiful country. But I'm still biased on the side of our slopes."

"They're different."

"Can't we get going, Dad?" Hilary said, speaking for the first time. "It's hot in here."

Hot and filled with a new threat for mildly insecure little girls—Libby herself. "You don't have to keep me company, Roger."

"I want to." Checking his watch, he said, "You two can carry on. You've got money for lunch. I'll see you back here for a visual check at two—"

"Ah, Dad!" Sonja balanced her weight on one leg. "Two? Just so you can tell us it's okay to leave again?"

"Two," Roger repeated, and Libby was glad to see how firm he was with his children. "And remember, you won't know when I'm likely to see you so don't do anything silly. Stay together. Don't stray from the runs."

"Yeah, yeah." Hilary crammed a fuchsia hat on her head, stuffed the pigtails inside and tugged her sister's arm.

"Bye, you two. Have a good time." Roger watched until the door closed behind them. "Kids have to be maturing earlier. Wouldn't you say that kind of behavior sounds more like fifteen than twelve?"

"I'm not a good judge." How could she be? "They seem like nice, well-adjusted girls to me." Even if they had exhibited symptoms of dislike-at-first-sight where she was concerned.

She caught sight of a flash of purple and black, and Aaron threaded a path between groups of skiers. His expression was grim.

"I've got to go to the office."

"That's what I thought," Roger said. "I tried to pinch-hit, but they wanted words with the Man himself."

"Damn nuisance." Aaron planted his fists on his hips. "Unfortunately I need to look over some files. Otherwise I could do this from here."

Libby pulled off her hat. "We'd better get going."

"I hate to ruin your day."

"Won't take you too long, will it?" Roger asked. "If Libby can stand my company, we could take a few runs until you get back."

"That'd be a nuisance," Libby said hastily. "Your girls will need you, and I don't want Aaron to have to spend half his day driving."

"Unfortunately my girls will be very glad if I stay out of their hair." Roger's smile did nice things for an ordinary face. "And I could drive you back if Aaron prefers."

"No need for that," Aaron said. "I'll do what I have to and come to take Libby to the ferry. I'm going over to see Mike and Susan."

"Are you sure? It wouldn't be out of my way to drive up."

"Yes, it would. I'll be back."

And so her decisions were made for her, Libby thought, looking from one man's face to the other.

Roger caught her eye. "That's if you'd like to stay. I'd certainly enjoy your company." He sounded hopeful, and she didn't have the heart to say she'd much rather return to Seattle with Aaron.

"I'd like that very much."

"I'll be back," Aaron said.

Libby watched him go, a tall, imposing man, undoubtedly aware of but totally unaffected by the attention he drew.

"You're fond of him, aren't you?"

She drew in a sharp little breath and gave Roger her full attention. "We've been through...Aaron and I have traveled a few stony paths in each other's company. I guess that's a pretty good way to put it. Thanks for agreeing to put up with me."

"Yes...I mean thank you for staying. Come on. Time for you to see how mediocre I am for a man who makes his living in this business."

Two less than exciting runs down an intermediate hill dubbed "Bum's Run" proved Roger to be exactly the skier he'd billed himself. But he was pleasant company. Libby couldn't help laughing at his stream of self-derisive comments.

"Roger," she yelled, passing him in a zigzag attempt not to outpace him too badly. "Spend less time criticizing yourself and more time getting down the hill."

He waved a pole. "I told you I was lousy." His voice faded as she moved away.

On the return pass she asked, "So why do you come?"

"Because I like it, of course."

Libby snickered, cut her traverse short and bobbed back in his direction, her posture upright. "If you like it, Roger, how come you're beating yourself up because you aren't satisfied with your form?"

"Grr. Exposed." He showed his teeth in a mock snarl. "Why pretend? I'm no better than an adolescent who wants to impress the prettiest cheerleader. I want to impress you!'' His shout echoed across the snow in her wake.

He was so *nice,* darn it. A sneaky doubt crawled into her brain. Had he and Aaron cooked up this so-called emergency? No, Aaron had been enjoying himself. She'd swear to that. If only she could want to be with Roger the way he was too charmingly admitting he wanted to be with her.

They decided on one more run before lunch and joined the lift line. Once off the chair, Roger moved ahead along the ridge. Libby heard the soft swish of skis behind her and kept to the side of the trail.

''No,'' a familiar voice said as the tips of neon-green Kastles drew level with her downward glance. ''It can't be Libby.''

She looked up into Dennis Falk's smiling face. His windsuit, slashed with black and red stripes, matched the blinding color of his skis.

''It *is* Libby. I can't believe my luck.''

There was nothing for it but to stop. ''Roger,'' she called. ''Wait!''

''Fancy meeting you up here.'' Dennis smiled engagingly, his teeth very white in a tanned face. Hatless, his blond hair curled wildly.

''Do you ski here every weekend?'' Libby realized she had no idea what the man did for a living. She couldn't remember from their previous meeting of years ago.

He leaned close. ''I'm a bad liar,'' he said, glancing in the direction from which Roger was now approaching. ''I admit I was hoping I might at least catch a glimpse of you up here.''

She bowed her head and smiled. ''You make it hard to be angry. But this is going to be hello and goodbye.''

Dennis spread his arms. ''I know. Which shows you

the depth of my regard for you. A moment was worth the effort.''

"Sure." She took in the overall, very professional, very expensive gear and laughed. "You don't even like skiing, do you?''

"Well…''

"What is it?'' Roger reached them, looked at Dennis and scowled.

Libby gripped her poles tightly. Roger really was scowling, an event she was sure would be rare with this man. *Roger was jealous?* Turning her face up to the sky, she wished she were anywhere but here.

"Roger Chandler. I'll be damned. If you aren't the last man I expected to see up here.''

"I ski regularly,'' Roger said stiffly. "We'd better move it, Libby. Time for lunch.''

"How's business, Roger?''

"Terrific.''

Dennis leaned on his poles and showed no sign of moving. "Glad to hear that. Did you get my message last week?''

"I don't think so.'' An ugly stain of red suffused Roger's face.

"Odd,'' Dennis said. "I had it delivered to your home by messenger.''

"That is odd.'' Roger's stare was vitriolic. "You ready, Libby?''

"Yes.''

"You know, Roger, I've heard a lot of good things about you.'' Dennis's conversational tone began to grate on Libby.

"I'm flattered.''

"I intended you to be.''

"There's always room for a talented man to move up.''

Roger shifted his skis. "Some men reach a point where they aren't interested in moving up."

"When they're dead, you mean?" Dennis's laugh was unpleasant. "I never thought of you as a humorist."

"I'm not."

Libby began to feel she was hearing a coded exchange.

"Really?" Dennis straightened and gave himself a forward shove. "I hope you'll rethink that. Sometimes choices about where we want to be are taken away from us. It's unfortunate to get caught in the middle of a situation like that."

"Those are the chances we all take." Roger's skin had taken on a pale hue.

"Oh, I don't know." The distance between Dennis and Roger widened. "I believe a winner can shape his destiny. You're a winner, Roger. There's always a place at the top for your kind and always someone who wants to help him get there. So we understand each other?"

"Don't hit any rocks," Roger said.

Dennis laughed over his shoulder. "I won't. Give me an answer, Roger. Do you understand what I've told you?"

"Sure. I understand."

"Good. Then the future looks bright for all the right people. Talk to you on Monday, Libby."

"Yes." Her faint response could never have reached Dennis.

As soon as he was out of sight, she turned to Roger. "What was all that about?"

He smiled, but she got the impression the result took effort. "Just business banter. Don't give it another thought." He set off, mumbling under his breath. One comment carried clearly on the crisp air. Roger said, "I hope the bastard breaks his neck before someone has to do it for him," and launched himself downhill.

15

The social cold front settled in the moment Aaron got into the Peugeot beside Libby. She felt his suppressed irritation fill the confines of the small car like the volatile stillness before a violent storm.

He started the car and floored the accelerator...with the predictable result. Despite chains the tires spun and the rear of the car fishtailed.

Libby looked at Roger, who sat behind the wheel of his own car in the next parking slot. His eyes had widened in surprise.

She folded her hands in her lap. "Didn't things go well in Seattle?"

"Why do you ask that?" For the second time in one day he sounded angry.

"I wondered, that's all. You seem..."

"I seem what? I'm fine. Everything went perfectly well."

Libby flinched but said nothing. This new side of Aaron was something she had no idea how to deal with.

Roger's Jaguar moved smoothly away. He waved and the girls followed suit. Their smiles, Libby was sure, came from their relief at having their father to themselves again. This had been a difficult day.

"Roger said you had a great time," Aaron said, negotiating easily into the line of departing vehicles this time.

"It was very nice."

As soon as Aaron had arrived back at the lodge—while she and Roger were finishing dinner—the two men had disappeared together. When they returned, from the suite Libby hadn't realized Aaron had on an upper floor in the lodge, Roger had been subdued and Aaron withdrawn.

"Roger tells me the two of you plan to do something together next weekend."

"If Susan doesn't need me." Roger had been so sweet and thoughtful. Looking into his hopeful eyes, she'd been unable to turn him down.

"So the two of you are really hitting it off."

"He's a special man. There should be more people like him."

The corner of Aaron's mouth jerked down. "That's good to hear. We cynical types like to have our faith in decency restored from time to time, even if it does bore us."

"Aaron—" She closed her mouth firmly. The mildest people had bad moods from time to time. Answering nastiness with nastiness would accomplish nothing.

"Aaron, what? Finish what you were going to say."

"I've forgotten." A small shudder traveled along her muscles. The antagonism made her uncomfortable and insecure.

"Maybe you were going to tell me I could take lessons from Roger in how to be good."

That kind of remark didn't deserve a response. Libby propped her elbow on the door and supported her head. Headlights swung along striated banks of snow as high as a one-story building. A never-ending line of giant firs, their heavily laden branches touching, reached into a star-speckled black sky.

"Thank you for bringing me, Aaron," she said when the silence twisted her stomach. "This is a beautiful place."

"You're welcome."

She sighed. "Are you sure nothing happened to upset you this afternoon?"

"Absolutely sure."

"Good. I had a very nice time."

He straightened his arms. "So you've already said several times."

Heat rushed over Libby's face and neck. "You must be tired. I'm sorry you had to drive all the way back to get me."

"I didn't *have* to." He sounded, what? Furious?

"No." Libby swallowed, growing more and more agitated. "But thank you, anyway."

"Damn!"

She turned to him, trembling inside. "What is it? Why are you angry with me?"

"I'm not angry with you. I'm angry with myself."

Her heart beat so hard that she pressed a fist to her chest. "Why?"

"Never mind. It's personal, okay?" He glanced at her, his features harsh in the light from the dashboard. "Is it okay with you if I don't explain every thought I have?"

"Of course." Hunching her shoulders, she wedged herself into the corner of the seat and closed her eyes.

"So now you're going to sulk. Typical woman. You can't get what you want out of a man, so you sulk."

Libby's eyes snapped open and she sat upright. "What are you talking about? I never sulk. And what am I supposed to want out of you?"

"Of course you sulk. All women do."

The shaky feeling made her teeth chatter. "I asked you a question. What am I supposed to want from you?"

He glared ahead. "I need to concentrate on what I'm doing here."

"In other words, back off." She crossed her arms. "That's fine."

"Good."

Snow slid from a tree and shot in a minislide across the road. Libby watched the way clumps rolled and bounced and glittered atop the hard pack left by many tires.

Suddenly her stomach seemed to fall away. "Did Mike call?"

"No."

"Oh, Aaron. Don't do this to me. Has something happened to Susan? I knew I shouldn't have left." Too late, she realized she'd grabbed his arm.

The car swerved. "I said no!" Aaron steadied the vehicle. "Stop being paranoid, will you? I would have told you if anything like that had happened."

"I'm sorry," she said in a very small voice. "I'm really so sorry."

"Please don't cry. I can't bear it when you cry."

Her throat constricted. "I'm not crying. I'm going to sleep if that's all right with you."

Fifteen minutes passed, half an hour, an hour. Libby kept watch on the clock through slitted eyes. When she dared, she peeked at Aaron—and quickly pressed her lids together. Something was wrong with him. He wouldn't confide in her, and she couldn't bear it.

"We'll be at the ferry in half an hour."

She didn't answer.

"I know you're awake."

"Yes."

"Is there anything you want to tell me about this afternoon?"

She straightened, wincing at her protesting muscles. "I already told you it was a good afternoon."

"Why didn't you say you saw Dennis Falk?"

"You didn't give me a chance," she said, incensed at his attitude. "And it was this morning. Just before lunch."

"You're going out with him."

Libby shook her head. "I haven't made any arrangements to go out with Dennis."

"He's calling you on Monday to talk about getting together."

"Yes. He's a pleasant man, and I think he's trying to be polite. Nothing more." She wasn't at all sure of that, but since Aaron had appointed himself her caretaker, she wouldn't add to the issues he thought he had to worry about on her behalf. "Surely Roger told you we barely said more than a few words to Dennis." What would be more interesting would be an interpretation of the remarks Dennis had made to Roger. Again this didn't seem the time to mention the subject.

"Why didn't you tell me about Dennis's call on Wednesday?"

The low-lying buildings in the center of the town of Anacortes lay on either side of them now, and Libby studied them while she tried to decipher what was going on.

"Why, Libby?"

"Mike told you about that," she said slowly.

He coughed. "Well, in passing, yes."

"A remark in passing was all it was worth. I wasn't thinking about it this morning. If you were, why didn't *you* mention it?"

"Let's drop it."

"Don't you like Dennis Falk?"

Aaron paused for a stop sign before taking a right turn at a Y intersection. "To be honest, I'm not particularly fond of the guy. But I don't have the right to choose your friends."

"I've given you the right to say whatever you feel like saying to me," she told him. "Is there a particular reason why I shouldn't have anything to do with Dennis?"

They reached the tollbooth for the ferry. Aaron paid and joined a line of waiting vehicles. "What I feel about Dennis is my problem. It doesn't have to affect you."

Libby sighed and leaned her head back. "You sound so irritated. Not that I blame you. Feeling responsible for someone else must get pretty overwhelming."

"What little you let me do for you...I like doing things for you." With the engine switched off the night closed in around them.

"When this is all over, I'm going to find a way to make a real difference to as many children in need as I can touch." She must let him know that she didn't intend to remain a burden and that she wasn't a woman content to live without purpose.

"I wish..." He averted his face. "You're trying to say that you don't want anything from me, aren't you?"

They never quite reached each other. "I'm not saying that, Aaron. I do want you."

"No. Not really." He laughed, a brittle little noise. "It's okay. We loners have to stick as far apart as possible, huh?"

"Is that supposed to be funny?" He was making her throat ache with wanting to understand him.

"No. It doesn't feel a bit funny."

"I always want to know you're there." Libby reached for and found his hand.

He squeezed and rubbed each finger. "What you really want is to be able to take me out of my box from time to time." Light caught his dark eyes. "My box is here in the States of course. So you'd like me to get out every six months and show up on your doorstep. Then you get to check me over to make sure I'm okay. And I do know it matters to you that I'm okay because you're so scared that something will happen to someone else you care about."

She tried to pull her hand away, but his fingers closed to trap hers.

"Then," he continued, "when you're sure I don't have any bad nicks or bruises, you're happy to pack me away again."

"No, I'm not. I'm—" She began to cry. Hateful tears. They choked her, gave away her weakness.

"Please, don't," Aaron said quietly. "Don't take any notice of me. I never was much good at handling people. That's why it's a good idea for me not to spend much time with them."

"You're part of my life." Why didn't he know without having to be told? And why did she feel this change, this slipping away that she was helpless to stop? "You're like the breath that comes into me so that I can breathe out again. One doesn't work without the other."

Libby bent forward and covered her face.

A strong arm, pulling her sideways, landed her with her nose pressed into Aaron's thigh. "That goes double from my side, kid." He sounded funny. "What d'you suppose we should do about that?"

Turning her cheek to rest on his leg, Libby closed her eyes and breathed deeply, trying to let the soothing strokes of his hand on her hair calm her. "I know you may not see it, but I've come a long way in the past few weeks.

I'm stronger than I used to be. Don't give up on me, Aaron.''

Gently he eased her up, brushed back her hair and wiped at tears with a thumb. ''Ah, Libby, I can't give up on you. Don't you know that?''

''I guess so.''

''All I need from you is a sign. Tell me what you want and you've got it.''

She wanted him to love her as a man loves a woman.

Libby's stomach contracted as if from a blow. Aaron was her friend, her best friend, nothing more. And nothing must change that. But it had changed. Fear and deep sickness swamped her. Blinking, scarcely able to breathe, she said, ''Just keep on being my friend. Promise me that.''

His hesitation frightened her. If he guessed how she felt, he'd run as far and as fast as he could. He didn't want permanent attachments of the kind she'd dared to think about.

''You've got it, friend,'' he finally told her. ''I promise.''

Libby couldn't stand being this close to him for another second. She turned the corners of her mouth up. ''I'll hold you to it.''

Aaron released her. ''That's great. Ferry's in.'' He switched on the engine.

MIKE TRUDGED in Aaron's wake along the beach. Sunshine for the second day in a row was a treat that lifted his spirits. Or it would if buddy Aaron weren't marching along, exuding an aura akin to that of an impending explosion.

Last night, after he'd brought Libby home and visited with Susan, he'd collapsed in a chair by the den stove and demolished three stiff bourbons—not Aaron's usual style.

Then he'd walked out without saying good-night, leaving Mike and Libby looking at each other in uncomfortable silence.

Libby had left moments later, and so far this morning Mike hadn't seen her.

"Hold up!" He broke into a loping run and fell into step with Aaron. "You invited me out here. If you'd rather walk alone, say so."

"I don't know what I'd rather do anymore."

Mike raised his eyebrows. Some might say he was a simple man, a man with only ordinary insight, but they'd be wrong. A rumble had been detected by his inner ear from the moment Aaron brought Libby back to the States. A storm was brewing between these two, and the only one who seemed to know it was him…unless Aaron had finally noticed that certain things were almost inevitable.

"Great day." Now that was an inspired attempt. "Look at the waves."

Sheets of crystalline green, glasslike and shot with trimmings of spume, rose to fall upon yellow sand. Folding, wrapping rocks and pebbles in a cold embrace, the water receded, only to paw the coastline again and again.

"You live in a great spot," Aaron said. "I envy you your peace."

"I didn't find it so easily," Mike reminded him. "If Susan hadn't come along and made me take a long look at my life, I might still be trying to find myself. Whatever that really means." He could always risk everything and just spit out what was on his mind. The thought made him shudder.

"Yeah. Well, at least there was something worthwhile waiting for you. It's a myth that there's someone perfect for everyone. Bunch of crap, in fact."

"You're in a charming mood." He was also ripe for

the kind of discussion Mike longed to have. Only the courage wasn't quite as strong as it needed to be.

"Dennis Falk," Aaron muttered.

"Oh," Mike turned his *oh* into a tuneless whistle.

"Son of a bitch." Aaron stomped on, driving the heels of his boots deep into the sand. The bottoms of his jeans were damp.

"Want to talk about it?"

Aaron turned on him. "If you don't want to hear, just say so. I don't want any favors from anyone. I can handle my own problems."

Mike lifted his hands. "Whoa. Cool off. I'm not the enemy."

Aaron sniffed, his eyes narrowed. "When Falk called here, he arranged to talk to Libby tomorrow?"

"Yes. That's what she told me."

"D'you think she didn't tell you what they really arranged?" he shot back.

"Good grief, no." Growing irritated, Mike walked on. "I don't know where you're coming from."

"I'm mad as hell." Aaron caught up. "That's where I'm coming from. You said you were there when Libby talked to Falk."

"I was."

"Do you remember if she mentioned going skiing yesterday?"

Mike thought. "Yes. Yes, she did. She said she was going with you."

"Hah!" Aaron picked up a rock and hurled it at the water. "Just what I thought. That bastard showed up at the Ridge yesterday and tracked her down."

"No kidding." And Aaron expected the world to believe that the only reason that made him angry was because of his business difficulties with Falk?

"She was with Roger. I'd already left."

"Huh?"

"I'm not going into all that." Aaron turned a fascinating shade of red. "Libby and Roger are getting along very well. She'll probably go out with him again next weekend. Isn't that great?"

"Great." For a man who usually managed his life well, Aaron appeared to be making one hell of a mess of it currently.

"It won't be great if that vulture Falk stirs things up. He approached Roger right in front of Libby. Not in direct terms. She wouldn't have known what he was talking about. But he more or less told Roger it was time to choose sides and the winning side was going to be Falk."

Mike stopped walking. "You mean he suggested Roger join his team?"

"You've got it. He made it clear that he intends to go after me and that he'd like Roger in his camp." He kicked up sand and squinted into the sun. "Roger won't go. At least, I don't think he will."

"You know he won't."

"Yes…although he's only human."

"Roger's your man. What do you think Falk's angle is with Libby?"

Aaron cursed vehemently. "The guy knows something special when he sees it. In other words he's got flawless taste, damn it. He took one look at her and wanted her. Falk goes after the best of everything."

"He knows you two are friends. Surely he'll expect you to warn Libby off."

Aaron shrugged. "I'm backed into a corner. If I tell her the whole story, she might think I'm encouraging this thing with Roger so she'll help keep him—and his stock—on my side."

"Don't be an ass." Mike grabbed Aaron's arms. "Libby knows you wouldn't use her."

"Maybe. But I have kind of—I've engineered the friendship with Roger. If Falk gets at Roger somehow, and Libby should decide she doesn't want to…she could decide Roger isn't for her. He's fond of her, Mike. This whole thing would blow up in my face if Roger got mad and told her what I've done."

"And you think Falk's worked all that out already?"

"No. I'm just telling you what I'm afraid of and why I'm not about to draw Libby into everything. Falk's pig-headed enough about his prowess with women to believe he can make her want him regardless of anything I might say."

"Look," Mike said, shoving his hands into his pockets, "I've never met Dennis Falk, but Libby's pretty much an open book to me. He's not her type."

"I hope not. She's definitely getting keener on Roger. But Falk's flamboyant, Mike. The quintessential lady-killer. Smooth. She could fall for him."

The sensation fermenting in Mike shook him. He swallowed and turned toward the sea.

"You think so, too." Aaron came to stand beside him, then leaned to look into his face. "Don't you? Damn. What am I going to do?"

"Stop it all!" Mike felt his temper snap. He threw up his hands. "Take charge, for crying out loud. Fix it once and for all."

"Mike—"

"Will you please be quiet and listen to me? Think, man. Buy Roger out."

"I can't. I haven't—"

"No, you haven't got the money right now. But Libby has."

Aaron's eyes stared blankly. Then he frowned. "Libby? I wouldn't borrow money from Libby."

"No, you wouldn't. But wouldn't it make sense to consolidate what the two of you have. You manage her affairs, anyway. Conrad's is a good investment for anyone. It would certainly be a good investment for Libby, particularly if she was your wife. You…you're very fond of each other. The two of you would make a fantastic team— financially and otherwise."

For seconds the sound of the waves was all he heard, the spray in the air all he felt. Aaron's eyes were black and expressionless.

Bone connecting with bone had a sound like no other. It had a feel like no other.

Aaron's fist caught Mike's jaw in a square uppercut that rattled his brain. He slipped, staggered and stopped his own arm in midswing. "What the hell—?" He shook his head. "Why did you do that?"

"I'm going to try to forget what you just said." Aaron turned on his heel. "But don't hold your breath in the meantime."

16

The man at the piano contrived to sound like Willie Nelson. Libby sipped her daiquiri through a fat straw. The not-quite-country sound fitted her mood.

Roger's hand rested on the table, a well-shaped, strong-looking hand with dark blond hair across the back. A slim yellow-gold Rolex rested low on his wrist. Hands fascinated her, good hands like Roger's...but most of all Aaron's hands.

Everything came back to Aaron.

The gravelly, harmonica-quality voice sang something about wanting one more chance, about never being able to forget. Where was Aaron at this moment?

"This was a good idea I had," Roger said, smiling at her. "I'm glad I got your sister on the phone. She thinks I have good ideas, too."

Libby looked through the windows of the bar at the resort restaurant at Roche Harbor. "She conspired with you, Roger, or I wouldn't be here."

"Come on, loosen up." He took her wrist in his long fingers, and she felt him gauging her reaction. "You're still on the same island as Susan. Less than a ten-mile drive and we're back."

"I haven't felt good about her in the past couple of days."

"Really? I'd have liked to meet her. The French-woman—Mimi Sedi...?"

"Mimi Sedillot. She's my companion in Madonna di Lago. And she suggested it wasn't a good idea for you to see Susan because that's what Mike and I have decided. No visitors except immediate family and staff until this is all over."

"I see." At least he didn't appear surprised or offended.

"What did Aaron say about you taking off on a Wednesday?" Whatever he'd said would be more than she'd heard from him since Saturday night. By the time she'd felt like facing anyone on Sunday, he'd left and Mike refused to say when or why.

"Aaron's in a foul mood." Roger rocked his glass back and forth, digging the base into a damp napkin. "I got the impression...well, how does he seem to you?"

A fierce need to protect Aaron made her say, "He always gets strung out at this time of the year."

"Of course," Roger said, and she realized he was too polite to tell her that he was in a very good position to know all about Aaron's seasonal moods.

Susan had indeed been enthusiastic about this trip. Evidently she and Mike frequently made the drive across San Juan to Roche. Formerly the home of John S. McMillin, founder of Roche Harbor Lime and Cement Company in the late 1800s, the old restaurant provided a view over Haro Strait. Sunny days had continued, and today the waters stretched like a sheet of silvery-tipped chips of indigo foil.

"There's a few million dollars-worth of seagoing real estate down there." Roger indicated the impressive assortment of boats bobbing against the docks. "If I ever have time, I intend to get into sailing."

''Not me.'' Georges had died aboard the yacht he'd bought for her. She never intended to own another.

''I understand Dennis Falk owns something resembling the *QEII*.''

Libby glanced at him sharply. ''You don't sound as if you like Dennis any more than Aaron does.''

''Aaron talked to you about that?''

''Not really. He only said Dennis wasn't one of his favorite people.''

Roger had kept his hand on her wrist. He patted her and withdrew. ''Did you get your promised call on Monday?''

She longed to ask exactly what the animosity between Aaron, Roger and Dennis stemmed from. ''Yes.''

''Are you going to see him?''

The carefully level tone didn't fool her. A small muscle twitched beneath his eye.

''We didn't make any definite arrangements.''

''But he did ask?''

She should resent the not very subtle interrogation, but Roger was gentle, and much as she wished it weren't so, his interest in her shone like a beacon. ''Dennis asked me to have dinner with him this weekend. I declined because I'm serious when I say I'm worried about Susan.''

''That doesn't sound as if the subject is entirely closed.''

Libby sighed. ''No, I don't think it is. We may get together one of these days.''

''I see.''

The piano man played a slow number with a heavy beat. Libby leaned back in her chair. Dancing with Aaron at the lodge was something she would never forget. Part of her wished she could forget. A stronger part ached with a longing to dance again, to close her eyes and let him guide her with his body....

"Are you up for a walk? Everyone's supposed to see the mausoleum here. Masonic-style construction."

She pressed her lips together and nodded. "Yes." The sooner she put distance between her and Aaron the better.

Roger, comfortably solid in a heavy gray sweater, jeans and a fawn parka, led the way from the restaurant to a narrow road that wound uphill. Gnarled madrona trees, strips of red bark peeling from their trunks overhung the way.

Libby tried to relax. With her hand tucked through Roger's she murmured in response to his comments. They walked past a tiny church, resort cabins and an airstrip.

"The mausoleum is something," Roger said. "Mc-Millin certainly didn't like the idea of being forgotten."

A rangy black part-Labrador fell companionably into step. They must look like a couple out for an afternoon stroll, Libby thought. Only they weren't a couple, and even to make Aaron happy, she couldn't imagine being more to Roger than a friend.

"I haven't enjoyed myself...I can't remember when I had such a good time," he said, turning a serious face toward her. "You make me feel very peaceful, Libby, very happy."

Her heart felt wadded tight. She smiled at him and watched her feet in the black après-ski boots Aaron had bought her. They were the most suitable thing she owned for this type of outing.

"You can see the harbor from a different angle over here." Roger left the road. Resting a hand at her waist, he walked them down a narrow track deeply covered with wet brown leaves to a point where they looked back across the water in the direction from which they'd come.

Libby shivered. She really must replace her thin jeans, but her shiver had nothing to do with being cold.

"Chilly?" Roger asked on cue. His hand moved from her waist to her shoulder, and he pulled her closer.

Not stiffening and moving away took more control than she'd known she had. This wasn't fair—on either of them.

Without warning Roger turned her into his arms and looked down into her eyes. "I don't expect you to fall in love with me, Libby. Not yet. But I hope someday… You and I could be very good for each other. I feel it."

She couldn't swallow, couldn't respond.

Very gently he wound a stray tendril of hair behind her ear and bent to kiss her lightly on the cheek.

Closing her eyes, she didn't resist when he held her against his shoulder. To tell him now, in this time and space, that she could never feel for him what he wanted her to feel would be cruel. There had to be a kinder way to disengage, and she'd find it.

"Roger—" with her hands on his chest she stepped back "—this has been good for me. Getting away. But I'm as edgy as a cat. Would you forgive me if I passed on the mausoleum?" She laughed and heard how forced she sounded. "Frankly it sounds more grisly than I'm up for."

"Of course," he said at once. "I'm being selfish, trying to keep you out longer. You want to get back, don't you?"

She let out a grateful, wobbly breath. "It's hard to explain. I've never believed in premonitions, but I keep getting the sensation that something's going to happen."

"Don't disregard premonitions." His smile was a little sad. "I get them sometimes and they're often right."

Libby didn't think she misread a hinted-at question in his words, but she avoided what she couldn't deal with now. Looking again toward the harbor, she seemed to see a subtle darkening over the water, and the air grew more still. An abrupt peal of bells startled her.

"Just the carillon of bells at the church." Roger lifted her chin. "Are you all right?"

"I don't know. Maybe this is part of what Aaron calls my paranoia...." Embarrassed at what she'd said, she caught his hand and scrambled back toward the road. "Susan needs me."

Roger didn't question the statement.

On the drive back across the island Libby's near-panic subsided. She sank low in her seat, overcome by a guilty conviction that she'd invented an excuse to escape what had threatened to become a sticky situation with Roger.

He smiled slightly as he drove. "The girls asked a few hundred questions about you, everything from whether or not I liked you to what it was like to live in Italy. I think they were entertaining daydreams of skiing in Italian mountains."

Libby thought it much more probable that they were more interested in the first question. "They'll have to come and visit me," she said, aware that she was implying that Roger should bring them.

"That would be wonderful."

This added stress had better be resulting in some satisfaction for Aaron.

"Who's car is that?" Roger asked when they turned the corner that brought Mike and Susan's house into view.

Libby sat forward. A blue Mercedes sedan was parked near the fuchsia hedge that bordered the property.

"I don't know."

A siren screamed. Roger pulled to the side of the road to allow an emergency vehicle, red and blue lights flashing, to pass.

"Oh, no!" She wrenched open the door and began to run.

The white van stopped behind the Mercedes, and what seemed like a swarm of men, one carrying a folded gurney, sprinted down the driveway toward the house.

THE ELEVATOR DOORS opened onto the third floor of the hospital, and Aaron saw Mike. He sat, his head in his hands, on the edge of a chair against the corridor wall.

"Mike. How's Susan?"

The face Mike raised was set in rigid lines of worry. "I don't know yet." A bluish bruise darkened one side of his jaw.

"Connie called my mother, and she contacted me to say you were here. They must have flown her to Seattle by Medevac."

"Yes. She was disoriented. I'd gone to the yard. Lester called, and when I got there the local doctor had already arrived. He said she needed to be here, so they brought her out by helicopter. Me, too."

Aaron looked around. "Where's Libby?"

"Not here yet. They're coming by ferry."

Mike stood up. He crossed his arms, then uncrossed them. "This is my fault."

"Mike—"

"No. I shouldn't have allowed it to happen, damn it."

Half expecting to be shrugged away, Aaron put his hands on Mike's shoulders. "It was meant to happen. Michael Georges was meant to happen. They're going to come through this."

Mike didn't reject him. "What's taking them so long?"

"I don't know. But they'd better hurry, or I'm going to lose it right with you." He wrapped Mike in a brief bear hug that was convulsively returned before they moved apart.

"I'm sorry if I said the wrong thing on Sunday."

"Forget it." He shoved his hands into his pockets. "I shouldn't have...well, I can't remember the last time I threw a punch."

Mike fingered his jaw, and a ghost of a grin touched his mouth. "You haven't lost your touch. Susan thinks I tripped over a rock and fell on a piece of driftwood." He looked away. "I can't take this."

"Neither can I. How long will it take Libby to get here?"

"Not too much longer I should think. Depends on the ferry schedule."

"She'll be frantic. I wish I was with her."

"You will be soon," Mike said.

Aaron looked at him sharply and turned to stare through a window. He'd had days to think about what had passed between them on Sunday morning. Mike knew his friend well enough to have picked up some of what he felt for Libby. But Aaron couldn't believe he fully understood the implications of what he'd suggested.

"Mike. You won't ever say anything to Libby—not anything like you said to me?"

Mike gave him a measured stare. "I hadn't planned to."

"She'd be horrified."

"Would she?"

"Good Lord!" He spun around and paced. "She thinks of me as her good old buddy. Never do anything to undermine that. Promise me, Mike."

"Okay, okay. I—"

He stopped as the elevator doors opened to reveal

Libby. She rushed straight into Mike's arms. "Where is she?"

"They're getting her settled. The doctor said he'd come out and talk to us soon."

"Soon?" She looked at Aaron with unfocused eyes. "How long have they been in there?"

Aaron made a move toward her and stopped. Mimi Sedillot had followed from the elevator, her arm through Lester Kinnear's. Roger was the last to appear. He went directly to Libby's side and settled a hand on her back. She bowed her head, and Roger gathered her against him.

"Mike," Aaron said, "I'm going down to the cafeteria. I'll check back after a while."

SUSAN'S EYES fluttered shut.

"She seems better," Libby said to Mimi, who sat on the opposite side of the bed. "Very quiet."

"It's the sedation." Mike leaned against the wall. "But whatever works is okay with me."

"You look worn-out," she told him. For the two nights since Susan had been brought to the hospital he'd slept on a rollaway bed in the same room.

"Mike's a strong man," Mimi said, as if he weren't present. "As his father says, his place is with Susan."

Libby smiled. These days Mimi rarely had an opinion that didn't seem to spring from some remark of Lester's. Even Marjorie Conrad—the Conrads had insisted that Libby stay with them until she returned to San Juan—had commented on how close Lester and Mimi appeared.

"I called home," Mike said. "Anne thinks she should be here."

"Maybe she should," Libby murmured.

"There's nothing she can do," Mike said. "And Susan wouldn't want her missing a lot of school."

And you want Susan to yourself as much as possible, Libby thought.

The door opened and a nurse popped her head inside. "Mr. Conrad wonders if he could spend a moment or two. I'll have to ask two of you to wait outside first." She looked with disapproval at the three of them. "We really should keep our visitors to no more than two at a time."

Mimi got up at once and Libby started to move.

"Stay where you are," Mike said. "I'll go." But as soon as the nurse and Mimi left, he sat on the windowsill. "We're not going to hurt her by being here."

Libby didn't necessarily agree, but she said nothing.

Aaron came quietly into the room, his attention immediately on Susan's peaceful face. He went to her, bent down and kissed her forehead. When he straightened, he didn't look at Libby.

Her eyes filled with tears. She got up and turned away—and found herself looking directly at Mike. His green eyes fixed on her. *He knew.* She opened her mouth to breathe and blinked rapidly to clear the tears. No, he couldn't know she was in love with Aaron. She was imagining things.

"What do they say about Susan?" Aaron asked from behind Libby.

"That they'd like to do a section," Mike said flatly. "She wants to wait as long as possible for the baby's sake."

"Does she have that choice?"

Mike shrugged. "In theory she always had that choice, I suppose. But the minute they say she can't wait, it'll be done. At that point the choice will be mine. Susan will do what I decide is best."

A rushing noise, like wind in her head, heralded the dizziness Libby had felt several times today. She sat down again. "Tell them to do it now," she said quietly. "Please."

"Libby," Aaron said sharply, "get hold of yourself. Mike doesn't need more pressure than he's already got."

She sat very still and straight, her arms wrapped around her middle. He was tired of her and what he saw as her phobias. "Aaron's right. I'm sorry, Mike." She'd have to cope with her fears alone and she was strong enough, darn it.

"You bet I am. I'll look in again later, Mike." Aaron opened the door. "I'm sorry to cut out so quickly. You know how it is right now."

"Don't give it a thought. Things are under control here."

"Libby."

She looked at Aaron.

"Roger said to tell you he'll be by this afternoon."

The door had barely closed behind Aaron before Mike was at Libby's side. He went down on one knee and held both of her hands. "Aaron's having tough times."

"What do you mean?"

"With his business. He wouldn't thank me for telling you, but he's struggling against a takeover bid. A serious one."

Libby tilted her head and frowned. "He never said anything to me."

"He wouldn't. You're…Aaron wouldn't want to worry you. I wish you could find a way to spend some time with him."

"So do I." Libby hadn't heard Mimi reenter the room. "Listen to Mike and to me, Libby. We know that you and Aaron are, well, very special friends. You can help each other now."

Libby looked from one to the other. "What can I do? He's angry with me all the time."

"Only because he's upset." Mimi turned her head, and her smoothly braided hair shone. "He's a man too much alone."

"Yes," Mike agreed. "And he's the last one to consider his own needs. He goes back to that condominium of his alone at night. No comfort. No one waiting to share the ups and downs of his days. There was a time when I might have laughed if someone suggested that was important. Not anymore." His gaze settled on Susan's sleeping form.

"You could make him a meal," Mimi said. "You're a good cook if you care to be. Be waiting for him when he gets home tonight."

Libby's skin heated. "I couldn't do that. I don't know when he's likely to be there and, anyway, I don't have a key."

"No sweat," Mike said nonchalantly, fishing in his pocket and producing a key. "Aaron leaves one with me in case he needs me to go in for something while he's out of town. And if the last two nights are good models, he'll visit here and leave for home around eight."

"But—"

"That's perfect," Mimi said. "If we should sense there might be a delay or a change, one of us will call you."

Libby raised her shoulders. "Don't you think we should find out how Aaron would feel about walking in and finding me there? Anyway, I should be here with Susan."

"Susan would want you to go to Aaron." Mimi turned up her hands and smiled. "And you have no adventure in your soul, *chérie*. He'll love the surprise, and it'll help him relax and feel cared for."

"Yeah," Mike said. "And the two of you need some time together."

"Yes, you do."

The thin voice from the bed brought all eyes instantly to Susan.

"Do it, Lib. For me. Aaron looks so tired, and I worry about him." She closed her eyes again.

Mimi gave Libby a triumphant smile. "Lasagna allows for flexibility in serving time. A green salad. French bread. Mmm." She kissed her fingers. "And don't forget a good red wine. Red wine is Aaron's favorite."

17

Tomorrow she was going to insist on making sure Aaron had something in his cupboards besides several boxes of soft crackers, a dozen cans of soup and a variety of store-bought cookies. And fresh items would replace frozen dinners and the rest of his horrifying selection of foods that could be heated in the microwave.

Libby moved around his very well-equipped kitchen—his too-clean, obviously rarely used kitchen—muttering at evidence of how careless he was about his diet.

She prepared a huge dish of lasagna—he could eat that for several days if necessary—and made a spinach salad. Of course, he probably ate out enough to get some semblance of decent variety into his food. Not that restaurant fare should become an exclusive habit.

The wine, a Beaujolais, was already on the table. The walk from the store at Pike Place Market had made the bottle too cold. If Aaron were much later getting home, it would be too warm.

Libby continued purposefully with her preparations. Clock-watching was a bad and nerve-racking habit.

But it was eight-thirty. Mike had been sure Aaron would be home by now.

The table, with its view over the lights of the city, looked striking. Red place mats and napkins, black china, crystal with black stems—the effect pleased Libby. She congratulated herself on her impulse purchase of a bunch of red tulips. Arranged in a low, shiny black vase with a fanned lip and narrow neck, they were the perfect final touch.

Where was Aaron?

In his front closet, hidden behind coats in a Nordstrom bag, were the clothes she'd worn when she left the Conrads that morning.

The Conrads!

Rushing, listening for approaching footsteps, she snatched up the living room phone and punched the numbers.

"Hello." Marjorie answered after two rings.

Libby felt breathless. "I'm at Aaron's. I'm sorry, I forgot to call."

"That's fine. You're calling now."

"Well, Mike and Mimi thought it would be nice if I came over and surprised him with dinner."

A small pause. "I think it's perfectly lovely. Does he want to talk to me?"

"Er, no. He isn't here yet." Libby exhaled a long, hissing breath. "Marjorie. He doesn't know I'm going to be here, so if he calls you, don't say anything, okay?"

Another pause. "Of course, my dear. That's so sweet. Just a minute."

Libby waited, jiggling on her toes.

"It's starting to snow again," Marjorie said when she returned to the phone. "I thought it had. How about there?"

Libby glanced through the windows. "Here, too."

"Mmm. And it's after nine already. It's so steep up here."

"Oh." Libby immediately understood Marjorie's concern.

"Don't worry. I'll just stay here. I'm sure Aaron won't mind."

"Yes." Marjorie coughed. "Excuse me. No, I'm sure Aaron won't mind a bit. That's a very good idea. Call me tomorrow. I'll check in at the hospital to see how Susan is. She was still quiet today?"

"Yes. Every day helps as long as she doesn't get worse."

"Don't worry too much," Marjorie said. "Talk to you tomorrow."

Libby hung up the phone and listened. No sound of approaching footsteps or a key in the lock.

She looked down at the bright yellow crepe jacket of the outfit she'd bought. Closed with tiny invisible buttons from a plain V neckline to a nipped waist, silk scroll embroidery in brilliant orange, purple and green edged the front. The bottom of the jacket flared slightly in a tailored peplum, and the skirt, orange with a yellow underlay, crisscrossed sarong-style. Too much, she thought frantically. It had looked beautiful displayed in the store, and she'd been short of time.

Where was Aaron?

If she hurried, she could either put on the navy slacks and tangerine safari shirt she'd also bought, or opt for the clothes in which she'd started the day.

But she'd bought the outfit to please Aaron. He needed to see that she still liked to look nice.

By nine-thirty the edges of the lasagna noodles were curled. Snatching up the phone, she dialed the number for the nurses' station on Susan's floor, asked for Mike and, within minutes, heard his voice. "What's up?" he whispered.

"You don't have to whisper," she snapped. "How's Susan?"

"The same. How are things up there?"

"Quiet. Did Aaron show up at the hospital?"

"Yes. Isn't he there?"

She lifted her hair from her neck. "No. Oh, Mike, how long ago did he leave you?"

"An hour and a half."

"Oh." Her legs suddenly rubbery, she sat on the edge of a low table. "Mike, it's been snowing for a couple of hours. The roads are awful. Do you suppose...?"

"No. I don't suppose. He must have decided to go out and eat, damn it."

Libby felt tears well, tears of impotent anger. "How could he? I've made lasagna. Everything's ready."

"Libby, Libby," Mike said softly, "he didn't know, remember?"

"Maybe if he came home and made himself proper meals he wouldn't look so tired. Wait till I see him."

A sound suspiciously like a stifled laugh came from Mike. "Well, stay there and wait, anyway, okay?"

"I don't think—"

"Keep it that way. Don't think. Stay and be cheerful when he does get there. Did you buy the wine?"

"Of course."

"Aaron won't turn down a glass of wine regardless of what he's eaten."

"Mike, maybe I should just—" She heard a scrape at the door. "Oh, I feel so silly. He's here. What am I going—?"

"Goodbye, Libby."

A click let her know Mike had cut her off. She scowled at the receiver and looked up in time to see Aaron in the entrance to the living room, his expression one of amazement.

"Libby? I thought I had a burglar for a minute. What are you doing here?"

"Nothing."

He advanced into the room, his dark overcoat hanging open, and the jacket of his suit. His blue tie trailed from beneath an unbuttoned shirt collar. "Who's on the phone?" He dropped a bulging briefcase.

"No one." She looked at the receiver and put it down as if it were hot. "Where have you been?"

"Huh?"

"Where have you been? You left the hospital at eight. Dinner's probably inedible, and I took a lot of trouble making it. And you look like an unmade bed."

"Thanks." He scratched his head. "I went back to the office. I don't get this."

"You wouldn't. I knew it was a stupid idea."

Aaron advanced, and Libby wasn't sure she liked the glint in his eye. "How did you get in?"

"With a key. Mike's."

His smile was thin. "I might have known."

"Everyone's worried about you because you look so tired. So I shopped, then came back here and slaved away in that kitchen you obviously never use. I laid a lovely table and bought the kind of wine you like and then all I could do was wait here and worry because of the roads."

He couldn't be...yes, he was actually smiling.

Libby felt the start of her own smile and pressed her lips together. "It's not funny."

"Yes, it is. You sound like a nagging wife. The poor old man crawls home from the office, worn-out and longing for some peace, and the old lady gives him the business because her meat loaf got singed."

"It's lasagna." She bit her lip. "I was trying to do something nice, Aaron. Wave a white flag. I really have been worried about how tired you've been looking, and we seem to have been at odds." The comments Mike had made about business concerns weren't something she intended to broach unless Aaron gave her an opening.

Aaron shrugged off his overcoat, keeping his eyes on her. "If I'd known, I'd have been here. This is the nicest thing that's happened to me in…probably the nicest thing that's ever happened to me." The jacket followed the coat, and he pulled off his tie and tossed it on top. "You look good enough to eat yourself."

Libby glowed. She spread her arms and pirouetted. "Like it? The salesperson said, yes, it was a size six, so I bought it. I didn't have much time and I know I look like a ragbag most of the time."

"You always look wonderful to me. But, yes, I like it very much. Dandelion-yellow—our color, I think." His gaze traveled quickly over her, but not so quickly that she didn't swallow and feel a dart of warmth.

"I suppose you already ate."

"Nope. Singed meat loaf will be fine."

"That's what you deserve. Sit down and I'll serve before it's a completely hopeless cause."

Aaron stopped her as she passed. "Thank you for thinking of me. You'll never know how I felt when I came through the door and saw you standing here." He lifted a hand as if to touch her face, but pushed her hair back instead.

Libby's breathing speeded up.

His dark eyes became somber and the smile disappeared. Her legs were suddenly weak. There was something in those almost black eyes, something different.

He stirred, rolled up his shirtsleeves and the smile returned. "Can I do anything?"

Libby took a shaky breath. "You can open the wine."

AARON PASSED the last rinsed plate for Libby to load into the dishwasher. "Done," he said, wiping his hands on a dishcloth.

"I think I drank too much wine." Libby opened her eyes wide.

"One glass is hardly too much."

His hair was rumpled, and she noticed that it curled over his collar. She also noticed that he seemed less rather than more tired than when he arrived home. "There'll be enough lasagna for your dinner tomorrow," she told him. "Just make up another salad."

"Yes, ma'am." His long, capable hands smoothed the dishcloth atop a tiled counter. "I don't want to let you go, but I suppose I'd better get out the jalopy and drive you back to my folks' place."

A sensation swept over her that seemed to press in on her lungs. "I called them earlier, before you came home...when you were late."

"Yes. Good. They would have worried about you. I should have thought of that."

"It's snowing."

"I know. Getting up those hills is going to be fun."

"Umm, I told Marjorie I'd stay here tonight. She thought that was a great idea. She's like me. She worries about you driving in weather like this."

Aaron raised his chin and stared down at her. "I see. Yes. That makes sense. Well—boy—I guess I'd better gather my things."

Words had never eluded Libby. Tonight they were becoming harder and harder to find. "I'm taking the couch," she said in a rush, giggling awkwardly. "And I insist, so don't try to argue, because if you do, I'm going to go find a hotel."

"No—"

"I mean it. Not another argument or I leave."

"Well, in that case—" he saluted "—I'll get you a pillow and some blankets."

By the time he returned she'd kicked off her shoes and was seated at one end of the couch. "Just put them down."

Rather than protest as she'd expected, Aaron set the bedding on the couch, gave her a last long look and turned back toward the bedroom. "See you in the morning, then."

"Yes. Good night."

His door clicked shut, and Libby fell back on the couch. Little by little she was going mad. Every nerve jumped. And it was all her fault. She'd come here and watched him, studied his every move and been unable to stem the mounting desire she'd forgotten she could feel.

Tonight she'd lie on this couch and feel him in the next room. If she was really unlucky, her ears would pick up the sounds of him turning, the sheets moving over his skin.

"Stop it," she muttered, putting her hands over her ears. This was all perfectly easy to explain. Aaron was the man, the person she trusted most of all on this earth. She'd simply mistakenly translated those feelings of trust into feelings of love...or lust. Her face flamed.

She'd make up her bed and lie in it. Here and otherwise.

The pillow was in place when she remembered that this time she didn't have an overnight bag. "Aaron!" She started for the bedroom door—and heard the shower come on.

Sleeping in her suit, or anything else she had with her, was out of the question. She'd borrow an old sweatshirt. After a hard knock on his door, she waited, an ear to the wood. Water gushing was all she heard. He must already be in the bathroom.

Cautiously Libby opened the door and peered inside. No sign of Aaron. On tiptoe she crossed the room, a knuckle raised to knock on the bathroom door—which stood wide open.

"Aaron."

He didn't answer.

"Aaron!"

Still he didn't say anything. Rising to her toes again, she entered the large bathroom with its white tile and accessories in black and gray and dark green. The shower was recessed into an alcove, but Libby knew the door was clear glass. With her head averted she sidled close enough to reach back and tap.

The water continued to stream, but she heard the door slide open. "Libby? What the hell?"

"I don't have anything to sleep in." The words tumbled out. "Or a toothbrush. Or anything. Could I...?"

A cool, wet hand closed on her wrist. "You could do whatever you want, Libby."

The timbre of his voice, low, different, the slight pull on her wrist, brought her face around. Aaron's hair streamed. He wiped his face with a hand...and his eyes never left hers.

"I thought maybe I could use... Oh, Aaron, I'm going to have to tell you something."

He put a finger to her lips. "Shh. Has something happened between us? Has it, Libby? Or am I way off base?"

She closed her eyes and felt his fingers slip from her lips, to her neck, beneath the jacket to her shoulder. Gently he urged her close. His mouth met hers in a caress, a feathery brushing that was more a tentative question than a kiss.

Then he withdrew and Libby opened her eyes. Waves of trembling passed over her. "Water," she murmured, feeling moisture through her hose.

"Who cares?" But he reached behind him to turn it off and stepped out of the shower.

She glanced down, but looked at Aaron's feet, not her own. Dark hair was plastered to their tops, and to muscular calves...and thighs.

His fingers slid from her shoulder to her neck, beneath her hair, and she sighed.

She let her gaze continue, and a great surge of heat almost buckled her knees. Her question was already answered. His arousal conveyed more clearly than any words that she no longer had to wonder if this physical yearning was hers alone.

Aaron's belly was flat, his hips lean and solid. More dark hair spread upward into a line at his navel and continued on to fan wide over a broad, wetly glistening chest.

Reaching up, placing a hand on each of his shoulders, she parted her lips and kissed him, first softly, then with all the urgency she could no longer hold back. Her tongue found his and he groaned.

"Aaron. What's happening?" With a racking sigh she dropped her forehead to his chest.

"You're trembling." His hands roamed wide over her back. It didn't matter if they were damp on her jacket.

"I don't want...I don't want you to think you have to make... You don't have to make me feel better."

His laugh was short and incredulous. "My lovely, sexy lady. If you mean what I think you do, you're a rotten judge of the signs a man gives when he's about to go out of his mind with needing you...wanting you. Libby, I want you. Is that okay?"

"It's okay," she whispered. Her hands went to the top button on the jacket.

Aaron moved to stop her. "I'll do it."

"I want to do it for you."

The little closures were resistant, but they popped free, one by one, until the jacket hung open.

"Kiss me," Aaron said. With a finger and thumb he tilted her chin upward. Nibbling, his teeth made a sweet, gentle foray along her bottom lip until she strained against him. Still he took his time, dipping the tip of his tongue into the corner of her mouth, sliding it inside, nuzzling her face higher and, finally, kissing her deep and hard until they clung together, panting.

Libby trailed her hands down his sides, hesitated, then spread her fingers to trace the lines of him until he captured her wrists. "I'm only human," he said, his smile more a grimace.

His fingertips grazed her throat, slipped down to the flesh above her bra and stopped. Libby took off her jacket, undid the side button on the skirt and unwrapped it.

Aaron dropped his hands and waited, a flush high over his cheekbones. His chest rose and fell.

Libby hesitated. "I'm too thin."

He shook his head but didn't smile. "You're beautiful. You always will be. Libby, we're going to make love. Is that what you want?"

"Is it what you want?"

"You know the answer to that. But I want it to be... Libby, do you really want me?"

She couldn't cry, wouldn't cry—not now. "I've never wanted anyone more."

The flicker in his eyes, the uncertainty, was unmistakable. Unhooking her bra, she slipped the straps from her shoulders and let it fall. Slipping out of what was left of her clothing took seconds. "Don't wonder if I mean it, Aaron. Don't question. This is now and it's right." She glanced at his hair. "You're still soapy."

He appeared almost disoriented.

Libby laughed. She stepped into the shower and turned on the water, flinching when cool water hit her skin, then drawing him in with her as it warmed.

Lovingly she held him beneath the stream and soaped his body, missing no millimeter of skin, relishing the parting of his lips to show teeth gritted in pent-up passion.

She rinsed him, following her hands with her mouth, her heart racing at the contraction of his muscle and sinew with each intimate caress.

Without a word she handed him the soap and waited. She heard his rasping breath, felt the power of the drive she'd unleashed within him, then felt the slick, sensual massage of his fingers over her skin.

They kissed beneath the water, his hands splayed over her aching breasts.

"I love you," he said against her ear. "I love you."

She couldn't make words. The tile was cold on her back, the spray warm on her closed eyelids.

Aaron encircled her waist, lifted, and she gripped his hips fast with her legs.

"I love you," she cried. "Aaron, I love you!"

The water beat down.

LIGHT FROM THE HALLWAY cast a straight-edged glow across the room and across her body. She lay on her back, the sheet barely covering her nipples.

Aaron propped his head on his hand. He'd never expected, never dared to really hope that she'd lie with him like this one day. But she had. She did now. Carefully he smoothed the long tangles of her hair spread on the pillow. They hadn't dried after the shower. When they made love again, here, still damp, she had spoken his name over and over and he'd felt what he'd never felt before—the total bonding he'd only heard about, the conviction that without Libby he'd never be able to find any purpose in his life again.

She opened her eyes. "Aaron?"

"Yes, my love. I'm here." He always would be if she'll allow it.

"What are you doing?"

"Watching you. I'm never going to get tired of that."

She smiled sleepily, her eyes gradually clearing. "You're going to be tired tomorrow."

"It already is tomorrow. I'm not tired."

The phone, its ring a vicious intrusion, jarred him to the bone. Libby sat up, the sheet slipping to her waist. "Aaron!"

He snatched up the receiver, but his eyes took in her body and he felt the returning leap of arousal. "Yes."

"It's Mike. I know Libby's there. Get her over here. Susan's in surgery."

18

"**I** didn't have any idea what time it was."

Aaron decided against touching Libby. She sat forward in the seat of the car as if she could help it move faster.

"The bedroom drapes are heavy," he said. "They cut out the light...and we were both tired."

The immediate brilliant wash of pink over her cheeks bothered him. "It's nine-thirty. I should have been at the hospital at least an hour ago," she said. "If I had, I'd have been there when they took her into surgery."

"And what could you have done if you had been?" He felt uneasy, uncertain.

"I should have been there," she told him, sounding obstinate. "Mike needs me."

Aaron parked the Peugeot in the garage opposite the hospital. By the time he'd locked the doors, Libby was already heading for the elevators.

"Calm down," he said as evenly as he could. "We're almost there."

"Hurry, hurry," she muttered, hugging her middle while she watched the lighted numbers on the panel over the door. He could see her tremble.

The elevator jolted to a stop, and they exited onto a catwalk above the street. Libby broke into a run, her hair flying. Aaron jogged to keep up with her. This morning she was again dressed in well-worn jeans, an antique sweater and her rust-colored parka.

Once inside the hospital they hurried to the obstetrical unit. In her rush to reach Susan's room Libby stumbled.

Aaron grabbed her arm. "Slow down! Libby, please, you're not going to be any good to anyone like this."

"She's not here." The bed was empty but made up and neatly turned down. "Cesareans don't take long. Where is everybody?"

"Libby!" More roughly than he'd intended, he jerked her arm and she half fell against him. "Get hold of yourself. Mike didn't say anything was wrong. Just that she was in surgery and he was going in to join her."

Tears gathered in her eyes. "She wouldn't be in surgery if nothing was wrong. She must have gotten worse while I was...I should have been thinking about her, about what she needed, not what..."

Aaron gritted his teeth, frustration and fury warring for control. "Not what *we* needed? Is that what you were going to say? Don't do it, Libby. Don't do the predictable and turn on the self-recrimination."

"If it's predictable, you aren't surprised, are you?" She tilted her head back, blinking away the tears. "What happened wasn't your fault. I was the one doing the pursuing."

"Oh, please." He spun away. "Spare me, will you?"

"But it wasn't your fault," she protested. "I was lonely. We've both been so worried. That's what caused it. I've spoiled what we had."

Fury was winning. "Don't say another word. You're irrational. What I said last night, I meant. I always will. And I believe you—"

"Libby!" Anne's high voice shocked Aaron into silence. "Where've you been? Come on." The girl, her hair and clothes mussed, stood in the doorway.

Before either of them could respond Anne disappeared.

Libby looked at him. Aaron grabbed her hand and strode from the room, following Anne's trotting figure. She looked over her shoulder. "One of the nurses said she thought she'd seen you come in. We're all down here."

"All" really did mean all: Lester, Mimi, Connie, Aaron's parents and even Jeff and Molly from Susan's salon. Molly sat with her bottom forward, shoulders back, visibly uncomfortable in her very pregnant state.

Libby drew slightly behind Aaron, and he glanced back at her. The flush had returned to her cheeks, and he longed to gather her into his arms. She stood, her eyes lowered. He was suddenly certain that in her mind everyone present knew they'd spent the night together—really together— and that they judged that to have been wrong.

"Sit down, *chérie*." Mimi smiled, and the French-woman's serene face and comfortable manner made Aaron want to hug her with gratitude.

"Sit here." Lester got up and waved Libby down beside Mimi.

"It's been a long time," Anne said. She bounced up and down on the toes of her sneakers. "Hasn't it, Connie? We've been waiting for*ever*."

"We've only been here half an hour." Connie wriggled inside her uncomfortable-looking blanket of a coat.

"It's been so long," Anne told no one in particular.

Molly sat forward, and Jeff automatically began to rub her back. His eyes met Aaron's and he grimaced.

"Is there someone I can ask for a progress report?" He couldn't stand this.

"Yes." Libby jumped up again. "Let's go and see what's happening."

Aaron smiled at her and held out a hand. She hesitated, and he thought she would ignore the gesture. Instead she smiled back, a soft, forgive-me smile, and slipped her fingers into his. His heart seemed to expand at her touch. He knew what he was going to do. Yes, somehow, no matter what it took, he knew what he was going to accomplish.

"Dad!"

Anne's yell brought every eye to the doorway. Mike, dressed in surgical greens, his hair standing on end, stood there with a smile on his face…and tears in his eyes.

"Mike," Libby said, going to him, "is she…are they all right?"

A second passed and another, and Aaron could see his friend was beyond words. He walked to Mike and Libby and enveloped them both in a huge hug. "It's okay, isn't it?"

Mike nodded and the tears coursed down his face. "She's fine now. It happened the way they said it would. As soon as they took the…him…her blood pressure went down."

"He's born!" Anne capered around them until her father freed an arm and pulled her in.

"He's born," Mike said. "And he's almost as handsome as his father."

"Geez." Aaron laughed, aware of a prickling in his own eyes. "That good-looking, huh?"

"Yep. Give 'em half an hour and you can all go take a look." He let out a whoop. "Thank God. He's so beautiful. Susan's so beautiful. They said he scored high on some sort of score."

"Apgar," Aaron's mother said from behind them. "That's good."

Aaron had eyes only for Libby. She cried and laughed through the tears. "Does he have hair?"

"Black, like his mom. And he's going to be bright. I can tell it by looking into his eyes."

Aaron began to laugh. "You're as bad as they say new fathers are. You'll make Anne jealous."

"No, he won't," Anne said fiercely. "I'm glad, too. I've actually got a brother. Do you know how long I've been an only kid?"

Mike ruffled her hair. "We might be able to work it out. You're going to love him, pumpkin."

A nurse, rubber-soled shoes squishing, approached from the corridor. "Your party can see the baby if they want to," she said, smiling broadly.

"If they want to?" Lester said in what sounded like a grumble. "*If* they want to? Let me at my grandson."

Outside the nursery they formed a jumbled, pressing crowd. On the other side of the glass a tiny, cross-looking infant with eyes closed in a puffy red face was placed in Mike's arms. Wearing a mask, he came close and indicated a speaker in the wall. "Talk. I can hear you," he said from his side. "What do you think? Isn't he cute?"

"Yeah!" they chorused.

"Hey," Connie said, shouldering her way to the fore. "How big is that kid? He doesn't look so preemie to me."

"Five pounds nine ounces," Mike announced in a tone that suggested no baby ought to be larger at birth. "The doctor thinks we were off on our dates. Not a thing wrong with this guy."

Libby slipped her arm around Aaron's waist. "He's all right," she murmured. "They're both going to be all right."

Aaron looked down into her pale face. "You look wiped out, sweetheart. I'm going to take you for some coffee and something to eat."

"I can't leave!"

"Yes, you can. Susan won't be back in her own room for a little while. Mike," he said into the speaker, "Libby's threatening to go into shock on us. I'm taking her down for a dose of orange juice."

"Do it," Mike said, but his attention was on his son.

Aaron led Libby away. She leaned heavily against him and said nothing all the way to the basement cafeteria.

He sat her at a table and went to buy a selection of whatever he thought might give her the energy she obviously needed.

Sliding the tray onto the table, he dropped into a chair and scooted it close. "Here." He gave her a waxed cup of orange juice. "Drink it all. You'll feel better."

For a moment she looked into the cup, then drank, first slowly, then thirstily until it was drained. "Isn't he beautiful?"

"Yes. Ugly but beautiful."

"He is not ugly." She looked so indignant that he laughed. "He's not."

"Of course he's not. Did you see the way Mike looked at him? Is he proud, or what?"

She studied the coffee he gave her. "He's proud. I don't think there can be anything as touching as seeing a man hold his baby. No need to be macho or anything anymore, just a tender thing."

"Why so sad?" he asked, seeing the corners of her mouth twitch.

Libby shrugged. "I'm happy-sad. Silly, really. Most of the time it doesn't bother me that I can't have children, but—"

He bit his lip and took the cup from her gently. "I'd forgotten for a moment. I'm sorry." Their eyes met, and he guided her head to his shoulder. "You've been a mother to hundreds of children in a way. Don't forget that."

"I don't."

"It's sad to want children and not be able to have them. Your own, that is. But there are ways of filling the gap if it's really important." Seeing Mike with little Michael Georges had awakened something Aaron had never felt before. Maybe fatherhood wasn't all bad, but not everyone was meant to know the moment he'd just witnessed.

"I've thought of being a foster parent," Libby said. "One day maybe. I don't know how easy that would be for me in Italy, but I can try."

Aaron's stomach fell, and his heart. He rested his brow on her shoulder. "Don't, Libby. Don't talk about that."

"Aaron—"

"Please." He couldn't break down here, but he was skating close to the edge of losing control. "Please, Libby. I can't listen to you talk about going away again."

"I don't know what to say," she whispered. "This is all so new and I'm scared. It was never supposed to happen, not between you and me."

"Libby," he said, raising his head, bracing her face between his hands. "I can't let you go. Do you understand? There's no way I can stand having you halfway around the world from me again."

"Oh, Aaron. You're so special to me. I—" Her eyes moved, glanced past him and widened.

Aaron straightened and swiveled, his hands still on Libby.

Roger stood a few feet away. "I heard the news about Susan and the baby. I'm glad."

"Roger." Aaron stood up. "I was going to call and tell you."

"Were you?" Roger's attention centered on Libby. His mouth drew back in a parody of a smile. "That would have been nice. I wish you had told me...about a lot of things."

He walked out.

"A BABY CAN ONLY WEAR one outfit at a time," Susan said. "This pile of loot is outrageous."

"It certainly is, Mrs. Kinnear." A nurse bustled back and forth, trying to take blood pressure and temperature over the piles of gift boxes on Susan's bed. "Ah, ah," she admonished when Susan attempted to talk around the thermometer.

Libby packed away small garments, examining each one before putting it into its box. She paused to look at her sister. Already the puffiness had begun to subside and her hair was regaining its luster. Susan made owl eyes and wiggled her brows, and Libby laughed. The nurse cast her an almost-serious frown.

"Anne made a fuss about going back home to go to school," Libby said. "I bribed her by saying that since tomorrow is Saturday, I'll arrange for her to come back to Seattle and spend the night so she can be near you."

The nurse removed the thermometer. "Good," Susan said. "She really is thrilled with Michael, isn't she?"

"Oh, slightly, I'd say. The only person more thrilled is that conceited husband of yours. You'd think he produced him all by himself."

Susan giggled. "I know. Isn't he sweet?"

Libby had never thought of Mike in terms of being sweet, but she nodded. "I'm going to pile all your goodies on the windowsill. Then I want to run over to Westlake and buy a book of nursery rhymes.''

''Oh, Libby. That's a great idea. I'll be needing them when I get home.''

Libby hid her grin. ''Well, maybe we've got a little while, but the thought appeals to me. And I could take back one or two of the duplicate gifts and get something down-to-earth, like extra crib sheets and receiving blankets. I called to start diaper service, by the way.''

''Mmm.'' Susan settled against her pillows, her eyes beginning to droop. ''That sounds lovely. I think I'll just take a little nap till Mike gets back. He and his dad went to look at plans for climbing sets for the yard. The big wooden ones you build yourself.''

''Ah. Good thinking.'' Libby shook her head and added, ''You're definitely going to need one of those in a day or two,'' but Susan was already asleep.

With two crammed carrier bags Libby made her way down to the lobby. Yesterday morning's encounter with Roger still weighed heavily on her mind. Aaron had said he would talk to him, but that didn't make Libby feel better. The pain in Roger's kind eyes was something she would never forget.

She didn't notice Dennis Falk until she approached a telephone to call for a cab. Dennis, dressed in business garb, rose from a chair in the lobby and came toward her, smiling widely.

Libby managed to return the smile. ''Hello, Dennis.''

''Congratulations, Aunt Libby,'' he said. ''I got the news when I tried to reach you at the Kinnears'. The housekeeper said you were here, and when I called, a nurse said you were with Susan, so I decided to stake out the lobby till I got a chance to see you.''

He'd called and left messages several times. Libby hadn't felt like returning them. "How are you, Dennis?"

"Good. Better for seeing you." He checked his watch. "Lunchtime. Can I persuade you to eat with me?"

She lifted the bags. "I've got some returning to do for Susan."

"You do have to eat," he said persuasively. "We could have a quick cup of coffee and a sandwich. My car's just across the street. Then I could drop you wherever you have to go. Do we have a deal?"

"I suppose so." He was so nice. And he was right; she did have to eat sometime. "But I can't be gone long."

"Great." He swiftly lifted the bags from her hands and ushered her to the door. "I'll tell you what. I'll even promise to cruise around while you do your errands, then deliver you back here again. That'll make it even faster than if you hadn't had lunch. How's that?"

"Wonderful." She laughed. "You strike a bargain I can't refuse."

Their coffee and sandwich turned out to be lunch at Palomino's, a new upscale restaurant at the top of an equally new upscale multilevel shopping center in the heart of Seattle. The Pacific Center, Dennis informed her as the escalator bore them upward past streamlined shops with a neon-lighted Art Deco stamp, was home to Barney's and Gucci among other big retail names and was becoming an in place to shop in Seattle.

"You aren't even a Seattleite, are you?" she asked, walking with him to the noisy, deliberately trendy restaurant. "How come you know so much about the city?"

"I know so much about a lot of cities," Dennis said, his hand resting negligently on her shoulder. "I make it my business to be at home wherever I am."

Compact, broad-shouldered, confident, Dennis Falk

gathered admiring glances on all sides. Libby believed he would indeed be very much at home wherever he went.

He took her coat, the new black cashmere she was grateful she'd bought, and hung it on a rack with his own vicuna. They were seated on facing banquettes, and in response to Dennis's question, Libby admitted to preferring white wine.

"A bottle of the Puligny-Montrachet," Dennis told the waiter. To Libby he said, "Their Focaccia is good. With Gorgonzola it's great. Pignolia nuts, basil...sweet red onions. Mmm." His nostrils flared. "Best bread in town."

Libby wasn't certain her stomach was ready for what he suggested, but she murmured assent.

"We have time to think about the rest of lunch," Dennis added.

"Euro-Bistro," Libby read from the menu. "Not exactly your typical coffee and sandwich joint."

"Somehow I don't see you as the coffee and sandwich joint type, Libby Duclaux. Maxim's would be a more appropriate backdrop, opulent rooms where names and connections count and where food is an experience rather than a necessity."

She smiled at his too-smooth loquacity. "I do believe I'm being snowed."

He appeared not to notice the facetiousness of the comment. "You make flattery a requirement."

The bread was as good as he'd predicted, spicy and crisp and a meal in itself. And the choice of wine couldn't have pleased her more, although she expected to feel tired later and wished she'd stuck with coffee.

"Orange is good on you." Dennis said of the safari shirt, which she was wearing for the first time.

"Thank you." She couldn't fail to be aware that his gaze lingered too long.

"You're a very beautiful woman. Georges had impec cable taste—in everything."

Libby's skin tightened. "Georges was a rare man, a rare human being. He saw people for themselves. His friends were drawn from all walks of life, and they loved him."

"And they miss him." Dennis breathed deeply, his lids lowered. "I miss him."

"You must have been a business acquaintance." She had been unable to remember Georges mentioning Dennis.

"I prefer the word *friend*," he said quietly. "And wish I'd known him better. If there had been more time…" He drummed his fingers on the table.

"Yes." A small rush of warmth for this man made Libby touch his hand impulsively. Quickly she withdrew "Thank you. I am reconciled to what happened, but it' still nice when someone speaks of Georges without being afraid I'll fall apart. Too often people avoid mentioning the dead for fear of upsetting those who are left behind."

"I know," Dennis said gravely. "Believe me, I know."

Libby looked at him quickly and reached to put he hand on his again. "Of course, your wife. Forgive me I'd forgotten. Unfortunately I never met her."

"An incredible woman," Dennis said. "But we have to go on. The ones we've lost would want that."

The waiter came to pour more wine, but they sti weren't ready to order lunch.

"You and Aaron seem to have become very close," Dennis said.

Libby found she couldn't meet his eyes. "We alway have been."

"Yes. But am I wrong in thinking…well, that isn't m business. You must be very worried about his recent, e business reversals."

She eyed him acutely. "I wasn't aware that Aaron's private business had become public knowledge."

"My dear, as we both know, there's nothing so public as, how should I put it? Reversals in a successful man's affairs?"

Libby pretended preoccupation with displays of glass fruit. Could Aaron really be in serious financial difficulty? He'd said he was doing well.

"How like you," Dennis said softly. "To be so loyal to a friend—particularly a friend who has obviously come to mean so much more than the simple translation of the word."

"What do you mean?" She felt cornered. Every word that came from Dennis's mouth was loaded with innuendo.

Slowly he swung his glass between finger and thumb. "Perhaps I should have the guts to say what I want to say and have done with it." His voice became harsh. "It's just damn awkward, that's all. And I'm not even sure if I'll be doing the right thing." When she started to speak, he gestured her to silence. "I'm going to follow my head rather than my heart in this. Has Aaron asked you to marry him?"

Aghast, Libby almost dropped her own glass. She set it down carefully. "No. What makes you ask? How do you know there's even anything like that? I don't understand any of this."

"He will." There was finality in the statement. "And I'm sure he's very fond of you. It'll be a good match."

"Dennis—"

"Please. This isn't easy for me, but for Georges's sake I know it's my duty to at least make sure you have all the facts. You aren't aware that there's a very real possibility that Alpine Ridge will pass from Aaron's control, are you?''

Her breathing became shallow. ''Well, I did know there might be some problem. Mike said he thought these were difficult times for Aaron. But I didn't think that meant catastrophic.''

''Mike Kinnear doesn't know everything. If Aaron can't keep control of his own and certain other blocks of stocks, he's going to become a minor player in the business he built from the ground up. No man can look that in the face and not do anything—and I mean *anything*—to save himself.''

''I had no idea.'' Distress numbed Libby. Poor Aaron, and he'd managed to say nothing and to be there like a rock for her and for her family.

''I didn't think so,'' Dennis murmured. ''What Aaron needs is a very large influx of capital. Capital that he doesn't have to worry about paying back until he's had several years to build up to a point where he's untouchable by any interested speculator. Preferably, in fact, capital that he never has to pay back.''

''Who are these people who are trying to take over?''

Dennis raised his brows. ''Some information is inviolate within certain circles. You know that from your life with Georges.''

''Yes.'' How well she knew. ''How much money are we talking about? How much would it take to make Aaron safe?''

''A considerable sum. Enormous. But I'm sure he intended to talk to you about that. Frankly—'' he studied his hands ''—I'm embarrassed that I appear to have spoken out of turn, although I suppose I must have had some premonition that it might be necessary.''

Libby set down her glass and gripped the edge of the table. "What exactly are you suggesting?"

"Suggesting?" He looked puzzled, then his blue eyes slowly cleared. "Ah, I see. You really don't have any idea. Libby, if I tell you what's troubling me, will you promise not to mention this conversation to anyone? Most especially not to Aaron?"

"I don't think I can." And she was beginning to think there was something she didn't like about Dennis Falk, something insidiously dangerous.

"For both of your sakes I think you must. It will be best in the end—unless you want to risk hurting Aaron."

She regarded him for a long time before she said, "Very well."

"It's well-known that Aaron Conrad is a loner by choice. His business has been both his wife and his children. Do I make myself clear?"

Libby could only nod. Whatever this man said to the contrary, she was becoming convinced he didn't like Aaron or wish him well.

"Again I tell you this out of respect for Georges's memory. It would, I'm convinced, not be in your best interests, or in Aaron's, for the two of you to enter into... This is so difficult. It would be unfortunate for a beautiful woman with so much to offer to find herself used."

Libby realized her mouth was open. "Are you suggesting—?"

"I'm suggesting that if your fortune became Aaron's, his money worries would be over. Libby, how do you think I know that you and Aaron are more than...this is appalling. All I want is to do what I think is right, no matter what it costs me. The hottest rumor on the grapevine is about Aaron Conrad. He's reported to have said

that a marriage license will be a cheap trade-off if it buys
him Alpine Ridge free and clear.''

ONE GOOD THING had come from Dennis Falk's outrageous suggestions—Libby had faced the need to deal honestly with Roger. She entered the building that housed
Aaron's offices and rode the elevator to his floor. Aaron
was out. When she called Roger and asked to see him,
he'd assured her they wouldn't be interrupted.

Roger met her at his office door and showed her to a
chair. Rather than sit behind his desk he pulled a second
chair close to hers. "You made it sound as if this was
urgent." She'd hurt him, but he could still find it within
him to be concerned.

"I need your help. Actually, what I need is for you to
tell me how I can help Aaron."

Roger turned his face away.

"You're a wonderful man. One of the best men I've
ever known. If we'd met—no, I can't say that. I think I
may have hurt you and I'm sorry. That's something I
never intended, and I should have realized soon enough
to stop it."

His eyes, when he faced her again, shone with unusual
intensity. "There are some things we can't stop. Usually
because they're meant to be."

"Still… Roger, Aaron and I are going to be together.
I'm not sure how or when, but I am sure we need each
other. I'm also sure that he's in some sort of awful trouble
that he's not telling me about because he doesn't want to
worry me."

"What makes you so sure?"

The flicker in his eyes confirmed her suspicions. "I'm
right. It's true. Roger, Dennis Falk told me Aaron's in
danger of losing the Ridge if he can't come up with a lot

of money. What I want to do is work out a way to help that won't allow Aaron to feel as if he's taking charity from me. A loan or something. I just don't know how to do it.''

Roger's laugh startled her. He got up and began to pace. "That's rich." He propped an elbow on his forearm and covered his mouth. "The ultimate irony. Did Falk say anything else?"

Libby wiped her palms on her coat. "He suggested that Aaron wanted... Dennis said Aaron would ask me to marry him to get my money." She felt sick. "How could anyone be that vicious?"

Roger muttered something. His eyes met hers briefly and what she saw there shocked her: rage...and malice?

"What did you say?" she asked faintly.

He took a visibly deep breath and flexed his shoulders. "I said I didn't realize Aaron had been so indiscreet. Okay, you might as well hear it from me as from anyone." This time he did sit on the other side of the desk, leaning forward, his hands flattened on the polished surface. "The block of stocks Dennis probably told you about, the ones that can make the difference between Aaron losing or retaining control, belong to me. Aaron found out that I was considering selling because, to be frank, I need the money."

"You're going to sell stock that would cost Aaron his life's work?"

"I don't want to, or I didn't." Roger pounded his forehead. "Let me say this quickly. Aaron sang your praises to me for months. Then he set us up to meet at that first dinner. I never did have a date. He said he wanted me to see if I liked you, and if you liked me. Then he pushed it, encouraged us to get together, kept telling me that you were falling for me. And I believed it, God help me."

He slammed his palm on the desk. "Aaron manipulated me...manipulated both of us."

Libby couldn't speak. She pressed shaking fingers to her temples. What Roger said was true, at least in part. She could see it all so clearly now. But did she really believe Aaron only wanted to use her? Maybe it would be better if she did...easier.

"Libby." Roger reached a beseeching hand toward her. "Aaron made sure I fell in love with you because you were the wife of his oldest friend. It's obvious he believed that if you and I got together, there would be no way you'd stand by and let me sell what he needed to a competitor.

"But his plan backfired. You fell in love with him instead of me. Isn't that right?"

"Yes," she whispered.

"Yes. So he's decided to sacrifice himself by doing the one thing he never wanted to do—get married." Roger made an irritable gesture. "I'm not being fair. I don't want you to think Aaron doesn't care a great deal for you."

Libby shook so badly that her teeth chattered. "But whatever happens between Aaron and me won't stop you from selling out to someone else."

"Yes, it will." Roger's voice rose. "He did his job well. There's no way I'd hurt you by ruining your husband. Aaron will get everything—the woman I want and his precious ski lodge, because, for her sake, I'll do nothing to harm him."

19

Nothing had ever felt as right to Aaron as this did. Without knowing it, all the years of waiting and being convinced he was a man intended to live his life solo had been leading up to tonight. As recently as six months ago, he'd have laughed at a suggestion that fate just possibly held some of the cards. He wasn't laughing now.

The yellow silk mums were a fright, but they were the closest he could get to dandelions, and Libby would make the connection and laugh.

Aaron wanted to see Libby laugh. He wanted to hold her, to make love to her again. Waiting was making him edgy. All afternoon he'd tried to call her, and when he'd finally reached her—in Susan's room—she'd been almost solemn.

He stared through the windows of the condo at an early-evening sky over Elliott Bay. No, she'd said, she didn't want to go out anywhere, and no, she didn't want him to pick her up. Libby had asked if she could come to him…at his place.

Like him, she must be almost afraid to believe this was happening between the two of them. But in her serious, direct way Libby had decided what he should have known was best: on what would be one of the most special nights of their lives, they needed to be alone in a place where there would be no interruptions.

The doorbell rang. Expecting the sound, he jumped and hesitated before striding to pull her inside.

He framed her face with his hands. "You're cold. You should have let me come and get you."

"I like the cold." Her glance moved from his eyes to his mouth, and he felt the pull of desire.

Pushing his fingers into her hair, he kissed her. The force of her response inflamed her. The sob that broke from her throat closed his eyes in mute, overwhelming joy. He slipped the coat from her shoulders and let it fall. Beneath his hands her skin beat back warmth through thin silk. His tremor was something she must feel.

"Libby," he murmured against her cheek, "I've been waiting for you." It sounded inane.

"I know." Ducking from his embrace, she picked up her coat and carried it with her into the living room. "It's been a long day." She threw the coat over a chair and stood before the windows, her hands clasped behind her back.

A little awkwardness was inevitable, particularly in so sensitive a woman. Aaron loved her for that sensitivity.

"Stay there," he told her. "Don't move."

Quickly he went into the kitchen and swept up the champagne bucket and glasses. Carrying them into the dining room, he said, "Tomorrow we're going shopping. Tonight I'm doing the best I can." He'd considered and discarded the idea of buying her a ring on his own.

She said nothing. Standing there with her back to him, her hair cascading over the shoulders of the bright silk blouse, she appeared smaller, more vulnerable. More than anything else he wanted to take care of Libby, to share his life with her and have her know that hers was everything to him.

The cork popped loudly, and he juggled a glass to catch

the foam. "I must be nervous," he said, laughing. "Shook up the bottle." Tucking the silk mums under his arm, he joined her, giving her a glass. Looking into her eyes he said, "To us, Libby. To everything we want and need."

They clinked glasses and she sipped slowly. "I'll always want the best for you."

With a flourish Aaron produced the flowers. "Knowing how you feel about expensive gifts and how much you like—" He regarded the too-bright silk. "You'll have to use your imagination. Yet again I had to use my imagination because the real article wasn't available. Accept these dandelions as a token of my regard. Every couple's supposed to have a song and a flower and those things. I never thought our flower would be the dandelion."

"It's a weed. But did you think ours would be anything?"

The still quality of her voice made him pause. "I guess not. But I'm very happy, Libby. Tomorrow, if you promise not to get uptight about expensive gifts, I'd like to buy you a ring."

"The other night…when we were together—" she looked at him "—that was good, wasn't it? It was a special time?"

He took her glass and set it down with his beside the flowers she hadn't taken. "You know it was. Libby, we've got a lot of shared history. You and I were friends for many years before we became lovers, and I think you're having a hard time reconciling the change. I admit I did, too, at first, but not now."

"You didn't initiate the lovemaking, Aaron. I did. If I hadn't, it would never have happened."

So much for female intuition. "I don't like telling you you're wrong, but you are. Some of us just take a little longer to work up the courage to get where we want to be than you do. What happened was inevitable.''

''I've made things difficult, Aaron, for both of us.''

He frowned and looped his hands loosely around her neck. ''You made things easier for us. Libby, will you marry me, please? Immediately? As soon as we can do whatever it takes in the way of formalities?'' He held his bottom lip in his teeth. ''Would you believe I rehearsed that and it still came out sounding like an invitation to borrow a lawn mower?''

When she raised her eyes, he saw the glisten of tears.

''Honey, don't cry. Or are those some of your happy tears?''

''No.'' Backing away from him, she bumped into the edge of a low table but didn't seem to notice. ''They're sad tears, but don't worry, I'm going to get over this. I do understand what's happened Aaron and I know you intended to try to make things as—as bearable as possible for both of us. That won't be necessary.''

He took a step toward her, but she backed up again. ''You could just have come to me, Aaron,'' she said. ''I wouldn't have let you down. We're friends. That's going to be tough to maintain but, if I have my way, we always will be friends.''

Words failed him.

''You told me you didn't have time for a wife or a family, remember? Your business is your life. I shouldn't have allowed what I felt for you to make me think I could change that.'' She bowed her head. ''I didn't really plan to try. What happened just sort of happened.''

''What are you talking about?'' He found his voice, but his words were only a dry croak.

She picked up her coat. ''I know everything now. If I hadn't been so preoccupied with myself and my problems,

I'd have figured out how difficult things have been for you or at least that something was very wrong. Aaron, I know all about the takeover bid and the stocks and how you need a great deal of money to put yourself on stable footing. And I know what you tried to do with Roger and me to make sure he didn't sell out.''

"Sell out?" Blood seemed to drain to his feet. "I don't know what you mean by that. What I did was wrong. I admit it. But I only wanted the best...for everyone.''

"Including you," she said, lifting her chin. "I'm sorry Roger had to get hurt, but I can't do much about that except hope he finds someone as special as he is.''

"Libby—"

"I'm going to have to leave now. I promised Susan I'd go back to the hospital for a while.''

"Libby!"

"It's all right, Aaron. I love you. I can't help that. Regardless of everything, I also know that you want me to be happy. I even believe you would have tried to love me the way you thought I needed and wanted to be loved by you. But we'll put all this behind us. In time we'll both forget this mess ever happened.''

"Libby, will you—"

"No! Don't touch me. There won't be any need for you to... We're going to find our way back to the friendship we had. It was suggested you wanted me because of my money—because you need money. I don't believe that, but what's mine is yours, Aaron. Whatever you need, you've got. Don't argue because I'm going to insist.''

He made a grab for her, but she darted from his reach. "You're going to listen to me." There could be no greater confusion and rage than he felt now.

"Not now," she told him. "I forgive you, Aaron. I understand... Both your personal and business motives.

Anyway, the money's there, so use it. You know it means nothing to me.''

Numb, he watched her go. Seconds passed and silence settled around him like a suffocating cloak. He was a fool, a clumsy, arrogant, manipulative fool, and he'd blown everything. But he wasn't the only one at fault.

Gritting his teeth, he picked up the champagne bottle and swung. The glass top of the coffee table split in half. Fragments of the green bottle rose, hung shimmering amid a spray of foam and scattered.

She'd been told a lie. And she believed it.

20

Michael Georges wriggled in Libby's arms. His eyes flickered rapidly beneath closed lids. "Isn't he going to wake up?" Libby glanced up at Mike and back at the baby. "I want to talk to him."

Garbed in matching blue gowns and masks, she and Mike sat side by side in the darkened hospital nursery. Michael Georges made a sound that was more birdlike chirp than hiccup and sucked on the splayed fingers that had found his mouth.

"Not for a while if he's on the same schedule he has been," Mike said. He touched his son's cheek and followed the faint, perfect line of a brow. "What's wrong, Libby? I've been trying to wait for you to tell me, but I never got any gold stars for patience. Susan knows there's something, too."

That was what she'd hoped to avoid, troubling Susan, or anyone. After leaving Aaron, she'd given herself an hour to calm down before returning to the hospital. It was time to pull herself together and face the future as she should have done a long time ago—head-on and without pretense. "Could you stand to have me hanging around your house for a while longer?" she asked.

"Whew." His eyes crinkled above the mask. "I hardly dared hope you'd say something like that. You know we want you there."

"I'll be what help I can…without overwhelming you this time."

"Libby, we've appreciated everything you've done."

"Thanks. You're very gallant. I've been a pain in the neck. It isn't that I didn't know it, but I wasn't sure how to be anything else and still cope."

Mike laughed. "Well, I guess I can't deny that you came close to getting your neck wrung a couple of times. But I do understand."

"I fought coming to the States. But it was the best thing I ever did. It's time I took a long look at myself and the way I tick." Even if she did feel more broken tonight than she'd ever dreaded feeling again since Georges's death.

"Will you—" Mike cleared his throat. "Umm, aren't you going to make some sort of announcement?"

Libby looked at him and the truth dawned. Aaron had told him he was going to suggest marriage.

"You did see Aaron?" Mike pressed, as if seeing her thoughts. "And you did say yes? I'm planning to be the best man, and Susan says she's going to starve herself into a willowy matron of honor."

Bending low over the baby, Libby closed her eyes. Her throat burned. She shook her head. "No. Poor Aaron. I know he wanted to do whatever it would take to keep me here. Even marry me if necessary. But, no, that won't be happening."

Seconds turned into minutes before Mike asked, "You don't love him?"

"Oh, yes. He was right about that. I love him, but I can't let him sacrifice himself for that."

"Sacrifice!" He shushed himself, peered around and dropped his voice to a whisper. "Sacrifice? What the hell are you talking about? He adores you."

"He's fond of me." How could she explain what she'd learned today without Mike thinking she no longer loved Aaron? "He's got serious financial problems. I think you already know that."

Mike nodded slowly. "What does that have to do with this?"

"He tried to pair me off with Roger." Swallowing hurt.

"Damn." Mike plunked his fists on his hips. "I knew you'd find out. I warned him, but he wouldn't listen. But—"

"Let me say this while I still can." Libby ran her tongue over dry lips. "I talked to Roger. He's upset and he has a right to be. Mike, at first Aaron wanted Roger and me to get together because he really does worry about me and wished I'd stay here."

"Yes. But is that so bad?"

"Please, Mike, let me go on." Her head ached and she wished she could lie down. "Later, when Aaron got worried about the company—the stock—he saw a liaison between Roger and me as a safeguard against Roger selling out."

"You've got it wrong."

Libby shook her head. "No. I had lunch with Dennis Falk today."

Mike became still.

"He as good as said the things Roger repeated to me later. He also said—although I don't believe it—that Aaron wanted to marry me himself so that he could use my money."

"That bastard!" Mike clapped a hand to his brow. "You can't be taking any of this seriously."

"For some reason Dennis Falk hates Aaron. Even I can figure that much out. But Aaron manipulated me—and Roger. When he realized I...when he realized I loved him rather than Roger, he decided to marry me himself. To keep me here so he wouldn't have to worry about me in Italy anymore and...and..."

"And what?" Mike's voice was low. "And so he could use your money to help him over a bad time? God, you don't know him."

"Maybe not." She lifted her chin defensively. "Aaron isn't perfect. No one is. And...maybe I don't want to love him!"

"So you're glad for an excuse not to?"

"I don't know. Don't push me anymore."

"I can't believe this." Mike got up and turned away.

"Please don't be angry," Libby implored him. "No with me, or with Aaron. He would have been good and kind to me. But he never planned on my falling in love with him instead of Roger. Don't worry. I am going to make sure he has whatever money he needs."

"Do you remember the bruise I had on my jaw?" Mike swung around, sat down and brought his face close. "Do you?"

"Yes. You fell over something."

"No, I didn't. Aaron did that because I suggested he do what you're accusing him of." He raised his head. "Oh, I wasn't serious in all respects. But I knew he loved you himself and I knew it was a rotten idea for him to try to match you up with Roger Chandler. I was half joking and half serious. Aaron decked me because he was disgusted that anyone would even hint at his using a penny of your money for his own needs. That man is wild about you and has been for a long time without letting himself admit it. Did you tell him this little theory of yours?"

Libby felt faint. "I told you what Dennis Falk suggested. I didn't believe him. But Roger said almost the same things. Roger wouldn't lie to me. He's loyal to

Aaron, too. Roger needs money, but he isn't going to sell to Dennis.'' She didn't add that Roger had said she was the reason he wouldn't do so.

"Roger's in love with you." Mike slapped his thighs. "Damn it all. Men—and women—have done a lot worse things for love. The guy's hurting and striking back. And who can really blame him after the way Aaron set him up. Damn, Aaron can be an idiot sometimes."

"I let Aaron know I believed Roger," Libby said in a small voice, holding the baby tighter. "Not completely, but more or less."

"I wish you'd come to me."

"Would it have helped?"

He laughed bitterly. "I'd have told you the facts that Aaron evidently felt too angry to tell you himself. Dennis Falk is the man behind the takeover bid Aaron's been fighting. He's been after Roger's stock. And, by the way, I don't believe for a moment Roger needs the money. He went to Dennis and fed him information about you and Aaron because he wanted to strike out at Aaron. I'd bet on that. And Dennis decided the worst thing that could happen from his point of view would be for Aaron to have access to your money, so he decided to spin his fairy story and try to make sure the two of you didn't get together."

Fury made Libby gasp. "I knew Dennis hated Aaron for some reason. I couldn't figure out why."

"You can now. He wants Alpine Ridge. I don't think Aaron means anything to him one way or the other except as an obstacle to be cleared."

Libby stared unseeingly at the wall. "Did I want a reason not to love him?" she muttered.

Mike ducked his head. "What did you say?"

"I don't know. I don't know anything for sure. Aaron wouldn't hurt me."

Mike snorted. "I don't even have to respond to that."

"At first I was afraid he wouldn't love me back, not the way I love him. Then, when he said he did, I was afraid all over again." Her throat hurt.

"Why, Libby?"

"Because...Mike, I was so lucky to have Georges. I got used to being grateful for what we'd had and I learned to cope with being alone, but the way it hurt to lose him is something I don't think I could handle again."

"You really do love Aaron, don't you?" Mike asked softly. "That's the whole story. You love him and you know he's innocent of anything wrong. Libby, think. Whether you're together or thousands of miles apart—married or not—if something happened to Aaron it would hurt just as much. Wouldn't you rather be with him, anyway, and work on getting over the fear?"

She closed her eyes. "Yes."

A nurse came into the small isolation cubicle where the baby was being kept as a routine precaution. "Mr. Kinnear," she said in a low, urgent voice, "there's a Roger Chandler on the phone looking for you...and Mrs. Duclaux. He sounds upset."

"I'll bet," Mike muttered, getting up. "Probably thought it over, and now he's trying to figure a way out."

Libby gently put the baby back into his isolet and followed Mike into the hall, pulling off the mask and gown. Her heart pounded. "Mike, let me talk to him." How could she ever explain to Aaron? Why should he even listen?

"Quit feeling guilty for something you didn't start. This is Aaron's fault. But Roger should have been above what he did." He took the phone from an orderly at the desk. "Yeah, Roger?"

Mike had removed his mask. Changing the phone from

hand to hand, he took off the gown, balling it as he lis-
ened.

"What is it?" Libby asked.

He shook his head, and the hardening of his features
urned her stomach. "Do something for me, Roger," he
said finally. "Call his mother and father. They'd want to
know." He hung up.

"What's happening?"

"He and Aaron had...they talked. Aaron was leaving
for the Ridge. He was angry."

"Leaving tonight?" A thud in her head joined her leap-
ng heart.

"Yes, tonight. I'm going out there now."

"Why?" She had to run to keep up with him.

"I'm going to make some excuse to Susan for leaving.
I don't want her worried. You stay here."

"I'm coming. What aren't you telling me?"

"You really want to know?" He stood still. "Early this
evening some ass decided to take off from the trails. By
he time Aaron arrived at the area, the guy had been reported missing and the patrols were out looking.

"The night manager just called Roger. Aaron insisted
on joining the search."

They were within yards of Susan's room. "Why would
he do that? That's the patrol's job."

"He'd do it because he is who he is. People are first
with Aaron. Money counts and his business, but they're
way down the list."

"But—"

"Libby, he went to help because they need every
rained hand. There's been a major avalanche."

THE LIFTS had stopped running, but the night-skiing lights
hed an eerie glare over silent slopes.

Waiting skiers stood in subdued knots. They knew that far above them a few skilled men and women were engaged in a desperate fight to beat a swift killer-menace.

Libby, dressed in gear gathered in the lodge shop, held Mike's hand and climbed to join a familiar group. Marjorie and Bill Conrad had somehow managed to beat Mike's almost reckless drive through the night. With the Conrads were Mimi and Lester. Libby had almost forgotten that to be close to Susan, they had also accepted an offer to spend a few days with Aaron's folks.

Roger Chandler stood a little apart, talking to a man in a ski patrol uniform. The latter spoke rapidly into a radio.

Stumbling, Libby rushed to the patrolman. "Are you in touch with Aaron?" She blushed. "Are you talking to the team?"

"No, ma'am. To the control center." He moved a few steps away, effectively cutting her off.

Roger put his hand on her shoulder. She stared at him and he dropped his arm to his side. "I was wrong," he said. "What I said today—I twisted it. But I was hurting. I still am hurting."

"I was wrong, too. I shouldn't have doubted Aaron' only motive for what he'd decided to do, not for a second." Libby walked to Mike, who stood watching, animosity etched in his cold stare.

A whoop went up from the onlookers and Libby strained to see up the hill. Barely she picked out a group of orange patrol parkas. As she watched, the formation took shape, two skiers guiding a toboggan from the front two behind, holding ropes and ranging wide to steady their human cargo.

"Is Aaron with them?" Marjorie Conrad took several steps forward as she spoke.

"Oh, God." Mike pressed a fist to his mouth and kept his eyes on the group.

"He wouldn't be wearing a patrol parka, would he?" Libby asked.

Mike shook his head. "I doubt it."

"Does anyone know how many went up?" Bill joined them, and Libby couldn't miss the gray tinge to his drawn features.

"You think he's the one on the toboggan," Libby whispered. She concentrated intently on the approaching group. "He'll be all right. He will."

"Yes, *chérie,* he'll be all right."

Libby hadn't noticed Mimi's approach. The woman slipped her hand under Libby's arm. Lester plodded over with Marjorie, and they drew close together.

The patrol members arrived in controlled order, sweeping to a stop, their attention focused solely on the toboggan.

"He's going into shock," a woman called. "We need to move him fast."

Libby heard the calls of "Move it! Move it!" and her body felt fused.

"They want to know if you need a chopper," the radio operator called.

"Let's get him inside," was the only response.

"Is it Aaron?" Libby managed to ask. "Is it?" Her legs finally moved, but Mike stopped her from running toward the toboggan.

Roger, who had kept a separate, silent vigil, jogged over. "It's one of the patrolmen," he said. "Slipped over a ledge. He's probably fractured both legs. He'll be okay."

Libby couldn't keep still. She grabbed Roger's sleeve. "Where's Aaron? If they've come down, where *is* he?"

"He's up there." Roger nodded. "They think they've located the missing man. Evidently he's wearing a beeper. Thank God for small mercies. Aaron and two others are trying to dig him out."

"Is there any danger of another slide?" She knew too well how a massive wall of snow, once loosened, could hover, waiting placidly, then drop with deadly speed in the wake of a previous avalanche.

No one answered her question.

"They don't have another toboggan?" She couldn't stand waiting, saying nothing.

"Yes, they do." The radio liaison had approached. "We weren't sure the guy was alone. If he's not, we're in big trouble now."

Half an hour went by, an hour. Libby passed beyond cold to a numb state that immobilized her. Some of the waiting groups began to disperse.

"Please let him come down safely," Libby muttered. "Please let me be able to tell him what a fool I've been."

Mike pulled her against him. "Make sure you do tell him. And make sure he listens. I can't take any more of this with you two."

She laughed, but the effort sounded pathetic. Why should Aaron listen...or forgive her? They'd known each other for years. There wasn't another man she could possibly know as well, yet she'd allowed herself to be swayed by lies about him...or had she simply been afraid to accept the truth?

"Anything?" Roger called to the radio operator.

Frowning, the man shook his head. "Seem to have lost contact."

Libby closed her eyes.

"Keep trying." Roger's abrupt command barely registered.

"I am."

"There they are!"

She was borne forward with the press of the little group. Skiing across the fall line, hugging a path close to the lift where the light was best, a trio of skiers surged downward, the second toboggan balanced between them.

Rather than orange, the man in front wore all black. He skied at a pace that kept the rear patrolmen leaning back into the hill as they strained to steady the load.

Libby swallowed and sagged against Mike. "That's Aaron in front."

"Yes. Thank God."

The man in black skidded to a stop amid flying chunks of ice. His voice carried through the frigid air. "Chopper! He was alone."

"How do you know?" It was Roger who reached him first.

"He told us," Aaron responded curtly.

Roger hesitated, then moved away.

"Aaron!" Mike broke into a run, but Libby hung back.

Marjorie and Bill rushed after Mike, who turned and called, "Come on!"

She shook her head.

Aaron gathered his mother in his arms and received his father's hug and Mike's. He tilted his head toward Mike, who spoke in his ear.

Straightening, he looked over his mother's head and located Libby.

She crossed her arms tightly. His face was a blur through her tears. While she blinked he turned and continued giving orders to the man on the radio. Patrol members swarmed around the toboggan.

"Go to him."

Libby was surprised to find Roger close by once more. "I can't."

"Sure you can. I'm going to have to and so are you. I'd rather be in your shoes." He walked away in the direction of the lodge.

Gradually the area closed. The few remaining onlookers dispersed to their cars and the toboggan was pulled to shelter only minutes before the sound of helicopter blades thrummed.

The scene unfolded before Libby. All attention focused on the injured man until he was loaded aboard the craft and it lifted away with its strange, half clumsy, half graceful sideways swoop.

He wouldn't forgive her.

Libby glanced around. Mimi and Lester had left, become part of the straggle of people heading for the lodge.

She would wait in Mike's car.

"Libby!"

Only one man remained, separated from her by a few yards of snow.

On legs that had no feeling Libby took a few steps toward him. "I'm sorry." Uncertain if he heard, she stumbled away toward the parking lot.

Aaron's labored breathing was something she heard an instant before he was upon her, swinging her around, his dark eyes glittering. "You owe me more than that."

"I know." His fury shook her. "But I don't know how to say it all."

"You'll get your chance. Inside. One case of hypothermia is enough for one night. Mike shouldn't have brought you."

"I made him."

Aaron, his hand a clamp on her arm, hurried her into

the lodge. Warmth hit, turning numbness to burning pain in her hands and feet.

Seated around the fire on the second floor, no one turned down the brandy Roger poured in huge measures.

"Damn fool," Aaron said in the middle of a lull. "Maybe he'll learn."

"Don't count on it," Roger said. "You know how that goes."

"Take Mom home," Aaron said abruptly to his father. "She looks wiped out."

Bill smiled. "Just this once you get to give me orders. The next time we meet you can be ready for my opinion of what happened this evening. Don't be shy with your two cents' worth on heroics, Libby. We'll warm up the car," he said to Mimi and Lester before leaving.

Mimi stood and Lester quickly joined her.

"I've got to get out of here," Roger said. "Aaron, can I talk to you for a few minutes?"

Without comment Aaron went to the bar and waited for Roger to join him. The two men spoke in lowered voices.

"Tough," Mike said quietly to Libby. "Maybe we'll all learn something from this."

Before anyone could respond Roger walked away from Aaron, his face set. "Good night," he said as he passed. "Drive carefully." He didn't look at Libby.

"We must go," Mimi said.

"Yes," Lester agreed, but he didn't move.

"Mom and Dad should have the car warmed up by now," Aaron said.

"Yes." Lester thrust out his chin and stretched his neck. "Mike, er, Mimi and I might as well mention this now."

"Lester," Mimi said, "perhaps—"

"Now." Lester pushed his shoulders back. "We've become, um, fond of each other, Mimi and I. Now we don't intend to do anything in a rush. We're too old for that. But we aren't dead yet.''

The silence was absolute. Libby had a wild urge to giggle.

Mike looked at his father through narrowed eyes. ''What does that mean?''

''We are…we're going to undertake a trial arrangement.''

The pretty rush of pink to Mimi's face delighted Libby. ''Trial arrangement?'' she asked innocently of Lester.

''You know what's being said,'' Mimi announced, her mouth determinedly set. She stood close to Lester. ''We'll live together. If we find we are, ah, compatible—then, well, then we'll see.''

Mike rose slowly from his chair.

''We'd like to be together in the cottage,'' Lester told him. ''Will that be agreeable to you?''

''I suppose…well…yes.''

''Good.'' Lester nodded. ''We'll be going, then.''

Libby became aware of a steady trembling within her body. ''We'd better go, too,'' she said to Mike.

''You and I have some talking to do,'' Aaron said. He poured more brandy into her glass and set the bottle down with a crack. ''Give my love to Susan, Mike.''

''I need to get back,'' Libby protested.

''No, you don't.'' Aaron leveled a stare at her before concentrating on Mike. ''But you do. Take it easy.''

Mike moved, but like a man in deep water. ''Yes, I will. You'll get Libby back?''

''Don't give it another thought. I'll take care of Libby.''

Nodding, Mike walked to the top of the stairs and paused. ''My father's going to have an affair.''

Libby covered her mouth. Even the jumpiness in her

stomach couldn't completely eclipse the humorous effect of Mike's stunned tone or his bemused expression.

"Think of it as a trial marriage," Aaron said. "A chance to find out if they can be good companions." He'd moved almost imperceptibly closer to Libby. She saw now his strong hands tensed into fists at his sides.

Slowly Mike clomped down the wooden stairs. His footsteps faltered once and he asked, "What am I going to tell Susan?"

21

"I was wrong!"

Aaron ignored her. He got up, collected his own park[ ]
and Libby's and crossed the room.

"Speak to me! I was wrong. I'm sorry. I'll always b[ ]
sorry."

He kept walking.

"Where are you going?"

"*We're* going upstairs. Bring your brandy. And mine.[ ]
A passageway led from the restaurant and bar. "Bring th[ ]
bottle," Aaron added as he walked from sight.

She stood and took up the two glasses in one hand, th[ ]
bottle in the other. Apprehension gathered beneath he[ ]
skin, and a kind of excitement. His every word held [ ]
challenge…and a threat. He expected her to do as he tol[ ]
her. She would. But she'd also expect him to admit hi[ ]
own mistakes.

The passage ended at a flight of stairs. Libby climbe[ ]
slowly, peering up through subdued light. At the top [ ]
door stood open, and she passed into a large room tha[ ]
was both sitting room and bedroom. A row of high, un[ ]
draped windows hugged a sharply sloping ceiling.

Aaron came from what appeared to be a walk-in close[ ]
and went directly to a circular black stove in the cent[ ]
of the room. He dropped to his haunches, and within se[ ]

nds flames shot up from the logs and sent sparks spiral-
ng into the chimney.

Libby advanced uncertainly. He behaved as if he were
eep in thought. Tonight he looked as he had that night
hen he came to her room in Madonna di Lago. Big,
owerful in the body-clinging black sweater and pants.

Had she loved him then? As more than a dear friend?
he probable answer brought a flood of heat. And the next
nemory deepened that heat: Aaron in the shower, reach-
ng for her hand, kissing her, his hair and face dripping—
ne intense dark of that night, its seething sensations.

He got up and faced her.

Libby looked away and set the bottle on a wooden
ench stacked with magazines. She held a glass out to
aron and he took it.

"I'm sorry," she said, and tipped up her face. "Why
n't I seem to say anything but sorry?"

"Do you love me?"

She shuddered and closed her eyes. "I love you, Aaron.
nd I shouldn't have doubted you." She shrugged, gulped
randy and coughed. "Maybe I didn't. No, I know I
dn't. I don't understand myself. Or maybe I do."

"I think I understand you—very well." His voice was
ry low. "Damn it, Libby. You're part of me. Do you
nderstand? Like my skin and my brain and my heart.
orny maybe, but true. When you walked out on me last
ght, I felt as if you'd torn out bits and pieces of me and
ken them with you."

The brandy warmed a path through her, and gave her
ourage. "You did some dumb things, Aaron Conrad."

"I know. So now I have to pay for them, huh? No
cond chances for this guy."

"Roger did and said things he had no right to do and
y. But you set him up. And you set me up. You treated

us both like children in need of the guidance of a brigh
grown-up.''

''I know, I know.'' Aaron spread his arms. ''Tonight
apologized to Roger. Does that count for something?''

The fire quickly heated the room. Libby lifted her ha
from her neck and plucked at her sweater.

''Too hot?'' He sounded...remote.

Without answering she peeled off the sweater an
windpants she'd put on over the orange silk shirt and nav
pants. Leaning down, she unzipped the après-ski boo
she'd borrowed from the shop and pulled them off. ''M
shoes and coat are downstairs. I can pick them up on th
way out.''

''Sure,'' Aaron said. ''Whenever that is.''

Breath stuck in her throat. ''Your parents will expe
me back.''

''No, they won't. My parents are smart people.''

Libby ran her eyes over the room. Covered with an ol
fashioned multicolored patchwork quilt, the bed wasn
large. Well-worn leather armchairs and a couch, studde
with brass, stood around the stove. The same burnishe
wood that paneled the walls and ceiling covered the floo
beneath a scatter of rugs trodden to faded rose and bu
gundy shades.

''Do you like it?''

She stared at him. ''It's beautiful. It reminds me
Madonna di Lago.''

''I knew it would. See?'' He indicated the room's hig
windows. ''It's snowing. Remember how it snowed th
night I came to persuade you to come back here wi
me?''

''I remember. I wanted to stay there, just the way w
were.''

''Will you go back now?''

She shook her head slowly. Her mouth worked, but she couldn't form the words.

"Drink," Aaron ordered. He tossed back the rest of his brandy and set down the glass. "Are you ready?"

"Ready?" Her throat closed. Even standing apart, separated by the width of a rug, she felt him as surely as if he held her.

"Ready to say the things that have to be said?"

Libby walked around the couch, trailing her fingers along the supple leather. She sat on the back, her head bowed.

"Okay," Aaron said. "I'll take that for a yes. We touched on this before. Georges was murdered by his nephew, a man you both trusted, maybe even loved. I don't blame you for losing confidence in the world, in decency. I don't blame you for being afraid of trusting again."

The brandy in her glass turned to a blurred amber swirl.

"You started to believe we could have it all together. Then friend Falk delivered his salvo. You didn't believe him, though, did you?"

"No," she whispered.

"Then Roger, who has every right to hate my guts at this moment, added some fuel from a slightly different angle. I tried to get something going between the two of you. That's true. I did. But I hadn't counted on what happened between us." He gave a short laugh. "Oh, if I'd been using my head and certain other indicators, I'd have known. But it happened in the end, anyway."

"Aaron—"

"Please be quiet. I have to say it all." Noiselessly he rounded her behind the couch, stood looking down into her face. "Whether you admit it or not, even as you were beginning to love me, you were getting frightened of how

much it could hurt to love and lose again. The things tho
guys told you weren't things you really believed abo
me."

"No." She didn't. He made it all sound so clear.

"We're not going to bring up the money issue agai
It doesn't count here. It never could between you and n
Roger and I will work things out and the business w
survive very well. There'll be rough times, but we'll sti
together, and in time I hope to God he forgives me 1
the rotten trip I laid on him. All I can tell you is tha
thought I was doing the right thing. And I'm sorry, Libl
sorry for what I put you through out of my own stupi
ity."

"I know." She trained her attention on his lean midd
"You were brave tonight. But...oh, Aaron, I was
scared."

The black sweater moved perceptibly closer. "I kn
what I was doing up there. Sure there was danger, b
waking up in the morning might be dangerous. You ca
live in fear."

Power surged into her and, with it, conviction. "I
not going to. No more being afraid from here on. At le
I'm going to take a good shot at it."

"Remember telling me that we would never have ma
love if you hadn't taken the initiative?" He was o
inches from her now.

She ached, deep in her belly. "Yes." Quickly s
pressed her fingertips to his mouth. "Shh, Aaron. Gi
me a minute to think."

He covered her hand, then shifted it to kiss her paln

Each breath became shorter. "Do you think we sho
sit down and talk for a while?" She swallowed and 1
him smile against her skin. "Would you like some me
brandy?"

Aaron shook his head. Now he kissed her wrist, but his dark eyes, eyes bright with laughter, never left hers.

"We could ski tomorrow if you like," she said, almost desperately. "I've always been able to think up there. Aaron?"

"Mmm. We'll ski tomorrow." Gently he cupped her chin and raised her head. "Tomorrow, my love. Not tonight." The possession of her mouth was softly erotic. Libby's lips parted beneath his. She reached for him, but he captured her wrist with his free hand and moved her face beneath his, rocking her head slowly from side to side with his lips, his tongue.

"You're playing follow-the-leader this time," he murmured against her ear. His fingers went to the buttons on her blouse. One thigh, pressed into hers, trapped her against the couch. "And diversionary tactics won't work."

He kissed her again and again while he stripped away the blouse, slipped her bra straps from her shoulders, smoothed her breasts with suddenly reverent care.

Twisting her, he pulled her to her feet. A few swift movements and her clothes fell to the floor. He kissed her again.

Breathing hard, he raised his head and stood back, his hands on her shoulders. "Do you still think I wouldn't ever be the one to decide to make love to you?"

"No...no." She couldn't look away from the heat in his dark eyes. But he looked away, swept every inch of her, used his fingertips in a slow, sensual line painting of her body.

Libby trembled. He pulled his sweater over his head, and the thin liner beneath, unzipped the tight pants and worked them off until he was naked.

Gripping her waist, he lifted her to sit on the back of

the couch and stood between her legs. She clung to hi
shoulders.

Adrenaline pumped through her veins and desire an
desperate raw need. "You aren't angry with me anymor
are you?" She felt the nudge of his arousal.

"Angry!" He raised his face and laughed. He held he
arms, stroked with his palms. "Love and anger don't g
together. Not our kind of love. Love and confusion pe
haps. Maybe love and desperation. But never anger."

Aaron nuzzled her neck, moved hands that trembled
her sides and kissed her breasts, dropped to his knees an
kissed her over and over. Libby leaned above him, whin
pering, and her hair swung across his shoulder.

"I love you." She ran her fingers over his scalp an
pressed his face to her.

Aaron stood then, lithe, a faint sheen of moisture c
his skin. "How could you even half believe I would us
you—for money?" His mouth descended on hers again

When she could speak, she said, "I didn't really believ
it. You were right. I was unsure and too ready to acce
any story that would take me away from the danger
being hurt again. I'm not afraid anymore."

He touched his nose to hers, slipped his tongue acro
her lips. "I love you. I always will."

"Yes."

Shifting closer, their bodies touched. "Are you su
you aren't going back to Italy?"

"No. But I don't want to go without you."

The touch became probing. She gasped and clung
him.

"Will you be my wife? Will you love and honor m
till death do us part?"

"I'll even obey in certain very exceptional circum
stances."

"Me, too." He grinned, but his chest expanded, giving way the cost of his control. "So, will you?"

"Will I what?"

"Take me...and the rest?"

Breathless, almost hysterical giggles tore from her, "Yes, I will. Will you?"

"Oh, Libby. I will. Tonight, on this spot, and for as long a forever as we're given." He entered her body, slowly, strongly, his eyes never leaving hers. "And you're going to have to wear my ring. And it's going to be as special as I want it to be?"

"Yes."

Lifting her, he carried her, face pressed into his shoulder, to the bed. They slipped down together and the words faded into breath and skin and small cries.

ARON STIRRED and opened his eyes. He drowsed, his body curved around Libby's. "It's still snowing," he murmured against her hair.

"Mmm. Lovely."

He saw the glint of her eyes. She was awake, too, and watching the soft drift of white in blackness beyond the windows.

"You will let me be part of the business?"

"As much as you want to be. But this is a case of what's mine is yours. Roger's not bailing out, remember. We'll be all right in time." He felt as sure as his voice sounded. With Libby he would always feel strong.

"Make love to me again."

Sighing, he turned her in his arms. "An insatiable wife. What a chore you're going to be."

"It'll be a small wedding."

"Nope." He brushed back her hair, kissed her brow.

"I want the dress, the bridesmaids, the whole works. S
do my parents.''

"You talked to them about it!"

He laughed. "They offered us their house. I decline
graciously. Are you going to marry me?"

"I said so."

"No, you didn't."

Her arms went around his neck and she pressed close
"Then, yes, I am."

"Dress, bouquet, reception, the whole works?"

She sighed. "I hate pretension, but for you…"

"Great… Good grief!"

Her warm, soft skin had already begun to work it
magic on his too-willing body.

"Why good grief?"

"Nothing. Leave everything to me. I'll pick out every
thing. You can sit back and enjoy. I think white orchid
and stephanotis would make a beautiful bouquet, don
you?"

Her laughter was honeyed. She urged him on top
her. "Nothing doing, Aaron. We'll start a trend."

He groaned. "No, no, no. No dandelions."

With their fresh joining she drew in a sharp breath. "N
dandelions, no deal."

She thought she heard him say, "It's a deal."

Stella Cameron

66615	ALL SMILES	___ $5.99 U.S.	___ $6.99 CAN.
66463	MOONTIDE	___ $5.50 U.S.	___ $6.50 CAN.
66495	UNDERCURRENTS	___ $5.99 U.S.	___ $6.99 CAN.
66795	7B	___ $6.99 U.S.	___ $8.50 CAN.

(limited quantities available)

TOTAL AMOUNT	$_____
POSTAGE & HANDLING	$_____
($1.00 for one book; 50¢ for each additional)	
APPLICABLE TAXES*	$_____
TOTAL PAYABLE	$_____

(check or money order—please do not send cash)

To order, complete this form and send it, along with a check or money order for the total above, payable to MIRA Books®, to: **In the U.S.:** 3010 Walden Avenue, P.O. Box 9077, Buffalo, NY 14269-9077; **In Canada:** P.O. Box 636, Fort Erie, Ontario L2A 5X3.

Name:_____

Address:_____ City:_____

State/Prov.:_____ Zip/Postal Code:_____

Account Number (if applicable):_____

075 CSAS

*New York residents remit applicable sales taxes.
Canadian residents remit applicable GST and provincial taxes.

MIRA®